THE DIRECTOR

THE DIRECTOR

Chris Marr

ROBERT HALE · LONDON

ISBN 978-0-7090-8719-9

Robert Hale Limited
Clerkenwell House
Clerkenwell Green
London EC1R 0HT

www.halebooks.com

Typeset in 11/13½pt Sabon
by Derek Doyle & Associates, Shaw Heath
Printed and bound in Great Britain
by MPG Biddles Limited, King's Lynn

To Barbara

CONTENTS

PART ONE

PART TWO

PART THREE

PART ONE

1

How Green Was My Valley (1941)

Every morning at seven o'clock Mrs Peavey took her Doberman pinschers, Mufty and Treacle, on a two-mile walk. The route never varied – and the dogs normally led the way – but on this June morning it was Mrs Peavey, bedecked in tweeds, who was striding ahead, her face set in an expression of determination.

The reason for her present mood lay in a documentary she'd watched the previous evening. The programme, about infidelity, had stirred up painful memories, and Mrs Peavey had poured a great deal of vitriol into her diary after she'd retired to bed. Her husband, Frank, had shown a disturbing interest in other women near the end of his life – a diabetic, he had died of an insulin over-dose a decade earlier – and since that time Mrs Peavey had taken a jaundiced view of those reneging on their marriage vows.

Her ill humour had resumed in the morning. Although thoughts of Frank had receded into the background, her mind had settled on the subject of her next-door neighbours' marriage. Mrs Peavey was the sort who, even if she'd resolved her own problems, was able to transfer her feelings to someone else. In this instance, she sympathized with Leonard, the husband, who for various reasons she suspected of being deceived by his wife.

The surrounding trees and hedgerows of the Essex countryside had hardly looked more beautiful. In true English summer tradition it had poured with rain for the entire night and the dew glimmered off the grass in the crisp morning air. A pair of robins fluttered overhead, adding a touch of colour to the spectacle, and no doubt Wordsworth, had he been present, would have dashed off something about sunbeams falling upon distant hills, the whisper of a passing zephyr. . . .

Mrs Peavey, however, was immune to such delights. Swinging the dogs' leads with grasshopper-threatening gusto, she pursued her own train of thought, a film of abstraction clouding her small grey eyes.

Oh, she was a right one, that Deborah. What was it she'd said the other day? Oh, yes – 'I'd prefer it if you left the bedroom cupboards and drawers alone.' The words themselves didn't amount to much – but honestly! The tone in which they'd been delivered, the whole body language! Mrs Peavey had been about to ask if she was addressing her – the person who so kindly offered to clean their house – but she'd already waltzed out the room.

'Cheap little tramp,' Mrs Peavey muttered.

Because – yes! – she *was* a tramp, even if the expression was somewhat surprising issuing from an Englishwoman of staid appearance. (Mrs Peavey more than a little resembled Clarissa Dickson Wright, one of the *Two Fat Ladies*.) Mrs Peavey had in recent years become addicted to watching films – inspired by having a film critic as a neighbour? – and so, inevitably, words and phrases – 'Cheap little tramp' had cropped up in *Chicago* – had found their way into her speech.

She continued on her morning's walk, still thinking, furiously.

What Leonard, dear, sweet Leonard, saw in her – Deborah – well, that was anyone's guess. *He* was quite different from his wife: much nicer, friendlier and funnier. Heh, heh! (She had to laugh.) The look on his face when she'd donned that mask from *Snow White*! Perhaps (you never knew) – perhaps he'd even spoken to Deborah about their long and interesting conversations; and perhaps Deborah (you never knew) had felt jealous about it, felt somehow under threat—

Jeepers, that was a thought! (You might be onto something

there, Agatha Jean!) Not that anything could happen between her and Leonard, of course. But there was that moment, wasn't there, when he'd stepped on his glasses? They were up close, face to face, and it would have been so easy—

But – no. Nothing had happened. She had resisted and so, too, had he, though the look in his eyes showed that he'd realized the danger. . . .

A key point in her deliberations had been reached and Mrs Peavey momentarily slowed her pace – before abruptly (as if to dismiss an idea) rubbing a mitten under her nose and leaving behind a snail-like imprint.

Yes, there you had it – there you had it all over: the difference between her and most of the population. Where was the self-restraint nowadays, the sense of loyalty? By gosh, even dogs had superior moral values. At least you knew where you stood with a dog. *And* – not forgetting the other thing about dogs – if they did get a bit frisky, you just took them to the vet's, dealt with the problem at source. Mrs Peavey negotiated a stile and squelched her way down a hill the other side. It was a pity in many ways you couldn't round up some of the young men today and—

Hold on a minute. What was that doing there?

A black sports car was parked at the bottom of the slope, at the turning. Mrs Peavey's thin lips pressed together, nostrils flaring. The previous night she'd heard a car coming up the road and had waited expectantly at the living-room window. But the vehicle, the same sleek black thing, hadn't been carrying a visitor for her. It contained Deborah Fleason, together with a man she didn't recognize. The car had screeched past her front gate on its way to the Fleason house, the only other residence further up the road.

And now it was back again, blocking the way. Perhaps it had got stuck in the mud, though it didn't look too boggy. Some people were so gauche, driving around in swish cars and littering the countryside. But – wait a second. Someone was still in it, slumped against the steering wheel. Drunk, probably. Treacle was already pressed against the door inspecting the occupant.

Lengthening her stride and plonking her size eights squarely in the mud, she rapped on the driver's window, receiving no reply. It was the same man all right, the one she'd seen driving past last night. She opened the door, jerking her head to one side. Dear heavens, what a smell. He'd been sick. She put one hand up to her mouth and, with the other, attempted to fend the dogs away, both of whom were now nosing around the insides of the car. The driver himself, though, seemed insensible.

'Mufty! Treacle! Sit!'

She tapped the man on the shoulder and, receiving no response, pushed a bit harder. Oh, jeepers . . . Oh, ohhh. He swayed over into the passenger seat, his mouth gaping open. Reaching out more tentatively this time, she touched his hand. . . .

Cold. Dead cold.

The old lady staggered back. The dogs were barking insanely, and she lurched forward again to shut the car door, gasping for breath.

The walk home passed in a blur. Mrs Peavey was hypnotized by the dead body she'd just encountered, a man cut down in the prime of life. The most terrible question was going through her mind.

Hadn't Leonard told her yesterday, with a gleam in his eye, that his wife's lover was coming over for dinner and that he intended to 'slip him something extra'?

Surely, though – surely – that had all been a joke? They had laughed over it for goodness' sake.

No, no, impossible. Just impossible. Leonard simply wasn't the sort . . . Wasn't the sort at all.

As a matter of fact, the subject of Mrs Peavey's thoughts was, at that precise moment, applying the finishing touches to the challenging assignment he'd set himself. He had been in turmoil for the last six weeks. But now it was over, finally over, the culmination of a sequence of events that had had their origin in the middle of April.

When he'd first suspected his wife of betraying him.

2

Man With a Movie Camera (1929)

Leonard Fleason looked more like a kindly uncle than a man of violence. He comported himself with a certain gentleness, belying his solid, nearly six-foot frame, and was invariably courteous and affable in his manners. Further enhancing this non-aggressive image, he wore horn-rimmed spectacles and generally favoured jackets or smart pullovers, lending him a donnish mien.

His suspicions about the soundness of his marriage had germinated after Deborah had arrived home late from a night out with some of her office chums. Not an uncommon occurrence – the two of them led separate social lives on the whole – but he had caught her out in a lie. She'd specifically told him she'd pop over to the gym after work with Carol and another woman called Kate, and then probably stay for a few drinks at the bar. Nothing wrong with that, of course, but Leonard, ever thoughtful, had noticed that a favourite programme of his wife's clashed with a film he wanted to video.

So he phoned the gym and asked the receptionist to relay a message to Deborah to ring him back, if possible, before 10.30. Then, the time approaching eleven (her programme started at 11.15, five minutes before his film), he decided to give this 'Carol' a call. Perhaps if she was in, she could supply his wife's whereabouts.

Fortunately a small phone book had been left on the bed, inscribed with a flowery 'D', and Leonard worked his way through it. Carol Something. Caroline . . . Carolyn . . .

Finally he found one, the only one. Carol Yateman. He dialled the number.

'Hello,' a woman's voice answered.

'Oh, hello. Is that Carol?'

'Yeah.'

'Oh, hi. I'm Leonard – Deborah's husband. Sorry to bother you, but is Deborah with you by any chance?'

The line seemed to go dead.

'No,' came the answer at last.

'Right. It was just a long shot. You don't happen to know if she's on her way home?'

Another long pause.

'I'm really not sure.'

'Well, not to worry. You did meet up, though, this evening?'

'Y-yes, that's right. But then I came back here. I'm not sure about Debbie. I expect she'll be back soon. I really don't know.'

'Well, I'm sure I'll track her down. Thanks anyway, Carol. Sorry to disturb you.'

He put the phone down. It was embarrassing to admit he'd lost his wife, but these things were bound to happen from time to time. All the nerves in any case had come from Deborah's friend. Those long pauses in response to perfectly straightforward questions! As if his wife was conducting an affair behind his back!

He and Deborah had been married now for five years. They'd had their differences, of course – some of them arising from the fifteen-year age gap – but they'd both slipped into a certain comfortable routine. Normally, for instance, it was Leonard's policy when his wife stayed out late to go to bed at midnight and not bother waiting for her return. On this occasion, however, he made an effort to stay awake.

He watched *Sliver* with Sharon Stone, a film he'd missed at the time of its release because he'd been on holiday. It was impossible, even in the life of a film critic, to catch every major film that came out and, although on returning to work, he'd read the reviews, other films had demanded attention. In characteristic fashion, off came his slippers, his stockinged feet rubbing together approvingly. Interesting idea, that. Very interesting. Of course only a

madman would set up surveillance cameras throughout an apartment block, but then who wouldn't – faced with all those TV
monitors – spend a minute or so examining the evidence?

It was now one o'clock and still no sign of Deborah. She could
have phoned at least. What was the betting she'd had too much to
drink and would get back at some ridiculous hour, falling all over
the place?

Well, he could have a laugh as well. It was a bit naughty really
– well, very naughty. But then hadn't she done something similar
once? Pressed record on the answering machine, then left the
room while he was turning the air blue scrambling around for the
remote? They'd both enjoyed that little prank at the time. And
so . . .

His last action before retiring to bed was to place a four-hour
blank tape in his camcorder, leave it on the dressing-table facing
her side of the bed, press record, and then slip into his dreams.

3.37 a.m. In little white characters in the bottom right of the
screen.

Waking up the next morning, Leonard hadn't given the affairs
of the night a moment's thought, and it wasn't till he was combing
his hair that he noticed the camcorder peeping out from behind
the mirror.

What was that doing there?

Oh, God, yes, that was right. Had he really filmed Deborah
without her knowledge? She was in bed now, so he must have. But
– how appalling! Talk about an invasion of privacy! Tiredness must
have affected his judgement, that was the only explanation. Still,
he didn't have to watch the tape, did he?

No. No, he didn't. And what was more, he wouldn't. He would
stand firm, retain his self-respect, knowing that in the end he'd
done the right thing.

Ten minutes later – oh, what the heck, just one little peek – he
was sitting in front of the television having just fast-forwarded
through over two-and-a-half hours of nothing. In the dimness of
their bedroom – he'd deliberately left one curtain open to improve
the lighting – he could make out his wife quietly and efficiently
disrobing. It was unusual to see her getting undressed in the

bedroom – lately she had taken to using the bathroom – and she seemed to be staring intently at the heaving mound in the bed that represented himself.

Apart from the preposterousness of the time, Leonard was perturbed at the sound of his own, rather elephantine, snores.

'Deborah . . . Deborah . . .'

He came closer to the bed and crouched down so that he was only a few inches from her face. It was ten o'clock. Deborah was lying on her side with the duvet tucked under her chin. There was something about her slumbering form that always touched him in a particular way. She looked so peaceful, and yet there was a firmness to her jaw, an irrepressible quality.

'H'm,' she said, her eyes still closed.

'You, er, feeling a bit fragile?'

'Hmmm. . . .'

'Can I get you anything? Like toast or – I don't suppose you fancy a fry-up?'

'Hmmm . . . Yeah. Fry-up.' She turned over so that he was facing her back.

He raised his finger to object but then let it drop.

Twenty minutes later – having fed Oliver, the cat, as well – he returned with a tray bearing her request and stood over her inert body.

'Deborah . . . Debbie . . .'

She managed to rouse herself, turning a bleary eye towards him.

'H'm? Oh, yeah. Put it over there.'

She waved a hand in the direction of the bedside cabinet. He deposited the tray and, sensing her moving about under the covers, turned and smiled, expecting some expression of gratitude. *Thank you, lover. You're so good to me.*

'Have you put the rubbish out?' she drawled. 'The place stank of cat food last night.'

He about-faced, gnashing his teeth a little, and padded downstairs. If she was having an affair, she wasn't lacking in chutzpah, that was for sure. Perhaps she was working towards the point where he was waiting on her *and* her lover.

And what would sir like? I believe you had a particularly taxing night. Perhaps a cup of tea and a cigarette would be in order?

Yes, well, good thing he wasn't taking all this too seriously.

He dealt with the rubbish and then retrieved his own meal. Then he made his way into the spacious living-room, a beautiful affair in yellow and white, and settled himself at the table at the far end overlooking the back garden. A film magazine had recently asked him to name his ten favourite movies and he wanted to come up with at least one unexpected title among the *Citizen Kanes* and *The Godfathers*. So what could it be? What could it be among the many. . . ?

Ahhh, yes. The honour would go to . . . *Breaking Away*.

Breakfast dispensed with, he was taking his empty plate back when he encountered Deborah coming into the living-room, still in her nightdress and clutching a herbal tea. She was a slim woman, the same height as himself, with a jaw-length strawberry blonde bob that was looking slightly dishevelled.

'Grease and fat,' she said, rubbing her stomach with her free hand. 'What a mistake.'

She switched on the television and his eyes darted to the screen. The camcorder was still connected to the VCR. Had he left it on? How would she react?

Fortunately he had turned it off – of course he had! – and a Saturday morning children's presenter grinned back at them.

'Good evening then?' he enquired.

'Yeah. Not bad.'

'Where did you go?'

'The gym.' A delicate line divided her eyebrows, her vision still fixed on the screen.

'So how was Kate? Still having problems with her husband?'

That was apparently the reason for yesterday evening's get-together, a full discussion of the latest goings-on in her friend's marriage. She finally gazed in his direction.

'Oh, it's very complicated, Leonard. I don't want to bore you.'

'Right. So, um . . . what time did you get in last night?'

She took a swig of her tea, turning back to face the television. 'One . . . half-one. . . . Something like that.'

He studied her profile for signs of embarrassment. Somehow he'd expected her to manufacture a more respectable time, but this was some way off the target. He wasn't her keeper, of course, but he did expect a more accurate version of the truth.

'I tried to get in touch—'

'Look at that big mouth. She really gets on my nerves.'

He gazed at the screen. The children's presenter had actually enhanced the size of the orifice in question with lipstick.

'That's the rule, isn't it, nowadays?' he essayed. 'Big mouths. Small noses. Extremely slim bodies.'

'And that's a good thing, is it?'

'I-I'm not saying it's good or it's bad. Perhaps in fifty years' time the fashion will be small mouths, big noses and thighs that rub together.'

She tore herself away from the television. 'Do you really think about what you're saying? Really think?'

How did this argument spring up? 'I was just— Look, never mind about that now. All I wanted to say was, I tried to get in touch—'

'Oh, for Christ's sake, belt up.'

She was addressing the children's presenter but for a moment he was thrown off his stride.

'Yes, well, anyway, I tried to get in touch—'

'Shut it.'

'—with you last night. I phoned up the gym—'

'Cretin.'

'—and because you didn't ring back—'

'Cretin!'

'—I phoned Carol. She was at home.'

She turned the television off, extinguishing the children's presenter and her all-pervasive lips for good. Perhaps now that he didn't have to compete they could have a sensible conversation.

'What?' she said unpromisingly.

'I was just saying . . . I can't remember myself now. Oh, yes, I tried to get hold of you. Last night, this was. I rang the gym, then spoke to Carol . . . Carol Yateman.'

'You—'

'She said she hadn't seen you. Not for a few hours. Didn't know where you'd got to.'

Her face looked blank for a moment – had her cheeks reddened ever so slightly? – before she exclaimed, 'Oh, yeah, that's right, I know! We left the gym early, then went to a pub. Just me and Katie. Carol didn't feel up to it. Why, what did you want me for?'

'Nothing much.'

'Huh! Well, sounds like I missed a riveting conversation.'

He let the subject drop. Even if he said he knew for a fact she hadn't gone to bed before half-three, she'd just say that Kate's watch must have been slow and – so what? – she was mistaken about the time. Blah, blah, blah.

It wasn't till later that day that his suspicions were confirmed. Deborah had left the house around lunchtime, saying she was going to drop some old clothes off at Oxfam. Somewhat unusually she hadn't invited him along – to carry the laundry bag and play the part of Parker to her Lady Penelope – but in this instance it suited his purposes.

Unable to resist the pleasure of secretly watching her again, within ten minutes of her departure he had set up the tape. Almost immediately, now viewing at his leisure, he noticed something strange. She was wearing what looked like a man's baggy jumper, unfamiliar to him. It was impossible to make out the colour but, in any case, it just wasn't her style (and he would have remembered if she'd gone out wearing it the night before). In a second, she had pulled it over her shoulders and stuffed it in the bottom of the chest of drawers. He rewound the tape, carefully wiped his glasses, and played the mini-scene again. He was determined to seek out the offending garment.

It had disappeared.

Of course, it could have belonged to Carol, or this Kate person if she existed (and was indeed a she). But Leonard didn't think so. His head was throbbing. What on earth was she doing with that jumper?

He slumped against the bed, his face encased in deep concentration. It was a mystery, certainly, but it wasn't the first time he'd been perturbed by Deborah's behaviour. One after the other, unpleasant memories surfaced from the last few months, of minor importance on their own perhaps, but collectively forming a more worrying picture. A couple of times Deborah had flinched when he'd touched her. On another occasion she'd walked out of the room while he'd been enthusing about a film. He'd discovered his Valentine's card to her lying in the bin a couple of days after the day itself. (He'd been searching for a lost receipt.)

Oh, God, this was just awful. Why in heaven's name hadn't he been more suspicious before? The signs were all there but he'd somehow managed to explain them away. Her offhandedness was because she was so absorbed in her work. The Valentine's card was disposed of because she didn't want to clutter up the house.

And perhaps – perhaps – he'd been right in his assumptions. Dear God, he didn't know anything at the moment. What if he'd seen one too many films about infidelity and become paranoid as a result?

She couldn't really be having an affair, though, could she?

No, no, she couldn't, just couldn't. She knew how much she meant to him.

If only, though, there was more evidence to go on. More evidence just to put his mind at rest. . . .

He closed his eyes, letting out a groan.

For God's sake. Not that. Surely he wasn't seriously contemplating . . .

No. He really was going to stand firm this time. Deborah trusted him completely, saw him as being upright and honourable. Besides, it would involve him behaving in a way he'd find distinctly uncomfortable.

So that was that.

The end.

The unhappiness stirring at the marrow of his being would just have to stay there.

3

Sleuth (1972)

'HVM Investigations Ltd.' The female voice, very Essex, twanged its way into Leonard's right ear.

'Hello . . . Hm-h'm . . . I wonder if you can help me?'

'We can try. What's the problem?'

'It's . . . hmm . . . it's matrimonial.'

He'd read the advert in the *Yellow Pages* – under Detective Agencies – and noted the word.

'Is she missing?'

'No.'

'Having an affair?'

'Well, I'm not exactly . . . I-I suppose that's why I'm phoning.'

'I see. So you want definitive proof.'

'Hm-h'm-hmm. Yes.' A frog was spawning in his throat. 'Can I ask why I should choose you to investigate the matter?' He asked one of his prepared questions.

'Of course. HVM have been in business for ten years, expanding from myself to a current staff of six. We belong to the Association of British Investigators, the only regulatory body in this country, and also the World Association of Detectives. We're what you might call a high-tech outfit, with up-to-date surveillance equipment and extensive computerized records.'

'Sounds very impressive,' said Leonard. 'And what about costs?'

'Well, we'd normally discuss that in a formal meeting. But as an outline, for this type of thing, we'd normally charge about £250 a day, plus expenses—'

'Eh?' Leonard's diffidence sloughed off in a wave of indignation.

'Which includes a full written report, together with an extensive breakdown of costs. You're paying, remember, for information that would be difficult to obtain by any other means. Most of our detectives are ex-policewomen who've been retrained to deal with a greater amount of undercover work. The only decision for you to make is between money and peace of mind.'

Leonard harrumphed himself through another couple of minutes but, since he'd reached essentially the same conclusion, he arranged to meet Hedda Marshall, the lady in question, later that afternoon. The main effect of the phone call, however, was to intensify his sense of guilt. What sort of person would countenance such an idea in the first place? It was dishonest, *cowardly* . . .

Yes, but hold on. As yet he hadn't agreed to anything. And he *was* concerned about his relationship with Deborah, very concerned. He couldn't say he trusted her any more, or believed anything she said, in fact. What was the point in discussing the issue with her when all he could expect in return were trumped-up stories? If he could only prove that at worst she was telling little white lies, it might make all the difference.

He made his way into Colchester. The detective agency was near the town centre and Leonard was able to walk from the car park. HVM, it turned out, shared half of the third floor of a four-storey complex with an insurance company.

'Ah, Mr Fleason.'

Hedda Marshall extended her hand. She looked about thirty-five, quite petite, with short hair and neat, vulpine features. She wore an elegantly tailored violet suit.

'Please sit down.'

Leonard took his place, facing the desk in interview style. There were no computers, at least in sight, and the only sign of modern technology was a fax/answering machine next to the phone. Thank goodness, though, it wasn't a seedy operation –

something out of *Blood Simple* or *Kiss Me Deadly*. The most noticeable feature was the number of certificates on the walls.

'Thanks for coming. We prefer it if clients do visit us. Gives us a chance to get to know you better and allows you to meet the operative working on your case. Would you like a coffee?'

'I'm fine, thanks.'

She walked over to a water bottle in the corner, wedged between a fridge and a filing cabinet, and yanked a plastic cup from the dispenser.

'Did you bring a recent photograph of your wife?'

Leonard rummaged in his wallet, retrieving two snapshots of Deborah which he placed on the desk.

'H'm.' She sat down, glancing briefly at the photos, then back at Leonard, in an apparent attempt to reconcile the two (a difficulty encountered by several people, including Deborah's parents). 'Would you care to tell me a bit more about your suspicions? I really need to know as much as possible.'

Leonard rehashed the business about the jumper and the late night out. His nerves were actually beginning to settle. It wasn't so difficult talking about personal matters once a start had been made.

'And does she often go out on her own with her friends?'

'Twice, maybe three times, a week.'

'Well, it all seems pretty normal, I must say. There's nothing else you'd like to tell me?'

Apart from the orgy the other day, you mean? 'I suppose she's been acting a bit cold lately. Dressing more provocatively. . . .'

Hedda Marshall sat back – she had evidently been perched on the edge of her seat – and intertwined her hands. 'Dress is important, that's true.' It was difficult to tell if she was being serious or ironic. After a pause she continued reflectively, 'We don't often get cases like this. Erring spouses. Not that it doesn't happen all the time of course. Just that contrary to popular opinion our services are rarely called upon. Mind if I smoke?'

'No, no, go ahead.'

'You see,' she continued, reaching into one of her desk drawers, 'with the cases we get, it's normally the women who suspect their husbands. They've found a phone number in a jacket, they've overheard a conversation. They might already have a name and just want us to collect conclusive evidence.'

'You think I might be overly suspicious?'

She lit up, blowing the smoke out of the side of her mouth. 'Maybe you're remarkably perceptive. Your wife hasn't spoken at length about anyone from work? You know, said so-and-so is funny, poor so-and-so's down on his luck, so-and-so was brilliant when he clinched the deal. Or' – her index finger struck out boldly – 'used to chat about some man-friend but now hardly mentions his name?'

'No,' said Leonard after a pause.

There was a knock at the door and a young, freckle-faced girl with ginger hair appeared. She was wearing a short skirt that displayed her long legs.

'Judy! Come in, take a seat. This is Mr Fleason. You haven't missed much. I'll bring you up to speed later.'

The girl, who looked about twenty, sat down next to Leonard and smiled coyly.

'Judy is one of my operatives in the field,' explained Hedda Marshall. 'She'll be handling your case if we reach an agreement, with me as the supervisor.'

Leonard was shifting in his chair, making various adjustments to his collar and tie. Telling one person his suspicions had been enough of an ordeal. Perhaps next a trolley lady would pop in and join the discussion.

Ms Marshall clearly felt compelled to defend her employee. 'Women, you know, in cases such as these, make much better investigators than their male counterparts. They can follow other women more easily – go to the toilet, look in their compacts while checking over their shoulder. The fact that Judy doesn't look like most people's idea of a private investigator is actually an advantage.'

'I see that, yes,' said Leonard. 'I was just hoping this interview was going to be kept as private as possible.'

'Everything you say will be treated with the strictest confidence. All my staff respect their clients' right to secrecy.'

Leonard nodded. The point she'd made about women investiga-tors was particularly convincing. Any Humphrey Bogart lookalike following Deborah would soon get found out.

Over the next few minutes he was asked a series of questions about Deborah's movements, the location of her office, her social activities. The irony was not lost on him that, whether or not she was seeing someone else, he was in effect making his own betrayal of their marriage. He also noticed that the two investigators, though sympathetic to his position, were trying to commit him to spending more money.

'You don't want your own privacy invaded?' Hedda Marshall queried, smiling.

'No, I don't.'

'I ask because some clients are open to the idea of having their telephones bugged.'

'No. Definitely not.'

'OK, fine.' She stubbed out her cigarette and reached for another one. 'You do realize, though, a lot of the work will involve shadowing your wife. If she's with you, it's more than likely we'll be trailing you both.'

'That's . . . fair enough.'

'Perhaps now is a good time to deal with costs.'

Outside on the pavement, Leonard mopped his brow. The humiliation! It felt as if he'd just taken down the top row of magazines at his local newsagent's, only to realize at the last minute that his mother was serving behind the counter. Hedda Marshall had said he could phone when he liked, and he had watched himself write out a deposit, but really he felt quite sick at heart. A year ago, a week ago, he'd never have dreamt of paying someone to spy on his wife, never imagined he could resort to such underhand tactics. Even now it wasn't too late to return to Hedda's office and say he'd changed his mind.

But no. The die had been cast. From almost nothing – an old jumper – events had acquired a momentum. For good or ill he had to know.

A little over a week later Leonard read HVM's report about his wife. His hands shook as they held the pages, smudging the margins, and his mouth moved in silent pronunciation of some of the words.

So that was it then, was it?
At last he had his answer.

4

The Way We Were (1973)

Before the advent of Deborah, Leonard had been married very happily to Shirley for twelve years. Their first encounter had taken place when Leonard, normally a careful driver, had backed into Shirley's car after seeing Wilde's *A Woman of No Importance* at the theatre. Climbing out of his vehicle to inspect the damage, he'd discovered, to add to his guilt, that the other driver used a walking stick to help her out of her seat.

He'd apologized profusely – there'd been some scratches and a small impression on the right rear of her car – but to his amazement she'd told him not to worry about it. With a queue of not-so-understanding motorists just wanting them to move, he'd insisted nonetheless on swapping details, assuring his fellow driver, despite her protests, to pay for any damage to her car. A week later he'd carried through on his promise *and* persuaded her – Shirley Bastable – to go out for a meal. It was hard to explain but never before had he felt such tender feelings for someone he'd just encountered . . .

Marriage, to Leonard's own incredulity, was soon under discussion – although Shirley was at pains to point out the implications. It turned out that her limp wasn't a temporary affair, that she'd recently been diagnosed with multiple sclerosis. To Leonard, of course, this was irrelevant. Advances in treating MS were being made all the time; in any case, he would take care of her, whatever the circumstances. In due course, however, the weakness of her legs was accompanied by problems with her eyesight and her speech. She also became tired easily – to the extent that, five years into their marriage, she was forced to give up her job and live at home. Shirley, as Leonard well knew, desperately wished to avoid being a burden; accepted with stoicism her physical limitations; did manage, for a time, to get by with help only from Leonard. Yet this relatively tranquil period, too, came to an end. It became necessary, eventually, to employ a part-time nurse to take care of her. Shirley, to her great embarrassment, had begun to suffer from incontinence. And, while Leonard tried his best to reassure her, privately he felt that her illness had advanced another step forward.

The cruellest blow, however, came from a totally unexpected source, precipitated by another car accident.

They were on their way home from the shops when a BMW had shot out of a one-way street the wrong way and crashed into the back of their car. (A split-second earlier and no doubt both of them would have died.) Their car, in consequence, had spun completely around and, by a process no one fully understood, ended up hugging a wall some distance away. Unharmed – yes, they might be – yet they were obviously in a severe state of shock. The other motorist, meanwhile, had driven off, leaving, as chance would have it, his number plate at the scene. Eventually the police were able to trace the owner. His story was that the car had been stolen.

In a way, though, it was academic. That night Shirley experienced her first epileptic fit. Leonard thought she was dying – her teeth were tightly clenched; her face had turned blue – and he'd rushed her to hospital, relieved beyond measure that by the time they arrived she'd recovered. According to the doctor, it was unusual for MS sufferers to suffer such a fit and, so far as he was aware, unprecedented for the attacks to be recurrent. No need, then, to worry unduly but, if necessary, if there was to be a future occasion, he would prescribe a course of drugs.

'Well, you can't say you're bored, can you, living with me?' Shirley had joked afterwards. And they'd gone home in the early hours, exhausted and shaken, 'to fight', as Shirley put it, 'another day'. Unfortunately, the next few days represented only a reprieve.

A week after her discharge from hospital, Shirley suffered a second seizure, followed, the next week, by a further two. Leonard was beginning to panic. Her body was so weak and these fits exerted such a vicious hold over her. Almost a month after the original accident, while they were watching the news on TV, Shirley let out a small cry, falling over to one side. Instead of pulling out of her convulsions, she seemed to go back in, again and again. . . .

Shirley was thirty-six when she died. After it was over, after the convulsions had ended, Leonard had held her limp body and smoothed the loose strands of her hair. Never to see her lovely smile again, to hear her lovely voice. Shirley, to him, had been everything, everything in the world. It seemed incredible, in hindsight, that he'd allowed twelve years to elapse without making more of their time together.

And now?

Well, what did life have to offer now?

Another three years passed before he met Deborah. The season of Christmas parties had arrived and he and his cronies, a small group of three, had been placed on the same table as *The Chronicle on CD-ROM*, a recent addition to the paper. His fellow partygoers were on the noisy side, but the atmosphere had stayed festive and, by the end of the evening, Leonard and his friend Andrew Dunstan were the last people remaining at the table. They were just making their way out when Leonard noticed a young woman slumped in a corner, legs stretched out before her, wearing a vacant expression. He lowered himself to her level and asked if she needed any help.

'They've all gone,' she said, almost to herself. 'They've just left me.'

He had ordered a taxi and with the help of Dunstan – nudging and winking away – they had negotiated her into the cab. Even then she seemed incapable of providing her address, and Leonard had climbed in beside her to interpret her ramblings. For most of the journey she had been huddled in a corner, tugging on her skirt to cover her legs, a habit that made Leonard, who had no intention of making any advances, feel quite sorry for her. She eventually alighted on the Fulham Road, leaving him to wend his way home.

That undoubtedly would have been that, but a few days later Deborah phoned up, thanked him for his kindness, and persuaded him to meet for lunch. She was totally different from how he remembered her: soberly dressed, far more upbeat. She assured him, wide-eyed, that she couldn't remember a thing from the party, but rejected his claim that she'd performed an impromptu striptease, ending only when she'd collapsed onto her boss's lap. She even laughed at that suggestion, and he found he was surprisingly disappointed when she mentioned she had a boyfriend. He quickly saw the lunch (as he had done originally) as a one-off event.

But she wouldn't let their new-found friendship pass by so easily and, early on in the new year, they went out again. And the following week, too – in fact, twice that week. Leonard found himself talking about things he hardly ever discussed, from the death of Shirley ('you poor thing') to his nervousness when talking on the radio ('but your voice is really sexy') and his wildest dreams on the career front ('yeah, go for it'). He hardly ever flirted with women, and yet with Deborah he seemed incapable of behaving in any other way.

Not that it wasn't strange being with someone else after Shirley. But, really, Deborah was quite different. Radical. She had ideas about feminism that after forty years on the planet changed his outlook on the world. He'd gone out and bought *The Second Sex* and was quite won over by its philosophy (although in Deborah's opinion Simone de Beauvoir was rather 'old hat'). Not only were things different in theory but also in practice. Whereas Shirley had let Leonard make most of the decisions, Deborah was more inclined to take control. She had her career, inhabiting a world connected, but quite dissimilar, to his. Although Shirley would always have a special place in his heart, Deborah had the power to make him look at life afresh. Her sense of humour, often at his expense, was also appealing.

Their lunchtime sessions developed into evening soirées, and then weekends away. Leonard discovered that the boyfriend was black – 'an experiment' as Deborah later termed it – and also that her father was Eddie Hornchurch, the gruff and dictatorial owner of the *Chronicle*. It appeared that Deborah owed her position as editorial director at *CCD* more than a little to his patronage. (When Leonard asked her how a CD-ROM was made, she replied, 'You get someone to do it for you, silly.')

Most incredibly of all, though, she obviously saw something in him. She seemed genuinely fascinated by his job, quizzing him about films and then making an effort to view his recommendations. She loved hearing stories about famous people he'd met and, unlike Leonard, loved being invited to parties and rubbing shoulders with the stars. Perhaps the single factor that advanced his cause more than any other was his assertion that if they were to have children, he would give up his job and become a house-husband. That a man could sacrifice himself this way – 'especially of your generation!' – she found quite remarkable (although the subject of children, funnily enough, was never seriously considered thereafter).

Another point in his favour, it appeared, was his house, a beautiful white-gabled pile in the Essex village of Quavering. Although not on a par with Deborah financially, Leonard had come into money through a landowning grandparent, and The Elms had been acquired upon his marriage to Shirley. The house was relatively remote, some way away from her set of friends, but Deborah loved the look of it and greatly admired the way it was kept, Leonard aided in this regard by the zealous Mrs Peavey.

And yet at no stage, despite these positive signals, did he feel confident the relationship would continue. After their first date it hadn't seemed possible she'd wish to go out with him again. But she had. Then it seemed absurd to think the relationship would continue for any length of time. But it had. Then the idea that Deborah would agree to marry him seemed quite preposterous. And she *hadn't* in point of fact, but only because *she* proposed to him first. Indeed, as Deborah expressed it, the only one to suffer from PMT – premarital tension – was himself. He could never quite overcome the idea he was betraying Shirley.

Everyone – his friends and hers – agreed that Leonard was a lucky man, his good fortune extending to the career front. At forty-one he was considered a little too old for a managerial role, but his writing talents were certainly treated with more benevolence. Within a couple of years he'd turned his back on the monolithic

Atex terminals with their unreadable green scrawl, endured by most of the other journalists, and was tapping away on a Pentium set up for him at home. The layout of his regular Friday column had also altered, bearing the slogan *Fleason on Film* together with a thumbnail picture of the author looking very boyish and thoughtful next to the by-line.

To be fair, this success, coinciding as it did with his propitious marriage, was not altogether a result of nepotism. Leonard had laboured away for several years now, achieving the respect of his fellow journalists and reading public alike. He enjoyed his work too, delighting especially in praising a film that might otherwise go unnoticed, being sure to name many of those involved in its production. On the surface at least, his life was near perfect, and certainly, only a few years before, he'd have been more than satisfied with his lot. . . .

And yet. . . .

And yet – incredible though it seemed – somehow it wasn't enough. Something was missing. It was just too cosy, too stultifying. Not quite what he'd visualized in his younger days. Perhaps he was having a midlife crisis – and that was the explanation – but, whatever the case, the fact remained that he wanted to break away from his current routine and start afresh.

Leonard wanted a bit more of a challenge.

5

Witness (1985)

Friday – the end of a slow week. With the afternoon to kill, Leonard was seated at his desk, answering letters sent into *Super8*, the magazine for which he contributed a do-it-yourself film-making column. The job at hand was not the most exciting and, in the last few minutes, he'd wandered off completely, recalling further moments of tension between Deborah and himself. Mrs Peavey was lurking somewhere – the desk faced outwards and she'd come into view occasionally – but her constant chatter had also faded into the background. Her refrain about this being the messiest room in the house wasn't one he would have taken issue with, anyway. Knick-knacks from various films filled two glass cabinets, ranging from a mock-up of a pistol used on a low-budget Brit flick to letters from such luminaries as Sir Alec G, congratulating Leonard on his wedding to Deborah. Reference books and magazines ran the length of one wall, many having to find space on the floor, and numerous collectables – puppets and props – lay in boxes or took up prominent positions on shelves. Above Leonard's desk were posters from *Sons of the Desert*, *The Shawshank Redemption* and *Double Indemnity* – 'You can't kiss away a murder!' Yet what did such possessions matter now? They were comfort symbols, that was all. Hardly a substitute for a happy marriage.

'*Heeeh*, heh, heh, heh, heh!'

Leonard shot up from his chair as a hideous old crone emerged from the other side of the desk, cackling wildly. His face had turned a dreadful pale and his eyes were wide with terror.

'Oh dear – oh dearie me! I got you that time, didn't I?'

Mrs Peavey removed her mask, revealing the old crone underneath, this one at least having the advantage of familiarity. Leonard had by now slumped back in his chair, his breath coming back in short gasps. His hands had instinctively raised themselves to his heart which in his mind's eye she was clutching in her outstretched claw, having plucked it from his chest.

'This is great, isn't it?' she said, holding up the mask. 'I was thinking I could borrow it for when the Jehovah's Witnesses call. Make 'em think the Second Coming's coming sooner than they expect. Heh, heh.'

'Heh,' Leonard added weakly.

'Are you OK now? I mean, you looked genuinely petrified.'

'I'm fine, thanks.'

'Wonderful film, though, didn't you think? *Snow White*.'

'Oh, well, yes.'

'What I would call good, wholesome family entertainment.'

'M'm. Although I believe Walt Disney used the studio to get away from his wife and child.'

Mrs Peavey stared at him for a second, then looked away, blowing her cheeks out in disgust.

'He took a big gamble with that film,' Leonard went on. 'He used a new multiplane camera, adding depth and detail. But it was hugely expensive.'

Mrs Peavey was still clearly experiencing her own train of thought.

'Clever tactic of hers,' she said, examining the mask once more. 'Poisoning that apple.'

'I suppose.'

'What is it about old people in films, d'you think?' She turned to face him. 'Why are they always depicted as mad or bad or just irrelevant?'

An avenue of conversation was opening up, but Leonard wasn't in a rush and he decided to give himself twenty minutes. As something of an amateur critic, Mrs Peavey had seen a lot of films and was never less than entertaining in her views. He'd even enlisted her help with research in the past, asking her to pop down to the library. She was extremely helpful, almost too helpful.

'I mean, the older woman has a lot to offer,' she averred, hitching up her bulky brassiere with no apparent irony. 'They've got more insight, more experience. D'you know what I think?'

And we're off.

'I think . . .'

Half an hour later she was still going strong, in a conversation that had taken in *Arsenic and Old Lace*, *Harold and Maude* and *Driving Miss Daisy*. In the meantime, Leonard had actually forgotten about his own dilemma, grateful for the distraction. That was the trouble with working mainly from home. Being alone meant you were more likely to dwell on your own problems. . . .

Leonard gazed at the manila envelope in front of him.

He had driven to Colchester to collect the report, coughing up the fee without question, returning home with the letter unopened. Throughout the week he had resisted the temptation to phone the agency, unwilling to reveal his true anxiety, and when Ms Marshall had handed him their report (her own expression conveying nothing), his ignorance had helped him remain remarkably suave.

But now it had come, the moment of truth. And, acutely aware of the terrible knowledge lying at his fingertips, he found himself strangely reluctant to take the plunge. A minute at least was spent in silent contemplation.

Then, resolutely pursing his lips and taking a deep breath, as if he were about to take an underwater dive, he took out the letter opener and ripped through the crease, pulling out the four pages cloistered inside.

Dear Mr Fleason
This is the report you requested into your wife's movements during the week, 25 April—2 May. The information contained within this document is not fully comprehensive – additional evidence, photos, receipts, etc. (not included in the original spec.), are available at HVM's offices for a small charge – but the findings below represent the task as commissioned. If you

are unhappy about any aspect of the investigation, or would like more background about the knowledge obtained, please do not hesitate to call us. A list of expenses has been attached and any enquiries about costings and future commissions would be welcomed.

We have determined that, as you suspect, your wife is almost certainly seeing another man. It has been impossible to ascertain the exact level of intimacy, but it would seem that for the last two to three months she has been meeting up with this gentleman outside work. The man's name is Nicholas Lasker and he works as an instructor at his brother's gym, Tiptop, in Phelan Street. During the week she was under surveillance, your wife visited the gym on Monday, Wednesday and Friday evening, and on two occasions, Wednesday and Friday, she stayed on with Mr Lasker. It seems likely that a couple of your wife's work colleagues are aware of the situation. The rest of the week she went directly home.

Mr Lasker is tall, about 6' 3", with short, slicked-back blond hair and blue eyes. He dresses in designer clothes, drives a black BMW, and lives in a converted farmhouse just outside Wickford with his older brother, Vincent. He is twenty-five, single, with apparently no previous marriages behind him.

On Wednesday Mrs Fleason left her office, accompanied by another woman, arriving at Tiptop just after seven. In order to maintain surveillance of the suspect it was necessary to obtain trial membership of the gym for a month (see expenses). Mrs Fleason and her friend worked out for the next forty minutes and then retired to the bar where they were joined by Lasker shortly after eight. The girlfriend left as soon as she had finished her drink, and the other two carried on for the next hour. He stroked her hair twice and held her hand, discreetly, for the last five minutes. They separated with a peck on the lips, him driving off and her gazing around with a worried expression, presumably checking to see if anyone was watching.

The following lunchtime the friend of your wife's visited the gym on her own, and the operative was able to engage her in conversation. Having gained her confidence, the operative professed her admiration for one of the instructors, 'the blond one'. This produced quite a chuckle, the friend saying that every red-blooded woman fancied him. The operative then said that she'd heard he was seeing some married woman. This produced an immediate reaction. 'Where had she heard that?' The operative thought she'd overheard it some time ago. 'Well, it hasn't been going on for all that long,' was the reply. A lot of details were consequently revealed. A friend of hers was having an affair with Lasker. The woman in question was married but 'the romance had drifted out of her life'. The operative told her confidante to warn her friend to be more careful but was informed it was quite hopeless, that she had tried. The woman was 'gone' (i.e. besotted).

The next day, Friday, Mrs Fleason visited the gym in the early evening with another friend, again waiting for the arrival of Lasker at the bar. This time the three of them stayed for only one more drink, your wife being the first to leave after a couple of anxious glances at her watch.

Mr Fleason, we regret having to confirm your fears in this matter. It's not often we express an opinion on such issues, but it would seem that your wife is consorting with a man she possibly knows very little about. The brothers Lasker seem quite interesting characters and from preliminary enquiries would seem to have some rather dubious confederates. If you would like us to make further investigations on your behalf, we would be more than happy to oblige.

It just remains to add that this report represents the facts as HVM are best acquainted with them at the present time. Any inaccuracies or exaggerations are the result of genuine misinterpretation and not the desire to mislead or deceive. HVM have not been working for any of the persons named in this report concurrent to the present investigation.

Yours sincerely
Hedda Marshall
Judy Taylor

Leonard looked up from the report, his basset-like eyes staring blankly ahead. For the past week or so he'd thought about this moment, preparing himself for the absolute worst. But now – confronted by reality – it was obvious he'd been holding out hope of another explanation. His face showed a dreadful grey pallor and a sick feeling gnawed away at his insides. Seven years they'd been together. Five of them married. In the space of a few minutes his life appeared pointless and empty.

He glared round the living-room, infested as it was with the spirit of Deborah. Staring at him in the most inscrutable fashion was the porcelain cat next to the hearth. It was a white, life-size figure, bought as a wedding present by Deborah's parents, with large almond-shaped eyes. He'd never liked the thing, but now it seemed more pleased with itself than ever, positively sneering at him, in on the secret. It wasn't a proper cat at all, not like Ollie with his low-slung torso and revoltingly bad breath. It was false, superior, flealess.

He needed to escape from the house. Everything reminded him of her and it was impossible to get his mind in any sort of order. Most of the rooms contained mirrors, inviting comparisons between himself and the new man in her life, and it was too tempting to take to the bottle or retreat to the bedroom in an attempt to find sleep. . . .

Donning his coat, he walked, almost in a trance, up to the shops. Why was Deborah seeing this other man? Why? He'd never been unkind or nasty towards her. True, their social life had tailed off a little since the *Chronicle* had set him up at home, but then that was hardly his fault, was it? Other film critics – he was by no means the first – worked from home. Anthony Lane even managed to work for *The New Yorker* while still living in England. And in any case, Deborah, whenever he'd suggested going out, had usually rejected the idea, saying she'd prefer it if he rustled up a meal instead. (After Shirley's death Leonard had enrolled on a cordon bleu cookery course.) Indeed, Deborah had her own circle of friends whose company she seemed to prefer. He'd wanted to join them, get involved in their concerns, but Deborah had effectively shut him out. He wasn't sure any longer about her brand of feminism. She seemed to believe in a division of the sexes. Whatever she said to the contrary, she wanted men to be men, while she on the other hand could behave how she liked.

Leonard stopped in the middle of the high street. (He had been pacing up and down for the last half an hour.) This would not do. He actually agreed with his wife on most issues. It was hard, but he would have to accept some of the blame for the present state of affairs. His dedication to his job, for example, was obviously a problem, watching up to fifteen films a week. A film required a lot of effort and he felt he owed it to all those involved, in spite of the time constraints, to provide a fair assessment of their work. Also, living and working in close proximity to the fridge had meant he'd started to put on weight. He had settled into his new lifestyle far too comfortably, automatically assuming that Deborah must be happy.

She had loved him a few years ago, she must have. So why couldn't she feel the same way again? Hopefully this business with the gym instructor was just an infatuation. (Leonard didn't want to think about *him* if possible.) For Carol, if it was her, to say that Deborah was 'gone', could just be a friend excited by the cloak-and-dagger nature of the affair. In any case, what if the investigator, Judy, had witnessed Deborah and Lasker's relationship at its most intense and nothing else had happened to place their relationship on a higher – in other words lower – footing? Saying that Deborah was 'almost certainly' but not definitely having an affair only prolonged the agony. It meant that he'd have to wait a little longer to resolve his fears.

Whatever the outcome, though, he had learnt his lesson. He would behave differently; make a fight of it. His decision to employ HVM had been made with a guilty conscience, but now that it appeared more justified, there was no reason not to turn his recently acquired knowledge to advantage. On his way home he bought some flowers. A plan was starting to take shape in his mind.

6

Blow Out (1981)

'So what's the deal, then, Leonard? First, the flowers, then you take me out to dinner. I'm starting to get worried.'

'What about?' he asked, smiling lamely.

'Well – you know! I'm beginning to wonder if you're angling for something, some sort of favour.'

He gazed at her for a second, organizing his thoughts. He could, of course, confront her about her overfamiliarity with another man. But that wasn't Leonard's style. In the first place he was embarrassed about revealing how he'd garnered the information about Lasker. And, secondly, he still hadn't ascertained the exact nature of their relationship. Perhaps the years of being a film critic had taken their toll and he was now, without thinking, a watcher.

'I just thought it'd make a change, that's all. One last blow-out before I get fit.'

A smirk appeared on her face, turning into a fully fledged laugh.

'You!' Another bout of guffawing. 'You . . . fit!'

'Yes – me . . . Mr Blobby.'

'Oh dear, I'm sorry.' She recovered herself. 'You mustn't spring these things on me.'

'We have a laugh, don't we?'

'So what d'you intend to do then? Go jogging three times a week? Do lots of sit-ups, that kinda thing?'

'Actually, I thought I could work out with you.'

That changed her mood. Her cheeks flushed ever so slightly in the dim light of the restaurant and she seemed to take longer chewing her food. It was ironic, but he felt more attracted to her than ever. She'd put on her Elizabeth Arden lipstick, particularly suiting her complexion, and he was fascinated by the sight of her lips moving. Perhaps in light of recent events she'd assumed a more independent, free-spirited air. Or possibly she'd acquired a more vulnerable quality, now that he possessed certain damaging information. In any event, she was undoubtedly hurting him, every one of her remarks fraught with meaning.

'Well, yeah, that'd be great – if you're serious. But you wouldn't wanna go into London all the time, would you?'

'I might. Or you could change gyms. Give up your London gym and come with me to the sports centre in Filchester.'

She looked at him quizzically, perhaps wondering if he was pulling her leg.

'Yeah, I'd like that. Thing is, I'm on a strict programme at the moment. Also, my membership doesn't expire for another nine months.'

'H'm. Yes, I see.' He pondered this seemingly insoluble dilemma. 'In that case, how about me spending a month at this club of yours, see how I feel? These places normally offer a discount for a trial period, don't they?'

She sat back, looking at him curiously. For a couple of seconds she was lost for words.

'You don't often surprise me, Leonard, but – well, once in a while . . .'

'H'm.'

Did she expect him to admit he was predictable? He sipped his red wine – his regular tipple on their evenings out – and continued, 'I just think it's time I got fit. I've been letting myself go recently. And, besides, exercise is meant to help with . . . you know . . . my problem.'

He glanced around at the neighbouring tables to see whether anyone was listening. This was not a subject he wanted to broadcast publicly. For the last few months he had suffered from recurring bowel troubles; in particular, he had been waylaid by constipation. It was a mystery how this state of affairs had arisen – Leonard not wanting to attribute it to age or decreasing mobility – but it had proved most irritating and not a little painful. His first stab at improving the situation had involved going on a high-fibre diet and imbibing lots of liquids. But the 'problem', as it was referred to, had not been entirely eradicated, and he'd eventually turned to the medically-minded Deborah for support. It was strange, but he still found the subject embarrassing, even with her. Nevertheless, it represented a perfectly valid reason to visit the gym.

'What problem?'

He didn't reply immediately and she suddenly realized what he was talking about.

'Oh, *that*.' She gave a cursory wave of her hand. 'You know what to do about that, Leonard. Take that magnesium hydroxide I bought you.' She leant forward. 'The chemist told me if you were all bunged up down there, that'd soon blow it open.'

He glanced around the restaurant again, feeling slightly queasy. She seemed to delight in such language and he found that he'd rather lost his appetite. He drew the conversation back to the subject of their working out together, and she eventually agreed to 'give it a try'.

Stage one had been achieved, without much difficulty.

'Good,' he added. 'We'll start tomorrow evening.'

The next morning Leonard made another trip to Colchester. When Hedda Marshall had alluded in her report to strange goings-on where the Laskers were concerned, he was quite aware she was dangling a carrot in front of him. However, the temptation to rake up some dirt about this friend of his wife's was just too much to resist, and he'd phoned Ms Marshall to arrange to meet and discuss terms. Now that the initial step with HVM had been taken, he felt more assured about his actions. He wouldn't use the detective agency to investigate Deborah any more, but in the case of the Lasker brothers, if they were really up to no good, it could even be argued he was performing a public duty.

In Ms Marshall's office he was quite startled when she opened one of her desk drawers and handed him a bundle of papers and photographs. On the top was a picture of a young man stepping out from the doorway of a house. He stared fixedly at the image, the face burnt into his brain. So this was *him*. He'd forgotten that

HVM had held onto some of the evidence.

Then, aware that he was being studied in turn by Ms Marshall, he forced himself to look up. This was no time to become maudlin.

'You said in your report that this, er, Lasker had some rather dubious associates.'

Even when he wasn't looking at the photograph he could still picture the face, the face that Deborah must know so well. Lasker looked so young, so . . . *virile*.

Hedda Marshall folded her arms. 'Yeah, going on some of the clientele he sees at the gym. Two of them at least are ex-cons. It's his brother, though, who seems on best terms with them. I'm guessing, but drugs could be involved. There's quite a business in steroids these days. Perhaps Nick, or Vince at any rate, is dabbling as a supplier or user. Up to you if you want us to check. . . .'

By the time he'd left HVM, the photograph tucked into his jacket pocket, Leonard had submitted to nearly all of Ms Marshall's suggestions. There was really no other choice. Recent events had demonstrated that, for better or worse, he was still devoted to his wife. She was part of his life, now and for always. The investigation would continue over the next month as a low priority, for a much smaller sum per day, concentrating on Lasker and his activities. The investigators would look into his job history, financial transactions, his whole statistical life.

The only sticking-point between them, in fact, was when Leonard mentioned he was going to Lasker's gym that evening, the PI querying whether that was altogether wise.

Leonard, though, insisted that he wanted to see things for himself.

7

Help! (1965)

Leonard, in fact, hadn't quite turned his back on the metropolis, attending press screenings at least once a week. Aside from the films themselves, these occasions were interesting for their insight into the world of his fellow film critics. Here were a group of people who'd gather in darkened rooms, each with his or her idiosyncrasies, some scribbling away for most of the film, some eating constantly (the rate of mastication depending on what was happening on screen), many of them insistent on sitting in a particular seat they saw as their own. Actually, you could set a camera up above the screen and learn a lot about human nature by focusing on this small band of people-watchers. What a critic thought of a film often revealed more about the critic himself, and these people weren't silent about their preferences, either. They gave themselves away in sighs and moans, the ultimate snub of calling somebody on the phone during a screening not unheard-of.

Would such a film – recording the groans and grimaces of those used to anonymity – be immoral? Well, the British government and police clearly didn't rate privacy highly in their battle against crime. Leonard recalled reading how Britain, with its four million surveillance cameras, was the most-watched nation in the world. Michael Howard, former Home Secretary, was, it seemed, primarily responsible for this situation. In the face of political opposition (but little opposition from a public stunned by shots of two-year-old Jamie Bulger being led away from a shopping mall to his death in 1993), he'd introduced government funding for CCTV. While Germany, Canada and other countries banned filming people on the street, Londoners, apparently, could now expect to be captured on CCTV up to 300 times daily. In addition, an estimated 70 per cent of CCTV camera operators, according to civil rights groups, were breaking the rules.

So Leonard, if he became serious about this clandestine film, would probably have to put up a sign to warn his fellow critics (though how big did the print have to be in this sign?). It was also interesting, he supposed, to speculate what his idea said about him and his current frame of mind. Control – yes: perhaps he felt he was losing control over his life. But not only that, looking at things purely from a professional standpoint, weren't there undeniable advantages to a covert approach? What better way, after all, to capture authentic emotion than to film someone in secret? That was certainly the view adopted by Norman Lear on the set of *Cold Turkey*. Unhappy about the reactions displayed by a crowd of extras, the director staged a fight with his star, Dick Van Dyke. As he screamed at Van Dyke, calling him stupid and incompetent, the cameras were rolling, capturing the stunned expressions of the onlookers, their astonishment growing when Van Dyke responded in similar fashion. Both men then suddenly stopped and smiled, Lear explaining that the argument had just been a ruse.

Sitting on Leonard's lap as he took the train into London was a bag with his PE kit inside, together with a copy of the *Chronicle*. He'd intended to read the paper during the journey, but the words blurred as soon as he looked at them and he found himself taking heavy breaths. Somehow he had to place his emotions on hold, analyse events later. Perhaps his baleful influence might even bring a dose of much needed reality to proceedings. Deborah and Lasker could hardly be misty-eyed young lovers in his presence.

It was unlikely, though, that he'd score any points. After all, he was entering his enemy's territory, a domain with which he was completely unfamiliar. Moreover, Deborah would probably be on the other man's side. She didn't want Leonard to come in the first place. She'd have warned her boyfriend in advance and assured him that Leonard's visit was just a one-off.

Things had built themselves up so much in his mind that, before leaving, he'd phoned Andrew Dunstan, who worked in the building next to Deborah's, and asked him to go to Tiptop with him – an invitation that had been politely declined. However, he was loath to leave it at that and, instead of going straight to the gym, he set forth in the direction of Chronicle House to speak to Dunstan again. He could stand it no longer. He had to tell someone else of his predicament, someone who actually knew Deborah and could provide impartial advice.

He showed his pass at the front desk and caught the lift to the fourth floor. The business, sport and features departments were on the third floor, home and overseas on this one. A minute later he was in a huge open-plan room, bustling with people. To his left, a bank of clocks told the time in various countries and, within view, six televisions stood on high shelves, tuned into various news channels. At 4.15 a sense of crisis was already in the air. Journalists punched away at their keyboards, squinting at their monitors, wrapped up in their own deadlines.

Andrew Dunstan's desk was at the other end of the room, and Leonard weaved his way along the aisles, exchanging a wave with the political editor, Cliff Jenkins, and acknowledging the greetings of two or three others who paused in their labours. He was just passing the pigeon-holes, guarded over by a gaggle of messengers, when he heard his name being called. He turned round to find he'd been joined by the tall, gawky figure of Sue Latchford, his replacement in the paper when he was away on holiday.

'Hel-lo, this is a surprise. It's lovely to see you.' She beamed at him, her outsize eyes peering through a pair of thick glasses.

'And you,' he replied, before explaining he'd come in to see Andrew Dunstan about going to the gym.

'You mean. . . ?'

'Yes, I'm going to the gym.'

'The gym?'

'Yes – that's right. You know, this conversation reminds me of the one I had with Deborah.'

'I'm sorry, Leonard. I didn't mean . . .'

'It's perfectly OK. I'm beginning to think only people in the peak of fitness actually go to gyms.'

'I mean, I wasn't referring to your . . .'

'Portliness?'

'Your physique, I was going to say. I just thought – well, you know – you were into more intellectual pursuits.'

'Ah, well!' he shrugged amiably. 'Actually, Sue, I was going to pay *you* a compliment. You know that review of yours – the one given my by-line by mistake? Well, my next-door neighbour said it was the best thing I'd written for years.'

She coloured violently. 'No! No, you're joking, she didn't really, did she? I don't have your range, your – your anecdotal approach.'

'Well, according to Mrs Peavey, it was a relief to read something of mine that was mature and perceptive, not guilty of my usual facetiousness.'

She was speechless, wringing her fingers.

'So if you ever need a reference . . .' he added.

He'd actually made up the comment about her article – Mrs Peavey *had* mentioned the write-up in favourable, if not quite so lavish, terms – but it was a harmless exaggeration. Since he was getting more and more used to deception, there was no reason not to use the technique for positive ends.

'Stop – stop it!' she remonstrated. 'Let's move onto something else. I don't believe a word of it!'

'OK, then, tell me what I'm supposed to be doing.'

'Well.' She collected herself. 'It's funny, Leonard, I was just about to give you a call. William spoke to me this morning. He wants to know whether you fancy a trip to California.'

'Oh, yes?'

'Not for a while, though. Not until you've recovered from Cannes. The Eastwood film about the female boxer. It starts shooting in June and he was hoping somehow you could muck in – perhaps spar a few rounds with the female lead.'

'I'll send you my story from intensive care.'

'He was hoping also you could talk to Clint.'

'Okey-doke.'

'And of course Morgan Freeman as well. Apparently, people trust you – or so William was telling me. You always get the inside info.'

Leonard laughed.

'Also,' she went on, 'I got a call from the University of Essex – they're organizing a film weekend. They were hoping you could give a talk about the film critic's role.'

'Right, OK.' They confirmed dates and times, before Leonard added, 'Being a film critic, eh? It's all about getting the inside info.'

Dunstan was on the phone with his back to Leonard when he reached his desk, his dog's-tooth check jacket draped over his chair. Although he hadn't seen much of Dunstan lately, the other had been best man at Leonard's wedding to Deborah, and the two went back a good fifteen years. Their paths had first crossed at a meeting of the Multiple Sclerosis Society, Andrew's wife, Chloe, suffering from the disease as well.

On the desk was a picture of the couple, Chloe seated in a wheelchair, beaming into the camera. Everyone liked the crime correspondent, his jovial manner, his rather chummy way of speaking. In spite of his wife's condition and the effect on his own life, he'd somehow managed to retain a youthful optimism.

He turned round, acknowledging Leonard with the flick of an index finger from a hand that was clutching a styrofoam cup of coffee.

'Yes, I know, I know. But if you can't find it, it won't just be your knackers on the block, old son. It'll be mine. Look in old-fea or even old-news. Some bugger might have binned it by mistake. . . . Yeah. . . . Yeah.' He looked up at Leonard. 'OK, Phil. Gotta go. This is vital, remember. OK, bye.'

He replaced the receiver in its cradle. 'One of my juniors has just lost a story for the pull-out tomorrow.' He shook his head in mock-despair. 'Anyway, Lenny, what brings you here? Not this gym business, I hope?'

Leonard cleared his throat. 'Can I talk to you, Andrew . . . in private?'

The other regarded him for a second, then stood up. 'Fifteen minutes? Canteen? You've caught me at a sticky moment, I'm afraid.' He reached for his jacket and led the way back to the lift.

This was definitely a good move. Dunstan had faced several crises in his life and been absolutely wonderful when Shirley had died. Leonard's only quibble about him, in fact, was his tendency to discourse on every subject as if he were an authority. But there were times, like the present, when he actually wanted to be put right.

In the lift he brought Leonard up to date with all the goings-on inside the paper, the temper tantrums, the sackings, and kept this up until they were facing each other in the canteen.

'So what's up then, old mate? You look a bit concerned.'

Leonard looked round to make sure no one else was within earshot. 'I think Deborah might be having an affair.'

Dunstan's face fell and he blinked a couple of times.

'I think,' Leonard added, 'she might be seeing somebody from her gym.'

Dunstan frowned, running his hand through his hair. 'No. . . .'

Leonard nodded grimly. He began explaining about the jumper – receiving a 'Very strange' from his companion – then with some hesitation spoke about how he'd hired a detective agency to spy on his wife.

'Are you insane?' Dunstan's elbows were on the table and his hands were massaging his face. If it wasn't colleagues at work losing stories, it was friends hiring private investigators. 'That's awful. That's appalling. How could you?' He was looking at Leonard as if he were seeing him in a new light.

Leonard gave a shrug. He hadn't yet mentioned his visit to HVM that morning and his authorization of more investigative work.

'Listen to me. I know this is all a bit confusing.' Dunstan scratched his head. 'But I really think, you know, you should have a word with Deborah. I mean, this hand-holding business. She's always been touchy-feely, your wife.'

'But what about the lies?'

'Well, what about them? Are you saying you never look at other women? Every marriage has its secrets. That's normal, healthy even. Let's assume for a moment Deborah *is* flirting a little. So what? It's probably just a bit of fun.'

'A bit of fun. . . .'

Leonard toyed with the words, trying and failing to give them an innocent context.

'Anyway,' persisted Dunstan, 'what's he look like, this bloke?

We'll soon knock this on the head.'

'Robert Redford's face in his younger days, with Jean-Claude van Damme's body.'

'There you go, then.'

'There I go . . . what?'

'Not her type, is he? She's into mature men.'

'Maybe.'

'Men with a bit more intelligence.'

'Thanks.'

'Men who can make her laugh.'

'Cheers.'

'As far as she's concerned, it's neither here nor there what you look like.'

Leonard frowned. 'Why, what do I look like?'

'I don't know. Just not like Robert Redford or Jean-Claude van Damme.'

'More like a horse's behind, you mean?'

'No, no, of course not. You always have to go to extremes. Look, let's say you and this bloke were dogs. Well, he'd be some thoroughbred greyhound, and you'd be a mangy old mutt with fleas who's been in the family for years.'

'Thanks for clearing that up,' said Leonard.

'What I'm saying is that she loves you. Think of all the years you've been together. Deborah's very loyal, you know. Ever since I've known her, she's always been wedded to the paper, almost as much as to you. I can't imagine her letting her parents down like that.'

'I suppose.'

'Besides, isn't she a Catholic?'

'True.'

In fact, Deborah only attended church on special occasions, and her religious inclinations certainly hadn't dissuaded her from holding feminist views – or taking the pill for that matter. But Leonard had a vague recollection that Dunstan was a Catholic himself and didn't want to offend him.

The other man had made up his mind. There was some mistake. The detective agency had got it wrong. Who, in any case, was she sleeping with every night? (Another good point.) He got Leonard to promise not to hire any more investigators, otherwise *he* might start to get paranoid. The thing to do was to talk to Deborah.

'I have been worrying too much,' Leonard said, as much to himself as to Dunstan. 'Sorry to bother you like this. You've been a brick.'

Dunstan opened his arms expansively in a 'don't mention it' expression, his attention diverted to the short skirt of a young girl passing their table. Although he had a roving eye, Leonard knew his friend cared deeply for his invalid wife.

' 'Least I know now why you wanted me at this gym,' said Dunstan, his gaze returning to Leonard.

'You still don't want to go?'

'No need, see.' He patted his midriff, which admittedly did look quite trim. 'Hey, you're not planning to confront this bloke, are you? Challenge him to an arm wrestling contest?'

'No, not at all. Just, you know, check him out.'

'Huh! Well, don't overdo it, he's probably gay.' He gave a little wink; his small eyes always looked as if they were laughing. (Deborah called them 'twinkly'.) 'Jesus, gotta dash,' he said, glancing at his watch. 'Good luck, old mate.'

He grabbed his jacket, rose from the table, and in a few moments was gone, leaving Leonard alone with his thoughts.

8

Pumping Iron (1977)

Outside the gym Leonard noted the presence of two BMWs, the registration plates displaying the legends, 'N1 CKO and 'V1 NCE'. Ever since the accident that had brought about Shirley's epilepsy, he'd developed an aversion, whether logical or not, to BMW owners. (He was quite sure the driver that day was the same man who'd claimed his car had been stolen.) Part of him as well had been hoping that Lasker wouldn't be around, that Deborah would have warned him away. . . . But – well, if it wasn't to be. . . .

The gym was situated in a small court of office apartments, quite near Gloucester Road tube station. Leonard filled in a couple of forms at the reception desk, signed a check for £45, and asked if Nick could be his trainer. (He'd heard good things about him.) Then he made his way along a balcony, overlooking a large room full of heaving, sweating bodies, to the changing-rooms. A few minutes later he'd reached the most naked state of his changing ritual – shirt on, trousers off – when he was accosted from behind.

'Mr Fleason?'

He looked round, and up, extremely startled.

'Hi, I'm Nick.' A young man in a T-shirt and trainer bottoms flashed his teeth at him. 'I'll wait outside for you.'

'Uh,' said Leonard in vague agreement. He hastily climbed into his Fred Perry tennis shorts. Lasker's intervention – their first meeting – showed him to be a cool customer if nothing else. Leonard had tried valiantly to shut out his nerves on entering the

52

building and getting changed, but now the butterflies had returned in force to his stomach. What exactly was he hoping to achieve by all this?

He left the room and discovered the other man outside. Lasker was flicking through Leonard's forms.

'All set then?'

He was chewing gum and Leonard noticed a gold chain around his neck. Tucking his clipboard under his arm, Lasker led the way along the corridor. On either side of them were saunas, steam rooms, solariums, spa pools, every modern convenience. They passed into the main amphitheatre.

To Leonard it looked like a modern torture chamber. The Nautilus machine had replaced the rack, the standing calf machine had replaced the pillory, but the real development in the last few decades was that people voluntarily subjected themselves to these forms of pain (before checking the results in the wall-to-wall mirrors). Incongruously, TV sets were placed at various vantage points, tuned to *The Hits* channel.

They walked across the maple-sprung floor to a warm-up area in one corner. Lasker seemed very casual, almost uninterested, speaking in a quiet Essex accent. One of his front teeth was slightly chipped but otherwise Leonard was hard-pressed to spot any other imperfections. A habit of pronouncing the word 'thing' with an 'f' but Deborah probably found this characteristic quaint. HVM had said in their report that he was dishy or words to that effect, and Leonard, who wasn't an expert on male beauty, was going to have to accept that fact. Did Lasker know he was Deborah's – Mrs Fleason's – husband for God's sake? If he *did* know, he was certainly not letting on. Arms akimbo, chin raised, he was peering down on his pupil, explaining about safety and how, before lifting any weights, it was important to do a series of stretching and loosening exercises.

Leonard was instructed to carry out knee bends, press-ups, squats, and all the time his supervisor looked completely unruf-fled, seemingly unaware of the irony in the situation. At one point, while Leonard was doing some sit-ups and Lasker was holding his ankles, one of the female instructors came over and struck up a conversation with him. It was all a little unnerving. Rather than treat him as a rival, the other man apparently believed, because of his physical prowess, in his own superiority.

Their next move was to go over to something called a power jogger. This could be set to various speeds and, after a small discussion, it was set to slow. Leonard found this very difficult to adapt to, seeming to take as much mental as physical effort. It was too fast for him to walk at a normal pace but too slow for him to run, and he found himself indulging in a sort of shuffle that looked as if his laces were tied together. It was at this point that he noticed Deborah (nearly falling off in the process).

She was on the other side of the room, looking very natty in a black-and-white striped leotard and black tights, sporting a matching headband. Alongside her was a friend. They both seemed quite involved in what they were doing.

'How d'you . . . stop this thing again?' he wheezed.

Lasker stepped forward and instructed Leonard to grip the parallel bars while he pressed a button.

'My wife's over there . . . with her friend,' he said between gasps. 'You don't mind if we pop over, do you? Won't take a minute.'

He led the way through the maze of heavy metal. He could see Deborah look up from watching her friend on the rowing machine. Her mouth dropped as she noticed who was beside him, and she blushed fiercely.

'Hi, Deborah.' He kissed her on the cheek. 'This is Nick. I believe you two know each other.'

The friend stopped rowing. Lasker and Deborah gazed at each other. The former smiled serenely.

'Everything OK?'

'Yeah, fine. So how's my husband? You haven't killed him yet?'

Lasker's smile broadened. 'Nah, we're taking it easy.'

Leonard was introduced to the friend, Carol ('the romance had drifted . . .'?), but he was perturbed to see Deborah had already recovered her composure. She had tied her hair in a short ponytail but a couple of strands had come undone and fell across her face. Every few seconds she brushed them back.

'So how's it going, Leonard?' she asked. 'Had enough yet?'

'I came over because I thought *you* might need a breather.'

'Ha! I'll survive.'

'I already feel it's doing some good.' He stretched his arms in extravagant fashion. 'Ooh – that's better. The old quadrupeds.'

This garnered a laugh from the assembled company.

'So,' said Carol, turning to the instructor, 'when can you next work your magic on me?'

'You've already had your introductory session,' said Lasker.

'Have *I* had my introductory session?' asked Deborah teasingly. 'I can't remember.'

She and Lasker exchanged a smile.

'Well, anyway,' said Leonard, breaking into this 'look'. 'It's *my* session right now. I think my gluteus maximus needs attention.'

Another laugh greeted this remark, though this time it owed more to Lasker's bemused reaction. Leonard said his goodbyes and trudged off, the other following on behind. Lasker hadn't seemed at all bothered by the interruption and, as for Deborah, she'd seemed . . . well, excited almost, like a little girl. It didn't help that she was looking quite lovely in her body-hugging outfit.

9

Pumping Iron II: The Women (1985)

They continued in a circle around the room, the women tracking them from the opposite end, trying out one piece of apparatus after another. Leonard was sweating now and took his glasses off between exercises to run his handkerchief over his forehead. Somewhat ridiculously he'd been trying too hard to impress Lasker – at one point on the bench press it felt as if he'd burst a blood vessel in his head – and he very much wanted to end this folly. Punishing his body to alleviate the mental anguish was never going to work.

'Are we done yet?' he asked.

'Well, we could do one or two more exercises. Depends how you feel.'

At death's door, now that you mention it. 'Next time, maybe. I really fancy a drink.'

'The snack bar's over there.' Lasker pointed to a spot along the balcony.

'Perhaps I could buy you one after I get changed? Just a quickie, I know you're busy.'

'Yeah, all right,' said Lasker after a moment's hesitation.

'Great. I'll just tell my wife.'

It would have been easy for the other to refuse but perhaps he felt secure in his position. Or just curious. Leonard walked over to Deborah and Carol, his spindly legs barely able to support his huge, flabby, grotesquely out-of-shape body. Having arranged for the three of them to meet up afterwards – he neglected to mention they'd be joined by Lasker – he retired to the changing-room. He sat down and almost instantly the room started to swim. Quick, toilet, now. For the next ten minutes he was leaning over the bowl, fully expecting to become reacquainted with his last meal. Why, oh why, had he eaten before leaving home? After lots of deep breaths he finally felt assured enough to leave the toilet.

This really was the limit. His body was losing its vitality, its parts rusting over, while another man's operated with greased efficiency. He had a shower and then got dressed. Looking at it another way, even if he lived to the age of ninety-two, he was already halfway there. He was, in a manner of speaking, half-dead already.

Deborah and Carol were waiting for him in the bar.

'God, Leonard, what took you so long? You been sick or something? You don't look well.'

She could talk. Her face was bright red, a beacon, as if all the red corpuscles were screaming for help on the surface of her skin.

'I'm fine, just fine. Can I get you another one?'

'Yeah, two more OJs would be good.'

He looked over at Carol, who nodded. She had large, imploring eyes and long dark hair, the fringe streaked with purple. He went to the bar, feeling as if he was the father of two independent-minded daughters with their own private secrets, and that he was somehow intruding. . . .

He returned with *four* orange juices, at virtually the same time as Lasker approached the table. 'Your husband asked me to join you,' he said by way of explanation.

They sat down, Leonard opposite Carol, and Nick opposite Deborah, and after a hesitation began talking about fitness. Carol for the first few minutes couldn't get over the other man's muscles, even asking at one point if she could 'cop a feel', a huge biceps plonked obligingly across the table.

Leonard was disturbed to find he was still taking heavy breaths. His recovery rate was slow to say the least. Beads of sweat were sliding down his forehead and, having left his handkerchief in his shorts, he was having to improvise with his hand. Not only that, but sitting down was making him feel nauseous once more. He was beginning to burp, very quietly, but attracting the odd frown from Carol.

Deborah was talking to Nick about her thighs. He was recommending that she was experienced enough to go beyond one exercise per body part and do two for areas in which she thought she was weak. Performing the lying side leg raise, for instance, as well as the standing side leg raise.

It was difficult for Leonard, in spite of the circumstances, to concentrate on what they were saying. He felt left out, the long-forgotten feeling of being back at school among confederates whose collective ethos was at odds with his true interests, yet whose opinions of him were still important.

'Has anyone seen the film *Pumping Iron*?' he asked at the first convenient break. 'There's a point where Arnold Schwarzenegger says that pumping iron is "a great feeling, like coming – but coming continuously".'

'Is that what he said, really?' said Carol after a lengthy pause.

'So I believe.'

'You mean coming as in reaching a sexual climax?'

'Yes.'

'Well, what a stupid thing to say.'

'Leonard's full of little quotes like that,' Deborah pitched in. 'It's really annoying.'

'Does he do it all the time?' said Carol, turning to her side.

'Oh, yeah, all the time. You wouldn't believe the rubbish he's got stored in his head.'

'I am still here, you know,' said Leonard. 'I haven't left the room.'

'Oh, I know what I wanted to tell you . . .' Deborah said to Carol, continuing the 'joke'.

Leonard shut up. This was obviously not the right company to make snide remarks about such a serious subject. Although they were in a gym, he didn't see why they had to talk about fitness all the time.

'Sounds like you found things a bit more hard-going,' said Lasker.

'I'll tell you when I get my breath back,' he replied.

'In future you can go round with your wife. I was just showing you the ropes. Or if you want, we can devise your own personalized work-out. Concentrate on toning up your stomach muscles.'

Leonard opened his mouth to reply but, to his mortification, the only sound emitted was a loud burp.

'Leonard!'

'Sorry, I-I do apologize. I've never . . . Must be the orange juice.'

'Oh, yeah,' said Deborah sarcastically. 'Vicious stuff, orange juice.'

Carol was regarding him as if he'd just done a quick impression of Arnold Schwarzenegger in excitable mood. He tried to move the conversation forward, turning to Lasker.

'So tell me, Nick. Does being so fit get you lots of babes?'

'As opposed to belching all over them,' said Deborah.

'Well, it helps, I guess,' the instructor answered, smiling.

'So how many have you got on the run at the moment?'

'Leonard, are you drunk? What sort of question's that?'

He kept his gaze on Lasker, not allowing Deborah to browbeat him into dropping the subject. The gym instructor glanced at Carol and Deborah. It looked as if he didn't mind having this discussion with other men but had reservations about ladies being present.

'Four,' he replied.

'Four?' This came from Carol.

'At the moment,' Lasker responded, unfazed. 'It's been more in the past. One of 'em doesn't really count 'cause I'm sharing her with Vince, my brother.'

Carol recoiled. She might object to Leonard's burps but now she was hearing something much worse. Men were such disgusting creatures.

Leonard was watching Deborah who was very quiet, hardly breathing. He assumed Lasker wasn't serious in his claim but, whatever the case, his remarks hadn't gone down well with her. The corners of her lips had dropped and her stare had become distinctly glassy.

'How about you?' Lasker asked Leonard, perhaps hoping to deflect the impending storm from across the table. 'Have you got a particular type? You must meet lots of actresses, being a film critic.'

Before he could reply – Lasker had evidently heard about his job

– Deborah stepped in with some asperity, 'Oh, Leonard's not into women. He's too wrapped up in his affair with Oliver. Our cat,' she added, in response to a couple of puzzled looks. 'The way he fawns over that cat, giving him the best food, making sure he's completely comfortable. Honestly, you've never seen anything like it.'

'You're not one of those who prefer animals to people, are you?' said Carol.

'He thinks they're really intelligent,' said Deborah, again butting in before he could reply. 'Remember that dog you once had, Leonard, the one that kept pulling on his lead? Leonard had this mad notion,' she explained to the others, 'that the dog might be trying to lead him to something – you know, like a dead body. So one day he decided to go just wherever the dog led him. I think they ended up going round this barn about five times.'

'It was three times, don't exaggerate,' said Leonard, responding good-naturedly to the mockery. 'Anyway,' he added, turning to Lasker, 'to get back to what you were saying, I'd very much like my own personalized regime.' He spent the next few minutes saying how he felt the work-out had done him a power of good and that he intended to come to the gym as often as three times a week. 'Not straightaway, though,' he finished. 'I'm off to Cannes next week for the festival.'

Lasker left shortly after. His departure was slightly awkward and not helped by Deborah's rather strained, 'Goodbye, Nick!' as the man strode away. Couldn't she make her feelings a trifle less obvious?

Nevertheless, Leonard was glad to see the back of him. There'd been no conflicts or dramatic announcements but he'd learnt a great deal. Lasker was at first sight a fairly normal bloke. Interested in sport, women, his own physical appearance. It was impossible to tell how affected his laid-back attitude was, but his great advantage over Leonard, and what cut through the latter's heart, was the ease with which – just with the power of his smile or the flash of his eyes – he could capture Deborah's attention. Leonard had endured all her little flushes at various moments and it was apparent who held the upper hand in their relationship.

A couple of minutes later they were in the foyer of the club, bidding farewell to Carol. The other two were spending some time discussing when they'd next meet up, and Leonard, feeling excluded, found himself examining his surroundings. For some reason his eye was attracted by a group of cards pinned up next to the payphone, and he wandered over to take a look.

'Big, busty nympho', read one. 'Needs satisfying urgently.' Another card with an illustration read, 'Experienced lady into leather. All sorts of naughtiness punished!' At the higher end of the market, a third, unadorned card read, 'Accommodation for Gentlemen. Call Yvonne.'

Leonard turned to his female companions to find both regarding him with quizzical expressions.

'Ready, Leonard?' Deborah enquired archly.

They stepped outside and finally waved goodbye to Carol, who was heading in the opposite direction.

Deborah's mood had completely changed. She was no longer full of wide-eyed excitement. It felt to Leonard as if he were with a teenager suffering the usual pangs of foreboding over love. He was still talking – doing his best to pretend nothing had happened – but she was merely grunting her replies. They arrived at the car park and Leonard climbed into the driver's seat of the Peugeot. Negotiating the car onto the street, he resumed the conversation.

'Deborah, I want to apologize.' He clutched the steering wheel. 'I've been too immersed in my work lately. It's not good. Not a healthy state of affairs.'

There was no sound or movement next to him. She was looking straight ahead.

'And,' he persisted, 'I was thinking I ought to set aside more time – you know, just for the two of us.'

There was a pause. He was desperately trying to think of some further comment to draw her out of her mood.

'I'm sorry, Leonard.' She was still not looking at him. 'I'm really tired all of a sudden. I've got this blinding headache. D'you mind if we don't talk?'

'All right,' he said quietly.

They drove through the industrial desert between Clapton and Walthamstow, a no-man's-land of second-hand shops, disused factories, boarded-up houses and roadworks. His wife was in love with another man, no matter that the man in question didn't seem as keen on the relationship as she was. Sitting beside him now in utter silence, her thoughts seemed to be screaming out to him. What did Nick mean by saying he was seeing four women? Why did he offer to devise a work-out for my husband?

This was going to be tough, very tough. If they had any chance at all of getting back together. . . .

But Leonard didn't even want to think about that tonight. Tonight, he felt depressed.

What in heaven's name was he going to do next?

10

To Catch a Thief (1955)

Leonard couldn't get to sleep. Imprinted on his mind were the events of that evening: the way Deborah had been gazing at Lasker; the way, moreover, Lasker had taken it all in his stride. The gym instructor was quite different from him, not just in terms of physical appearance. He was able to provoke another aspect of Deborah's character, make her feel excited and young again. Perhaps in the scheme of things Leonard was just another experiment, like the black boyfriend, at a time when she was going through an older man phase. Now, though, she had moved on in life, eschewing men who reminded her of the grave, as a new beefcake era began.

When they'd arrived home he'd asked Deborah if she wanted any headache tablets, but she said she just wanted to go to bed. It was now just after midnight. She was lying next to him but she might as well be a thousand miles away. How he wished he could just forget the whole evening. Close his eyes and—

What was that? A door creaking? He lifted his head off the pillow, staring into the gloom, straining his ears for any sound. . . .

No. Nothing. Nothing at all. He breathed out again. Phew, that was a fright. Amazing how many little reverberations disturbed the calm of the night.

Jesus. What on earth. . . ?

Something heavy had crashed to the floor. He sat bolt upright, his hair poking up at odd angles. Oh, heavens alive. Someone was moving about downstairs.

Climbing out of bed – thankfully Deborah was still asleep – he donned his dressing gown and slippers. Could this have anything to do with the gym? Someone following them home? No, surely not. Not all that way. But Lasker was meant to know some dubious people, wasn't he? Leonard opened the bedroom door and peeped out onto the landing. Security in the house was lax to say the least. They'd lived in this mini-mansion for five years in the middle of nowhere and not even installed an alarm system. He tiptoed downstairs. Tomorrow, he'd definitely see to it. Assuming he lived till then of course. . . .

A *thud* came from the living-room. Leonard paused at the foot of the stairs, gripping the banister for dear life, his mouth pinned back in a ghastly rictus. There was no mistake now. Someone else was definitely in the house, rummaging about. Breathing heavily, he grabbed an umbrella from the stand in the hall and crossed to the living-room. The door was already slightly ajar, and he pushed it open. . . .

No one was there. Thank God.

Ah, and there was the reason for the disturbance. A terracotta oil burner had fallen off the mantelpiece and was lying on the floor, miraculously intact. Still, no sign of any other activity. The only place left to look was behind the door. Advancing slowly, umbrella at the ready, he caught sight of something in the corner of his eye, jerking his head upwards. From the top of the door a black shadow plunged down on him, the claws of the beast setting fast to his shoulders.

'Aaargh! Oliver! Gerroff!'

The cat scampered away, leaving Leonard in a heap on the floor, his heart pounding furiously inside his chest, his face bathed in sweat. It took him a good few minutes before he managed to recover his breath.

'Leonard, wake up!'

The heaving mound in bed made an indistinguishable grunt expressing his reservation about the idea.

'Get up – c'mon! We've been burgled.'

She did a fair job of wrenching his arm out of its socket,

dragging him half out of bed.

'All right, all right. Just a minute.'

His body felt in a state of civil war, the effect of yesterday's work-out still exerting itself. His joints had seized up, his muscles were sore, and any movement caused him varying degrees of pain. His arms, in particular, seemed to have frozen into a sort of bear hug position, turning him overnight into the Tin Man from *The Wizard of Oz*.

Deborah led the way down the stairs, avoiding the decapitated mouse that lay on the hall carpet next to a small pool of vomit, and entered the living-room.

'There!' she exclaimed.

'What?' His eyes still felt heavy.

'There! Over there! The break in the glass. Someone got in through the door to the terrace.'

He gazed at all the pieces of glass lying on the carpet, then cast his eye around the room. The television, VCR and stereo were still in their rightful places.

'They've taken my cat.'

'What, Oliver?'

'Not Oliver, Dummkopf. Lotte.'

Leonard still looked puzzled.

'Lotte, my porcelain cat. The one Dad bought for me.'

'Oh.'

' "Oliver", he says. Yeah, that's likely, isn't it? The burglar could nick Ollie, then head over to Mrs Peavey's for those killer canines of hers.'

'So did anything else get taken?'

'Oh, just some stuff from the sideboard. The silver tankard and the man with the fishing rod, the one you thought was tacky. I just can't believe it . . . Can't believe it.' She looked on the verge of tears, tugging distractedly at her hair.

'It's a shame, a real shame.'

He looked at the space on the hearth. What could he put there instead? A bust of Alfred Hitchcock?

'Why don't you show a bit more emotion?' She rounded on him.

'Sorry?'

'Well, it's a bit more than a shame, isn't it? If I was you, I'd leg it down to the basement. See if they've nicked anything there.'

'Yes . . . Yes, you're right. God, I hadn't thought. Still trying to wake up. This is – this is absolutely shocking. I'd better call the police.'

'Yes, do that.' She pulled herself together. 'Oh, and clean up that mess in the hall.'

The day had been devoted to tightening up security at The Elms. The police, Constables Toms and Fletcher – the former a young man with a distinctive bald pate – had shaken their heads at the state of *glasnost* that existed between the Fleasons and the criminal fraternity but otherwise had been sympathetic. Had anything else been stolen, they wanted to know. Had there been any strangers at the door recently, or phone calls where the caller had hung up? A further twenty minutes had been spent taking fingerprints and then they'd been replaced by a window fitter who'd secured a new pane in the door, a task carried out while Leonard rang the insurance company. The next to arrive were two men in a large van from Southern Security, bringing with them a battery of equipment. Deborah had taken the day off work and decided to go shopping, unable to withstand the thought of staying in the house after the overnight invasion, and Leonard had been left to turn the place into Fort Knox.

He had certainly taken his responsibilities seriously. The workmen had left just after five and Leonard had spent the next hour conducting a series of tests. He was eagerly looking forward to Deborah's return and, at 6.30, the Peugeot could be heard pulling up in the drive. He opened the control panel in the hall and went out to greet her.

'Hi, how's it been? Had a good time?'

'Under the circumstances.' She was carrying two bags of shopping. 'There's two more of these in the boot, thanks, Leonard.' She stared up at the bell box fitted to the front wall. 'Oh, great, you've done the alarm system.' Her eyeline shifted to one side.

'We've got a camera as well,' he announced.

'Yes, so I see. Is that really necessary?'

'I thought it would come in handy.'

'Yes, Leonard. But the cost.'

'Ah, well, you see, I've got round that. It's a dummy.'

She gazed at him as if he were raving, then turned her attention back to the camera.

'A dummy? It looks real enough to me.'

'That's because it *is* real. It's just missing its component parts. No one'll guess.'

'Ha!' She gave an ironic laugh, shaking her head. '*You're* the dummy, Leonard, if you ask me. Oh – Leonard. . . ?'

He was just heading off.

'Leave Billy in the boot, OK? I'll deal with him.'

She stomped inside with her shopping as he went round to the garage. *Leave Billy in the boot?* That sounded like a line out of *Goodfellas*. Awaiting his services in the car were *three* more bags, but what immediately caught his attention was a porcelain cat sitting in their midst. This one was smaller and more colourful than the last, altogether happier. (But of course she was in love!) Leaving it there, he trooped inside with the rest of the shopping. *She* could talk about costs. It had been a very expensive day and he reminded himself to check their bank account later in the week.

'What's going on here then?'

Deborah was standing in the hall, passing a critical eye over the control panel.

'Ah, you noticed. Let me explain.'

'Just briefly, please, Leonard. I don't wanna know the number of kilohertz or whatever.'

'Well, this is the control panel, the brains of the operation. It covers a range of zones in the house.'

He took her through the essentials of how the system worked.

'Hold on a minute,' said Deborah, making one of her many interruptions. 'A motion detector?'

'Over there.' He pointed to a small white case mounted high up in one corner. 'The other ones are in the living-room, the bedroom and the basement.'

'The bedroom?'

'That's where crooks head first, apparently.'

'I'm not gonna set off an alarm during the night, am I, if I go to the loo?'

'No, no. Don't worry about that. We'd only have it on for holidays.'

A quick tour of the ground floor followed, during which Leonard pointed out all the door and window sensors, including a glass-break sensor on the picture window in the living-room. On their return he went through how to activate and deactivate the alarm.

'All right,' she said when he was finished. 'How much did it cost?'

'Just over six hundred pounds.'

'Well.' She let out a sigh. 'So be it, I suppose. No birthday present for you, though, this year, Leonard.'

She gave him a mischievous look before walking off, leaving him where he was, standing alone in the hall. He gave his face a rub, then glanced over at the motion detector in the corner, adopting a sort of half-smile.

'All right, Mr De Mille,' he murmured, 'I'm ready for my close-up.'

11

My Brilliant Career (1979)

Leonard had always loved movies, from the moment he'd seen *Some Like it Hot* at the age of nine. The whole experience had been magical: the escape into another world, the feeling of eavesdropping on larger-than-life characters. But what had really made an impact at the time was the knowledge, a breathtaking realization brought on by the closing credits, that the actors weren't making it up on the spot, that the film had actually been written and directed by Billy Wilder.

From that day forth Leonard had wanted to be involved in films. He'd read everything he could find on the subject, seen as many movies as he possibly could, and signed up to numerous fan clubs. His earliest ambition had been to become a director and, with that object in mind, he'd transformed his bedroom into a film set. An old 8mm cine camera (no longer working) was his main piece of equipment, and two pairs of his mother's expensive stockings wound tightly over a garden rake acted as a boom mic. ('Good!' he said to his mother when she came into his room and looked aghast. 'Keep that emotion. Don't lose the moment.') At night he would curl up with the blankets tucked under his chin and imagine himself on the set of his latest film, making decisions about camera placement and lighting, chatting away with such luminaries as Olivier and Orson Welles. ('You've got a point there, Lenny. I hadn't thought of that.')

Ah, yes, such lovely visions! But while such fantasies did not entirely abate over the next few years, an element of reality found its way into Leonard's career plans. Directing wasn't a job one could apply for or get promoted to, and nor did the opportunity exist, with the camera technology of the time, to make a cheap film of one's own. Leonard's prose style had been receiving praise at school and, since he enjoyed writing, he'd decided instead to become a scriptwriter. Up until that point his only real attempt at creative composition had been a billet-doux to his English teacher, hoping to persuade her to leave her husband and come and live with his parents (his sister could move out).

For you, Mrs Medlam, my little heart beats.
You are the Fanny to my Keats.

But now, with a literary fire burning within him, and with the help of Mrs Medlam (who inexplicably seemed to like him), Leonard began to write ten- to fifteen-minute playlets. One of these, *Cut!* – about a hairdresser who unthinkingly fashions her clients' hair in the style of her favourite movie stars – had even come second in a national playwriting competition.

This early promise, though, hadn't fully materialized. Leonard had left university and gone into journalism. (It was unfortunately necessary to prostitute himself in this way before the real writing could begin.) Here he had stayed. His reputation as a columnist hadn't yet been established and, without the necessary contacts, ideas about entering the film industry were doomed to failure. (He'd attempted to join the Association of Cinematograph Television and Allied Technicians – virtually the only way to get involved in films in those days – but discovered he could only become a member of the union if he already had a job in the industry.) He could still write a treatment or a screenplay, of course, but as somebody who'd read extensively about the film business, Leonard was more aware than most of the chances of success. Only one in five screenplays that were bought or commissioned ended up being made, and these successful scripts still had to undergo development hell, tampered with by other writers. In any case, because Leonard had been more concerned with taking care of his first wife at the time, thoughts of an alternative career had

had to be postponed. Shirley had overridden everything.

But now these thoughts were starting to drift back. In the space of fifteen years Leonard had progressed from his local paper, the *Filchester and Grimstone Mercury*, to the *London Chronicle*, making the transition from feature writer to TV reviewer to film critic. Aside from being a contributor to various film magazines and journals, he had also gained kudos in the literary world, writing two biographies about Alexander Mackendrick and Michael Powell (the latter 'vastly entertaining', according to *The Times*). The film industry, meanwhile, had opened up considerably, and Leonard, who took his responsibilities seriously and felt that he was fortunate to be in his present job, had recently attended a course run by the National Film and Television School. He'd particularly enjoyed making several shorts, and perhaps the most pleasing aspect of the whole exercise, given his rather reticent personality, was the rapport he'd developed with the cast. It appeared as if many of the actors preferred his approach of asking for their opinions over the dictatorial antics of some of the other students.

Yet in terms of actual scriptwriting, he still hadn't written anything longer than a few minutes. Leonard was beginning to wonder whether, despite all his experience, he was capable of writing a feature-length film. Yes, the excuse of work was valid, of course, but, in truth, was the real reason for the delay related to self-doubt? Unlike some film critics who believed their own impeccable skill and judgement allowed them to criticize others, Leonard questioned his own ability all the time. His marriage had bolstered his self-image for a while, but he was still left with the feeling that Deborah's father – only eight years older – looked down on him. . . .

One day, though! After all, his years in the industry had to be worth something, and examples abounded of film critics who'd gone on to write screenplays. James Agee, for one, had helped pen *The Night of the Hunter*. Paul Schrader (*Taxi Driver*) and Dario Argento (co-writer of *Once Upon a Time in the West*) were others. Perhaps Leonard's favourite story involved film critic Peter Bogdanovich. He was at a showing of a film in Beverly Hills when a friend introduced him to the producer Roger Corman, seated behind him. Corman told him that he liked his writing for *Esquire* and asked him if he'd ever thought about writing for the movies. 'I'd love to,' Bogdanovich replied and, wasting no time, Corman had hired him to write a screenplay.

Yes, certainly it was a little far-fetched (even more so since Bogdanovich had gone on to become a director), but everyone was entitled to their slice of luck, weren't they? And why couldn't that happen to Leonard?

And then, one glorious evening a couple of months ago, it had. At least a start had been made.

It was a few days after the premiere of Augustus Dorry's latest film, *The Plot Thickens*, and he'd met up for an exclusive interview with the veteran director at the Savoy. Dorry had been a significant buttress of the British film industry for many years but was generally considered to be past his best. Fortunately, though, Leonard still admired his work and the two had had a nice dinner before retiring to the bar.

Dorry was incredibly open, revealing how much the criticism had hurt him, to the extent that he'd even started to question whether his powers were on the wane. Leonard had sympathized. They had ordered more drinks. Then, very uncharacteristically, Leonard had confided in Dorry his thoughts about writing a screenplay.

Much to his surprise, the other man had responded enthusiastically. He'd told Leonard that if he sent him a script showing sufficient promise, he'd get Geoff – Geoff Hartnell, the producer on most of Dorry's films – to sort out the money. This wasn't all, though. Leonard, by now somewhat under the influence, had gone on to describe his childhood ambitions, and Dorry had said there might be a consultative role for him – say, as his assistant – if the project got the green light. Even at the time Leonard was aware that there were a lot of ifs or buts in what he was hearing . . . But all the same! He knew Dorry was very respectful of scriptwriters and that it wouldn't be the first time he'd given a writer a major input on one of his films. Whatever his rational side was telling him, it was also a fact that you only needed one person with sufficient clout to make your movie.

And with the directorial talent of Dorry attached. . . .

*

The next few weeks, however, had been desperately disappointing. Every idea Leonard had come up with seemed to overlap with something he'd seen already. He hadn't told anyone about what he and Dorry had discussed – not even Deborah – in case it jinxed his success. But it was clear that, although he'd waited so long for this moment, he had nothing to offer should it arise.

12

A Place in the Sun (1951)

The quiet resort of Cannes had undergone its annual transformation into Hollywood on the Riviera. Thirty thousand people from the entertainment industry had arrived, jamming the Croisette, the tree-lined boulevard that hugged the Mediterranean, and all eyes were led to the parade of stars making their ascent up the red-carpeted stairs of the Palais des Festivals, the main convention centre. Everything was bustle and billboards and breasts, the latter displayed with uncommon frequency and tanned to a crisp.

Festival goers, as Andrew Sarris, the film critic, had pointed out, could be divided into moles and moths. The moles – of which Leonard was a foremost example – would watch as many films as possible, starting at eight in the morning and finishing around midnight, venturing out for the odd press conference, and staying up in their hotel rooms until two at night finishing their copy. The moths, on the other hand, hovered around the bright aura surrounding the stars, attended numerous gala dinners and cocktail parties, and avoided any of the fifteen hundred films it was possible to see.

Every year Leonard swore he'd never return to Cannes, and every year since 1998 he'd reneged on his vow. Deneuve, DiCaprio, Schwarzenegger, he'd missed them all. And, anyway, he had more pressing concerns now. As the plane dived out of the clouds towards the picturesque Nice-Côte d'Azur airport, surrounded by beaches and palm trees, he leant back on the headrest and gazed out of the window.

Everything had gone according to plan with the burglary and he was confident Deborah had no idea he was responsible. The operation had literally been a spur of the moment decision. He'd been sitting on the floor of the living-room, having been scared half to death by Oliver, and suddenly noticed their *other* cat, staring at him out of its porcelain eyes, wearing the same scornful expression it had worn while he'd been reading HVM's report. There was no question. He had to get rid of it.

In the same spirit of fervency as the crusading knights of old in their attempts to expel the infidel hordes from the Holy Land, he'd heaved the wretched thing all the way down the back garden and through several fields, before depositing it in a ditch covered by brambles and undergrowth. Then he'd popped the tankard (impractical) and the man with the fishing rod (simply revolting) in a plastic bag and thrown them in the dustbin. It just remained to break a pane in the living-room door which gave out onto the terrace – the only really risky part of the endeavour – for which he used a hammer from the garage. Then, with still no stirrings from upstairs, he'd finally made his way to bed.

Leonard had never committed a serious crime before and he was struck by how relatively straightforward it was. Certainly he'd felt very nervous lying to Constable Toms about the break-in – his knees had started shaking uncontrollably – but these emotions simply accorded with how he was meant to feel, and couldn't have looked terribly suspicious. The only real problem was the guilt that assailed him every so often – hurting Deborah's feelings far more than expected, wasting the time of the police – leading to the strange desire to confess. But otherwise there was little chance of being apprehended, and he'd continued on his duplicitous course.

Deborah had believed everything he'd said about the alarm system and, so far as it went, he'd told her the truth. The camera on the outside of the house *was* a dummy. The motion detectors would do exactly as he'd said they would. There was one thing, however, he hadn't told her. The idea had come about in conversation with the technician, Roy, who'd installed the system. Much to the other's surprise, Leonard had already prepared for him a floor plan of the house, and actually knew what Roy meant when he referred to PIRs.

'Passive . . . infrared . . . motion sensors.'

'Correct.'

'And they trip an alarm, is that right, when they sense movement?'

'Spot on, my friend. You can even, believe it or not, hide a camera inside one.'

'No-o!'

'Yep. Part of our service.'

Leonard's excitement was growing. True, he had been meaning to ask about the feasibility of setting up cameras – hence the reason for the burglary – but here was someone providing him with a foolproof method.

'And that's perfectly legal, is it?' he queried.

'It's your house, squire.'

'Wouldn't I have to stick a notice up – you know, to alert people?'

'You can – but you're not obliged to.'

'This is a revelation,' Leonard murmured, his mind racing.

'You want us to rig something up here?'

'Yes – well, possibly. We've got a cleaner, you see . . .'

'Say no more. Lingers a bit over the Crown Derby, does she?'

'Well, you know! – I suppose.' What was he waffling on about? 'Anyway, to get back to these hidden cameras, what about wiring? Isn't that a problem?'

'Good question. Very good question. We can hard-wire it for you, that's not a problem. But listen to this. If you want, just by paying a bit extra, we can make the whole system wireless. How it works, you see, is that the signal's carried by radio transmission – very reliable, very easy to install. What you could have is a motion detector in the living-room, another in the bedroom—'

'One in the basement would be good. I've got a lot of technical equipment down there.'

'Oh, yes?' said Roy, who gave every appearance of viewing Leonard as a long-lost brother.

Leonard explained that he'd turned the basement into a home theatre.

'Awesome,' said the technician. 'Matter of fact, I've been toying with a similar idea myself.'

'I'll show you round if you like.'

'Well!' said the other, rubbing his hands. 'I don't see any problem here. I'll pop back to the office, pick up everything I need. Reckon I'll have you sorted by four or five. How about that?'

Good Leonard, as he was only too aware, had turned into Bad Leonard. Hiring the detective agency had merely been a prelude to this monstrous exercise in paranoia. Yes, he'd been devious, but at the same time his self-disgust was complete. He wasn't an automaton. He possessed a conscience. He recalled the look of distaste on Dunstan's face when he'd revealed he'd hired a detective agency. But it had simply reached the stage where he had to know the whole truth about Deborah's activities, whatever the method. The point, the only possible justification for his behaviour, was to catch Deborah *in flagrante delicto* with Lasker. If they really were having an affair, they were almost certain to see each other while he was away, and there was a reasonable chance they'd use The Elms for their purposes. To put the matter beyond any doubt, the germ of an idea was starting to form in his mind about a film for Dorry, for which this exercise might prove useful. . . .

In his heart of hearts, though, he felt that no excuse or manner of circumstance provided sufficient grounds for his behaviour. As soon as the plane touched down, after returning home, he would pack up his equipment, he really would.

After all, how would he like it?

Having settled into his room, collected his pink pass, and made straight for the bar, Leonard was still wrapped up in thoughts about his home life when he heard a couple talking behind him.

'What d'ya want, doll?'

'Bloody Mary, thanks, Joe. Easy on the tomato juice, though. You'll sober me up.' Some inane giggling broke out.

The male half of the couple stood next to Leonard, and the latter stole a glance to his side. Yes, it was definitely Joseph Koski, the architect behind such classics as *P* and *Blood Before Dawn*. Leonard took in his companion, a bleached blonde, no more than eighteen, sporting a viscous creation which merely hinted at clothing. The director rapped on the bar.

'*Garçon!* Hey, *garçon!*'

The barman glanced over and shrugged his shoulders. He was serving someone else.

'Er, Mr Koski. Hm-h'm.'

The famous director gazed at Leonard, his face registering nothing.

'Mr Koski, I don't know if you remember me. Leonard Fleason? I work for the *Chronicle* in London. We spoke once on the phone.'

Koski's expression remained a blank. He sniffed.

'Any idea how to get served round here?'

It was more of a closing statement than a question, and Leonard found himself addressing the great man's profile again.

'Mr Koski, I've got this idea for a film. I think you'll—'

'Ahhh!'

The director threw his head back. At that moment the barman arrived.

'Can I get you anything, sir?'

'Yes. A scotch for me, better make that a double. A Bloody Mary for the lady. Oh, and any suggestions for how I can get rid of this idiot would be appreciated, too.'

Leonard's hand eased itself off his glass. His face was suffused with embarrassment. Swallowing the phlegm that had gathered in his throat, he brushed past the blonde – 'Oi! Watch it!' she cried – before making his way out, away from the hotel, not stopping until he reached the boardwalk on the Croisette. The ghost of John Wayne looked sadly on, shaking his head.

'*Excusez-moi, monsieur!*'

A young woman on roller skates flew past him. Oh, God, what was happening to him all of a sudden? He was just getting in the way, just annoying other people. Did his life now, as well as his job, simply consist of interfering in others' more important lives? He leant against a palm tree, not far away from a man standing stock-still with a white-painted face.

Mr Koski, I've got this idea for a film.

What had he been playing at, talking about his plans to the celebrated director? It was obvious Koski wouldn't be interested. And, anyway, he'd already spoken to Dorry, so there was no need to approach anyone else. His trouble, plainly, was that he was terribly insecure, anxious to know he was on the right lines. *That* wouldn't be so bad but, unlike those who'd come to Cannes having given up their job and remortgaged the house, *his* idea was simply that: an idea. He hadn't written anything down. Not a treatment. . . . Not a scene. . . . Not even one word of script.

13

Great Expectations (1946)

'Hello. *Bonjour.*'

Somebody was addressing him, standing a yard away. He had curly brown hair, turning grey at the edges, and a crooked smile. Leonard regarded the speaker, unable temporarily to put a name to the face.

'Geoff Hartnell!' he exclaimed at last.

'You looked miles away,' said the other.

'Yes, I was, er, just admiring the view.'

'Ah, yes, the famous view.'

He turned to share Leonard's field of vision. Leonard had probably only exchanged about twenty words with Geoff in the past, barely enough to claim acquaintance with the fellow.

'You see that boat over there, the largest one?' Geoff pointed to a spot somewhere on the horizon. 'Well, it's owned, apparently, by the porn industry. They're hoping to stage a non-stop orgy on board.'

'What, for the whole festival?'

'So I've been told. Crazy, isn't it?'

Leonard shook his head resignedly. 'You don't get that sort of thing in Margate.'

'No,' agreed the other. 'Difficult to picture, anyway.'

They fell into step along the Croisette, having decided to go for a spot of breakfast. It seemed that Geoff shared a lot of Leonard's views. He laughed at Dirk Bogarde's remark made to Barry

Norman about why the former used to avoid the festival each year – 'Because it's always full of all the people I'd hoped were dead' – and indeed Leonard felt that he'd had the good fortune, to use the modern parlance, to bump into a fellow homey. They might not be from the same ghetto or street gang – Geoff probably hailing from somewhere in the home counties – but there was something innately British about him. Maybe it was the Jermyn Street shirt that marked him out. In the next few minutes they'd probably be talking about Millwall's recent run in the FA Cup, and then they'd be friends for life.

To cement things in Leonard's mind, he suddenly recalled after a few minutes that Geoff was the producer on Augustus Dorry's films. Why this hadn't occurred to him straightaway was a mystery, but the point was that here, opposite him in La Mère Besson, his regular eatery in Cannes, was the most important man in his nascent career plans. He was just pondering the best way to introduce the subject when the other brought it up himself.

'So, Leonard, what's this I hear? Gus Dorry was telling me you were interested in writing a script for us, maybe even getting involved on the directing side. That's quite a departure, isn't it, from your normal terrain?'

Leonard spent the next five minutes delivering the pitch he had been hoping to deliver to Koski. To his amazement, the idea seemed instantly to appeal to Geoff, the latter nodding away in appreciation.

'Yes, yes. I like it. I like it a lot. This whole business of setting up cameras to spy on people is very in vogue right now. There's so many reality shows around, but no one's really explored the issue in a film. Apart from – oh, what was it called?'

'*Final Cut?*'

'Yes, that was one of them!'

'That was quite experimental; largely improvised.'

'M'm, big, big mistake. But I was thinking of another film, with Albert Brooks . . .'

'*Real Life?*'

'Yeah. Now that was *really* ahead of its time.'

'Though it was actually based on a TV show called *An American Family*. The idea of using hidden cameras probably goes back at least to the 1920s, with King Vidor and Dziga Vertov.'

Hartnell smiled, yielding to Leonard's knowledge.

'My idea,' Leonard went on, 'is that filming, rather than being conducted in documentary style, will take place in secret. So it's much darker.'

'Right! I particularly love your main character, the film critic. He sounds completely bonkers.'

'Well,' said Leonard dubiously. 'Not completely.'

'No, not on the surface maybe. You could make him superficially attractive. But then this obsession of his could take over until he totally flips, goes out of his mind.'

'Well . . .'

'Yes, yes, that's definitely the way to go. Perhaps – I know you haven't worked out the ending yet – but perhaps he could end up killing somebody.'

'H'm,' said Leonard vaguely.

'It's a possibility, isn't it? That would add a dash, a *soupçon*, of violence. And – yes, now that I think about it – there're opportunities for nudity.'

'It's not really that sort of—'

'Oh, I know, I know! But – well, you know! It'll make the younger audience sit up a bit.'

'I suppose,' Leonard agreed, deciding to play along. 'You're not planning to go on board that boat we were talking about – to do some casting?'

'Ha! I don't think so,' Geoff responded with good humour. 'But now that you mention it . . .'

'I envisage three main character actors,' Leonard continued (just in case the other was serious). 'There's just one main location, the film critic's house.'

'Good, good – nice and cheap. What we British specialize in. Tell you what, we can even say, can't we, that we *want* the film to look cheap, to make it look gritty and real. Yes – blow me! I'm getting into this idea more and more. We can actually say we made a brave artistic decision not to spend any money. Ha, ha! What could be better?'

Leonard smiled benevolently.

'So how far have you got in writing it?' the producer asked.

'Oh, it's . . . coming along. I'm nearly there.'

'You've done it?'

'It just needs an extra draft or two.'

'Excellent. So you could send Gus or myself a copy? I don't know – by the end of next month?'

'Sure. I think so.'

'Great. That's great. You know, it sounds funny – and you'll probably think I'm mad – but I've got a good feeling about this.'

Before Leonard's eyes the other man was turning into an angel, sprouting wings and a halo. Yes, there it was above his head. If he and Leonard weren't two Englishmen in a public place, he'd probably have kissed him. . . .

And then the moment of euphoria passed. After all, this was all too good to be true, wasn't it?

'Sorry, you'll have to forgive me,' he said. 'I know we haven't agreed to anything, but – well, why are you being so nice to me? I'm a film critic. We're not the most popular of people.'

Geoff let out a chuckle. 'Actually, I was hoping, believe it or not, to meet you here in Cannes. When Gus talked to me about your interest in getting behind the camera, the first thing that entered my head was something Cliff Carney said about you. He said that the short you made for him at film school was the best he'd ever seen.'

Good old Clifford. There was another Englishman Leonard could kiss.

'The other thing, of course, is your writing. We obviously share a certain empathy, shall we say? You were virtually the only critic who gave *The Plot Thickens* a good review.'

Without somehow casting a negative light over the conversation, Geoff then went on to talk about the difficulty of raising finance. He enquired about Leonard's agent and explained why he couldn't talk about option agreements until he'd seen the completed script.

'The key thing here,' he added, 'will be to get an attractive package together. If Gus likes the script and wants to be the director, that will be wonderful.'

'Absolutely.'

'He's very experienced, stays on schedule, knows the cinematographer.'

'Oh, he'd be ideal.'

'However, if you're interested, and if you stay on the set, I'm sure there's a chance you'll be brought in at some point. Gus might want you, for example, to take charge of a second unit to shoot some exteriors. I don't know how you feel about that?'

'Oh, I think I can muck in,' said Leonard.

The conversation moved onto other projects Geoff was working on, but Leonard, in a whirl of suppressed excitement, found it difficult to concentrate, actually envisaging himself on the set of his screenplay, perhaps even taking over the reins if Gus Dorry couldn't make it in one day. . . .

'Catch you later,' he said to Geoff as they were parting. 'Oh – and thanks.'

'Not at all. Perhaps I'm a bit biased towards people roughly the same age as myself. Nothing wrong with that, is there?'

Leonard shook his head in a wide arc.

'In any case,' the other added with a smile, 'I can say I discovered you.'

It was 11.30 p.m. exactly, 10.30 in Britain, his second Wednesday away. Leonard dialled his home number. Four rings. Then his voice on the answering machine, interrupted by Deborah.

'L-Leonard. You woke me up. I was spending a quiet night in and just dozed off.'

'Well, I won't keep you then, darling. Everything all right?'

'Yeah. Everything's hunky' – she yawned – 'dory. How 'bout you?'

'Fine. I saw a Bulgarian film today, all about infidelity. Called *She Had It Coming.*'

'Interesting,' came the bored-sounding voice at the other end of the line.

'So how's the house? You've remembered to feed Ollie?'

'Hardly any point, is there? He seems to do very well on his own.'

'What do you mean?'

'Look, I'm joking. If you don't believe me, ask my lover. He's here beside me in bed.'

Leonard laughed. 'That's funny because I've got Cindy

Crawford next to me.'

'Has she heard your snoring yet?'

He was about to say he didn't snore but then recalled listening to himself on tape.

'You always have to have the last word, don't you?'

'You keep feeding me lines, that's why.'

Leonard chuckled away, enjoying himself. This was like the early cut and thrust of their relationship.

'Well, night then, darling. When I get home we'll have to go out – you know, somewhere nice.'

'OK, we'll do that.'

'Sleep well. I love you.'

There was a click as the handset was replaced.

'I suppose sometimes I have the last word,' he said to himself.

14

Romancing the Stone (1984)

Leonard had no idea what to expect when he got home. It was possible, if unlikely, that Deborah had discovered the cameras, but she certainly gave no indication if that was the case. Then it was terribly frustrating waiting for her to leave the house so that he could check the results of his covert plans. He'd programmed the VCR to record in time-lapse mode (set to one frame every four seconds instead of the standard thirty frames a second), allowing a six-hour tape the potential to record continuously for up to thirty days. (For the sake of simplicity he'd decided to use only the camera in the bedroom.) The brilliant aspect of all this was that whenever Deborah entered the bedroom, the motion detector would automatically send a signal to the VCR to start recording in real-time, which it would continue to do for the next five minutes (and longer if she – or they – were still moving about), enabling perfect playback.

As soon as he'd arrived home, Leonard had gone down to the basement to turn everything off – noting that the LED counter on the VCR showed 6:04:21 (so the tape had been fully used) – but because he and Deborah were on the point of going out, there was no time to look at the results.

They sat facing each other in the restaurant. It was quite balmy outside and Deborah was wearing her red summer dress, simple and elegant, straps looping over her shoulders. Although Leonard had only spent just over a week away, everything seemed different.

Deborah looked so much younger than her thirty-one years. He noted the delicate colouring of her skin, the graceful swaying of her long fingers in the candlelight. As they chatted about the paper and his trip to Cannes, he pictured her locked in an embrace with Lasker, hands caressing each other's hair, heads bobbing up and down. . . .

She was talking excitedly about her friend Kate's unhappy marriage, the way her husband was mistreating her – driving her into the arms of another man – but Leonard was only half paying attention. *He'd* never beaten Deborah up. On the contrary, he loved her. Whatever problems they were going through, he could still – after seven years – feel his heart swelling with affection.

They drove home and, as he took Deborah's coat off in the hall, she said, 'Thank you, Leonard, that was really nice.' She went upstairs, the smell of her perfume, of jasmine, lingering in the air.

He followed a couple of minutes later, finding her lying on the bed, eyes closed. When was the last time they'd made love? Four, perhaps five, months ago? Was that normal? He really wanted to trust her, really wanted to believe Dunstan's view that she was having at most an innocent flirtation. After all, Andrew was normally a good judge of character. And maybe her involvement with Lasker *had* been appallingly exaggerated. . . .

In a way, if something sexual was to happen now, between himself and Deborah, it would be an act of faith on his part. It would be saying that he didn't need to look at the tape. . . .

Deborah opened her eyes and smiled at him. Was she ever so slightly drunk?

'Bathroom time,' she murmured.

'Deborah?'

'H'm?'

'When you're finished I thought we could . . . you know . . . talk.'

She sat up, frowning slightly, a gentle chiding expression. 'Yeah, we could, you know, talk, after I've been to the, you know, bathroom. If you've got something to say, Leonard, spit it out.'

He hesitated a while longer. Of course he shouldn't really have to say anything. It should just happen. It wasn't just the act itself, anyway. His desire to make love to her was more of a spiritual than a physical need, as if it would put right all the wrongs in their relationship, atone for all the mistakes.

'Well, all right then,' he began. 'I just wanted to say I've had a really lovely evening. What would really make it perfect – not that it's the be-all and end-all—'

'Would be if you could shove your thing up me.'

'I wasn't going to express it in quite that way.'

'Do you really like sex, Leonard?'

'Yes . . .' He cleared his throat. 'Yes, I do.'

'Do you? Really?'

'Yes,' he replied, feeling somewhat on the spot. 'I like everything about it. From the point where you say, "All right then, if you really have to go through with it", to the point where I say, "Well, I enjoyed it even if you didn't".'

'That's what I mean, though,' Deborah went on, maintaining a serious expression. 'Sometimes I think men and women were never meant to be together. Or at least they should recognize their differences. Do you know what Andrea Dworkin calls marriage?'

'No.'

'She says that marriage is rape.'

'She sounds like a barrel of laughs.'

'I don't suppose you ever feel institutionalized?'

'No.'

'That's because,' Deborah said, getting up and heading towards the bathroom, 'you're a man. You're one of the oppressors.'

She closed the door on her yellow-tiled sanctuary.

'Well, thanks for a lovely evening,' said Leonard.

With Deborah installed in the bathroom, he had the next half-hour at least to contemplate the ignominy of his rejection. He changed into his pyjamas, turned off the lights, and climbed into bed.

Next door he could hear the rush of water as she ran the Jacuzzi. The L-shaped bathroom – based on a 1930s design – was a paragon of luxury and size, with gold-plated taps and handrails. It was coloured in various soft shades of yellow, and the lighting, cut away in the walls, gave a subdued, warm effect. Most of Deborah's potions and powders were situated on oak shelves running along one wall, starting at the sink and finishing short of the curtains half shielding the toilet and bidet. She was always experimenting, always looking for the ultimate experience in aromatherapy. (Leonard had once pointed out, without gaining her wholehearted agreement, that the bathroom fulfilled the same role as the basement for him, representing her sanctuary from the outside world.) A legion of medicines were here, bottles of prescription drugs lined up in neat little rows. Deborah, at some time in her life, had suffered from an uncommon number of ailments and disorders. Apart from remedies for standard complaints such as headaches, indigestion, sleeping problems, skin conditions, anxiety – a whole shelf devoted to eyes, ears, mouth and throat – there was a plethora of vitamin pills and alternative medicines, to be used even when her body was operating at maximum efficiency.

At last she emerged from the bathroom and slipped into bed. Rejection in any form always depressed him inordinately and he wanted reassuring he wasn't deficient in everything else. All his insecurities were reappearing from the depths.

'Deborah?'

'What?' She sounded as if she were on the verge of sleep.

'Can I have a chat? About my career. About the direction it's going in.'

This was not the first time he'd engaged in a discussion about his job at some late hour. It made him feel better to talk out his problems and he spent the next few minutes trying to explain how frustrated he felt.

As usual, Deborah had listened for a few minutes, given her advice, and then grown impatient when he hadn't immediately accepted it.

'Leonard, we'll talk about it tomorrow, OK? I've told you what you need to do. Devise a plan. Then when you've got one, act on it. That's my last word on the subject. Just do it.'

She turned over on her side, leaving him to face her back.

15

sex, lies, and videotape (1989)

Finally! Deborah had left for work – he'd watched her all the way down the drive – and he was alone in the house. (Of course he could have watched the videotape last night after she'd dropped off to sleep, but this approach was safer.) Strange, but now the moment had arrived, he didn't feel like rushing down to the basement. The seriousness of the situation demanded that he carry everything out with the same care and foresight he'd shown thus far.

He filled the kettle with water and plugged it in. Then, while waiting for it to boil, he went downstairs to collect the tape. If there was any incriminating material to see, he had no desire to view it on the hundred-inch screen in the screening-room. He poured out his coffee – calmly, methodically. Then, once established in the living-room, he inserted the tape.

For a while nothing happened. There was a slight flicker due to the time-lapse setting, but otherwise the picture quality was at least satisfactory. The motion detector was also performing its part, as witnessed by a gory piece of action.

Oliver had caught a thrush. Leaping onto the bed with his victim and activating the real-time mode (which should have been set to a less sensitive trigger), he carefully deposited the bird onto Leonard's pillow, and then waited patiently for the bloodied corpse to move. This was presumably a token offering in response to Leonard's leaving him by himself.

That evening, a few minutes of viewing time later, Deborah came into the room, gave a little scream when she saw the dead thrush, and after some scrambling around – Leonard normally dealt with this sort of problem – retrieved a pair of his underpants from the chest of drawers (unless he was mistaken, the ones he was wearing at the moment). She then wrapped up the bird and walked out with the bundle held as far away from her as possible.

A little later, terribly embarrassed, he watched her getting changed for bed. He wasn't used to all this gratuitous nudity in the bedroom, and it was clear he hadn't thought through all the implications of his actions. What if she decided to indulge in a spot of self-abuse? Oh, God, he hoped for her sake she was contemplating nothing of the sort. He hadn't gone to these lengths for voyeuristic reasons. For a large part of the time he gazed at the carpet, feeling renewed remorse at the wickedness of his actions.

Fortunately the next few days rolled by on film uneventfully. Mrs Peavey, who did for the Fleasons on Fridays, came and went. At one point she took quite an interest in the motion detector, standing on the stool and peering into the lens, even swivelling it back and forth on its bracket, making Leonard feel a little sick. Thankfully, however, she put everything back to where it was and continued with her work, reminding 'Agatha Jean' not to forget certain chores. She was just returning a book of Leonard's from the dressing-table to his bedside cabinet when Deborah entered. (She must have taken another day off work.)

'Agatha, I'm going now—' She stopped in her tracks. 'Is it really necessary to clear out those drawers?'

Leonard knew that his wife found their neighbour intrusive at times and obviously felt this was a good time to say so. Mrs Peavey looked up blankly, very surprised.

'I don't know what Leonard's told you,' Deborah continued, 'but I'd prefer it if you left the bedroom cupboards and drawers alone. Do you mind?'

Mrs Peavey nodded her head dumbly.

'Good. I'm just a bit funny that way. Anyway, I'm off. The money's on the dining table. Bye.' She swept out of the room.

The book in Mrs Peavey's hand slid into the drawer, and slowly, methodically, she closed it. She then stood in the same position, hands on hips, for the next few minutes, staring solemnly at the bedroom door, her chest heaving with large breaths. Leonard found the whole scene engrossing. What was she thinking? Her appearance reminded him vaguely of Boris Karloff. Suddenly she clicked out of her reverie and started pacing up and down next to the bed.

'Do you mind? Do you *mind*?' Her eyes were wild-looking. 'Little Miss Madam! Little Miss Hoity-Toity! Well, perhaps I *do* mind.' She was nodding vigorously, her face ablaze. 'I was just putting your husband's book away, lady. That's all I was doing. Is that all right? Is that all right, lady?' She opened the drawer again and took the book out before flinging it back. 'That's all I was doing. It just takes some manners, that's all.'

Leonard sat glued to the television. He'd never seen anything so riveting in his life. Unfortunately she made her way to the bathroom.

'That's very *neighbourly*,' he could hear in the background. He turned up the volume. 'I mean, is that a *neighbourly* way to speak to a neighbour? Is it?' The taps were turned on. It sounded as if she were cleaning the sink. 'Spoilt. . . .Stuck-up. . . .Self-obsessed. . . . And she's got *me* to do for her, out of the kindness of my heart.' There were lots of grunts. Leonard turned the volume up to full but it was difficult to make out anything now. At one point he thought he heard the word 'tramp', but he wasn't sure. She left the bathroom a few minutes later and walked straight out of the bedroom.

'Well!' he murmured. He'd always regarded Mrs Peavey as a trifle eccentric, but it appeared that she was totally batty. There was a look in her eye that boded ominously for anyone who crossed her path and, though she was no longer a young woman, to judge by her movements, there was still a lot of strength in her sturdy frame.

However, nothing happened of a sexual nature.

Deborah didn't always return home before midnight, but Leonard had taken that into account, fitting an infrared illuminator to the camera beforehand. Everything from the technical as well as the marital viewpoint was going swimmingly. The tape didn't have long to run now, and then he could jettison these horrible suspicions for good. Put the whole business down as a lesson about the lengths he was prepared to go to secure his peace of mind. His wife, it appeared, was quite conventional. No singing or prancing around. No personal habits he didn't know about. Most importantly, she was always on her own. . . .

Until virtually the last day.

She'd come into the room, wearing the red dress she'd worn the previous evening – it was about ten o'clock at night – and was sitting at the dressing-table while combing her hair. It was clear from an early stage that she wasn't addressing herself but someone a fair distance away. Her voice was raised.

'Don't worry, there's no chance of being discovered.'

A voice responded – a man's – but it was impossible to make out any of the words.

Leonard sat a little more upright on the sofa. This was wrong, surely. Why was there a man – on his own? – in the house at this stage of the evening?

Deborah unhooked her earrings. 'Yeah, it's a dummy. He assured me.'

The camera outside, she was talking about the camera outside. Now what? She was standing up and – oh, *ohhh* – lifting her dress up over her head. She was in her underwear with another man roaming around the house! His eyes drank in the screen, a pink spot radiating from each cheekbone.

The man was speaking again – louder than before – but still difficult to—

Was he coming up the stairs?

Leonard had turned to stone, barely breathing. So help Lasker if he laid a finger . . .

'Well,' Deborah replied, sitting down and examining her coiffure again, 'even if it *is* real, we can just say you popped over for a social call.'

Why, oh why, was she fiddling with her hair when she was wearing next to nothing? If she intended to change her clothes, she was leaving it perilously late.

'I suppose,' said the man. His voice was distinct now. He must be on the landing at least, about to enter. No . . . *no* . . . NO—

Then he was there, standing over her, gazing into the camera, one hand clutching a bottle of wine and a couple of glasses, the other stroking her head. The first thing Leonard noticed was the dog's-tooth check jacket he was wearing.

'You look magnificent. I don't know about you, but I could really do with a work-out right now.'

Leonard's blood had stopped pumping, frozen with shock. He was looking into the face of Andrew Dunstan.

PART TWO

Revenge is a dish best served cold.
— Old Greek Proverb

16

Don't Look Now (1973)

So the world was flat after all.

Dunstan placed the wine and the glasses on the dressing-table and began gently massaging Deborah's neck to her sighs. Leonard's head swung up to the ceiling as he let out his own, almost inaudible, groan. He wanted to turn the sound and pictures off, but his arms and body felt terribly heavy and his gaze returned inevitably to the screen. The massage was continuing – she was sucking one of Dunstan's fingers – but somewhere out of shot a door opened and closed. Surely they couldn't have invited someone else? There was a shuffling of feet in the hall. . . .

It seemed to be an age before he realized that the sounds he was hearing weren't coming from the television, that someone else was in the house at that moment, and that this person was just the other side of the living-room door. Desperately he lunged for the remote control. . . .

Just in time.

He frantically wiped at his eyes as Mrs Peavey came bustling in, carrying something large which she dumped in the middle of the room. The television was now showing *Trisha*.

'Hello, hello! Thought I'd do a morning shift today. Wanted to show you what I found yesterday, lying in a ditch.'

The cleaner was puffing and panting away, her face a delicate shade of purple. She smoothed her hands on her cardigan and turned to face Leonard on the sofa. Through a watery haze, he regarded the porcelain cat he'd recently dispensed with.

'Your eyes are all red!' Mrs Peavey exclaimed.

Leonard looked up from the cat. 'I'm so glad you've brought it back.'

'Yes, well, I knew it'd be worth something. It's Meissen, isn't it?'

'H'm.' He needed to escape from her as soon as possible, re-establish his privacy.

'I've cleaned it up. I suppose the burglar must've got tired of lugging it around.'

'H'm.' *Really do with a work-out right now. . . .*

'Frank and I saw a lot of these in Germany. You can tell it's Meissen by the crossed-swords mark. Unless I'm mistaken this one was modelled by Kändler.' She suddenly noticed the other cat by the hearth. 'What is *that*?' She frowned at Leonard.

He shrugged helplessly. She was like a salesperson who forced a response in order to continue her pitch. 'Something Deborah bought the other day.' Deborah the finger-sucker.

'Well.' Mrs Peavey shook her head pityingly. 'I hope she didn't pay much for it. Straight off the conveyor belt by the looks of it.'

She prattled on as Leonard battled to regain his composure. Deborah and Andrew. In the bedroom. *His* hands caressing Deborah's neck.

'So have you heard any news?'

'Who?'

'*News*. About the burglar. Remember him, Mr Sleepyhead?'

She rocked her head on her shoulders with her mouth gaping open, in what was meant to be a good-natured impression of Leonard.

'No. No, we haven't.' He had to get out. Get the tape and go.

'Wouldn't happen in my house, no offence or anything. My dogs'd tear the burglar apart.'

'Yes, I can imagine. Anyway, better be—'

'Strange, don't you think? That someone should steal something valuable, then just abandon it like that. I looked around but I couldn't see any footprints.'

'Thanks,' said Leonard. He hadn't even thought of footprints. 'I'll get in touch with the police. Tell them you've found Lotte.'

'I suppose they'll want to see me, won't they? Find out where I found her.'

'Possibly, I guess. The important thing is she's back. I don't think we'll have another break-in.'

Mrs Peavey nodded. 'Is that what the cameras are for?'

Leonard started to get up. Questions, questions. He'd just retrieve the tape in the VCR and make his departure. 'The one outside, yes.'

'I was here last week,' said Mrs Peavey, glancing around the room with about as much casualness as a hawk. 'I couldn't help but notice a camera hidden inside the motion detector in your bedroom.'

Leonard sat down again. They stared at each other for a second. She knew about his covert surveillance operation. At least, she was aware that something was going on.

'Your wife'd taken the day off work. I was going to have a word with her, but – well, I think she was in a rush. Obviously I didn't think you were filming at the time, but for future—'

'Oh, no, don't worry. Everything's switched off.'

'I'm sure you'll understand, though, if I just speak—'

Leonard raised his hand. 'No, no! Just – just let it be our little secret. Please.' His forehead was damp with sweat.

'Our little secret,' Mrs Peavey repeated, raising her eyebrows and folding her arms. Her whole demeanour suggested that further explanation would be required if she wasn't going to talk to Deborah.

'Yes. You see, I thought my wife . . . that there was a slim chance she—' He gazed forlornly into her eyes. He knew she wouldn't believe anything else, but why was he trying to explain at all? Judging by her earlier outburst, she hardly sympathized with Deborah. 'Oh – it doesn't matter. Forget I said anything.' He climbed to his feet. 'I'm really sorry, Agatha. No filming will take place on Fridays, I promise you. Anyway, I'm thinking of taking it all down.' He walked over to the VCR and collected the tape – how much more suspicious could it look? – then left the room.

'I know a little bit about CCTV.' She started to follow him but, as tactfully as possible, he closed the living-room door.

*

He quickly made his way to the basement. God strewth, what in the world was he playing at? That woman was just the sort to winkle information out of you. Next she'd be saying, 'I know somebody who works for a detective agency and she happened to see you the other day. . . .'

He locked the door behind him and slumped in his favourite couch. Oh, Jesus. Oh, God Almighty. He'd told Dunstan about hiring a private investigator, hadn't he? Perhaps Dunstan had decided not to mention it to Deborah on the grounds it might worry her unduly, but the fact remained that the man knew virtually everything. Leonard had trusted him absolutely, confided in him, made himself look like an idiot. Instinctively his fists began to curl up, the nails digging into his palms.

The devil. The complete and utter snake in the grass.

What was it Dunstan had said when Leonard had expressed his deepest fears about Deborah? That she was into older men, wedded to the paper. Leonard took a long intake of breath. Dunstan had advised him to speak to Deborah presumably because he'd calculated he'd be able to warn her of Leonard's suspicions before Leonard had a chance to see her himself. It was even possible at the gym that she'd played up to it a bit with Lasker, deliberately acting coldly to Leonard afterwards.

Everything was gradually falling into place. The old jumper that Deborah had been wearing all those weeks ago wasn't Lasker's, it was Dunstan's. The reason she'd been toning up her muscles wasn't for Lasker's benefit – after all, he had plenty of other women – but for the new journalist in her life.

Leonard felt heartily sick.

And now he had the final and most important shred of evidence in his hand: the tape. He was going to watch it to the end, however upsetting it might be. It was still theoretically possible, of course, that Dunstan might be impotent, that his relationship with Deborah was purely platonic. . . .

17

Pillow Talk (1959)

The screening-room was actually the scene of some of Leonard's happiest memories, allowing him to escape into another, more fantastical, world. Thousands of videos and DVDs lined the walls, from short clips dating back to the beginning of the century to advance copies of films sent to him by the *Chronicle* to review. There was a comfortable settee down here, which he was presently occupying, together with an armchair with a leg-rest. A popcorn machine stood in one corner and a Mutoscope – a 'What the butler saw' machine – in another. The highly superior DLP projector was housed in a spacious wooden alcove; the surround sound speaker system was scattered around the room; and the screen, occupying most of one wall, was framed by curtains that had once covered the French windows in the living-room.

Leonard watched them having sexual intercourse.

It was extremely hurtful and he'd had to stop the tape on several occasions. While Deborah was still sitting at the dressing-table, Dunstan had transferred his hands from her neck to her breasts, kneading them slowly, the two of them indulging in a long, tongue-filled kiss. Then she had stood up, unfastened his shirt buttons, before concentrating herself on his chest. This was simply a prelude to the main dish, as she had lowered herself down, and down. . . .

The tape continued its sick progress. In point of fact Deborah and Leonard had never practised such high jinks, an attitude he had been at pains to understand, and yet here she was choosing different (flavoured?) condoms to taste. There were moments when he could not bear to watch.

The most revelatory aspect of their lovemaking, though, was the incessant talking and joking around. Apart from looking extremely aroused, they appeared to be having fun as well.

'You're gorgeous,' said Dunstan.

'You're absolutely huge,' she said, rolling her eyes – to their mutual amusement – in the direction of a certain part of his anatomy.

'You've got lovely, long legs.'

'It's massive. I've never seen one so big.'

'Your breasts are perfect.'

'Will it even fit?'

Leonard and Deborah, whenever they'd found themselves in the same situation, weren't silent, of course, one or the other making the occasional grunt, but this was ridiculous. At the point of climax, when Dunstan had established that it would indeed fit, the noise was deafening. He was bellowing, 'Oh, no! Oh, *no*! Please *God*! *Oh, no*! *Jee-suss*! *Oh, oh*! *Yeeeaaaahhhhhhhhh*!'

Leonard sat alone in the closed atmosphere of the basement, surrounded by the heavy granite walls, his mouth drooping open disconsolately. He felt dead from the neck up, overcome by a dreadful depression, unable to think coherently and just wanting to escape from reality. Dunstan had returned from the bathroom and, after some heavy petting, had engaged in an animated conversation with his companion's private parts. At least after the excitement of her lover's orgasm, Deborah had been more restrained in her expressions of ecstasy – not sounding too dissimilar to normal.

After it was over, they lay on the bed stroking each other's hair. It all looked so natural, as if they'd made love many times before but were still not past the first flush of their relationship.

'You're special to me, Debs, you know that, don't you? I've never felt this way before, the way I feel about you.'

She wasn't saying anything, just grinning at him.

'It's funny. I always used to look at women with a view . . . Well, let's say with one object in mind. But now . . . now I don't do that any more. I guess this must be the real thing, eh? I must be really falling for you.'

Leonard rushed to turn the tape off. About the only thing that would have given him any satisfaction at that moment was to take an axe to the man's head. He returned to the sofa and started pummelling the cushions, stopping a few seconds later when he ran out of breath, his chest rising and falling, a hand raised to feel his heart.

A minute passed, and then, still feeling dazed, he turned the tape back on and resumed his seat. His whole body was bathed in sweat and he placed his hands flat on his legs in an attempt to stay calm. They were still lying there looking into each other's eyes.

'You don't mean that,' she murmured. 'I know you don't.'

'Yes, I do.'

'No . . . No, you don't.'

'I do. You're wrong.'

'You don't.'

'I do. I really do.'

Deborah folded her arms, regarding him tolerantly. 'Are you saying if some stunning nymphomaniac came along—'

'Not interested. Not remotely.'

'Oh . . . yeah!'

'No. Really.'

'You'd be interested, I know you would.'

'No, I wouldn't.'

'Yeah, definitely.'

'Swear to God I wouldn't,' Dunstan protested. 'There's more chance of you going off with someone else.'

'No, there isn't, not at all.'

'Yes. I think so.'

'No.'

'Yes.'

'No.'

'Yes.'

'Oh, for heaven's sake,' said Leonard, twisting about on the settee.

The phone rang on the bedside cabinet. They both sat up, startled.

'Don't answer it,' said Dunstan.

'I have to. He's been phoning me about this time.'

The answering machine clicked into action. Oh, God, this was *him*, wasn't it? Phoning from Cannes. She picked up the receiver.

'L-Leonard. You woke me up.' She smiled at Dunstan. 'I was spending a quiet night in and just dozed off.'

The other man grinned.

'Yeah,' she continued to Leonard. 'Everything's hunky' – she pretended to yawn, playfully pinching Dunstan's cheek – 'dory. How 'bout you?'

There was a pause.

'Interesting,' she said, pulling a bored face.

'Look, I'm joking. If you don't believe me, ask my lover. He's here beside me in bed.'

Dunstan buried his head in his hands.

'OK, we'll do that.'

She placed the phone back in its cradle, picking it up again briefly to check for the dialling tone. Leonard remembered his feelings during that phone call. He'd thought she'd sounded a little unnatural, but he was actually missing her and experiencing some remorse over setting up the cameras.

'Strange, isn't it?' she said, straightening out the cover. 'I always feel closer to him when he's not here. I think he cares about me in his own way.'

'Feeling guilty?' asked Dunstan.

'Perhaps. Perhaps a little bit, I don't know. It makes me feel better somehow, knowing you feel the same about Chloe. Does that make sense?'

'No,' came a voice from the couch.

'The thing is with Leonard, he does have his good points. He always has a meal ready for me when I get home. He always makes sure the place looks clean and tidy. I'm sure most women would love to have him as their husband.'

'But you – you're not one of them?'

Leonard's fingers, clinging to the armrest and the edge of the settee, tightened slowly.

'Well, sometimes I feel a certain fondness for him. Just before he left he took me through how to operate the alarm. The number to activate it is one-four-one and the number to deactivate it is one-seven-two. I didn't get it immediately, but if you put them together – fourteen-eleven-seventy-two – that's the date of my birthday.'

'Oh, God, now I feel guilty,' said Dunstan.

'Ah, baby!' said Deborah, leaning across and giving him a kiss, provoking a less generous epithet from the couch. 'No, it's true that Leonard can be sweet at times. The problem with Leonard,' she resumed, moving back to her side of the bed, 'is this love affair he's got with films. I used to think it was really fascinating – this burning interest of his – but ultimately it just takes him away from me. I look at him sometimes when he's watching a film and he's totally wrapped up in it, totally transported. I've got no idea what's going on inside his head.'

'And you resent it?'

'Yes. Yes, I do.'

'Well,' said Dunstan, shaking his head, 'all I can say is it's his loss. If he wants to spend his whole life watching films. . . .'

'Yes, but that's the interesting thing.' Deborah turned towards Dunstan to make her point. 'Just when you think that he's gone for good, lost in this celluloid world, back he comes into the frame. He actually tried to reach out to me the other day. We were on our way back from the gym . . .'

'And?'

'Well, I just couldn't talk to him. I couldn't.'

Dunstan nodded sympathetically.

'I didn't realize I could be so cold and distant,' Deborah went on. 'I think it was the shock of the moment, the idea of the two of us having a frank and open conversation about our feelings.'

Dunstan took Deborah's hand in his. 'What's to become of us, d'you think?'

'What's to become of you and Chloe?' said Deborah, glancing to her side.

Dunstan let out a sigh. 'Oh, I really don't know. She's getting worse, I think. It's this steroid treatment. Nothing I do seems to get her approval. I know I shouldn't say it, but it'll almost be a relief once it's over.'

Deborah nodded slowly, immersed in her thoughts.

'How about Leonard?' Dunstan asked. 'You ever thought about leaving him?'

She gave a little smile. Leonard glared at her intently.

'Leaving good ol' Lenny, now there's a question! It's crazy, I know, but I actually believe marriage is for life.'

Leonard snorted with derision.

'There's only three exceptions, I think, to the rule. Adultery, of course: if Leonard were to go off with someone else. . . .'

They both laughed, appreciating the irony in the situation. Leonard uttered an oath.

'Secondly, if Leonard was violent – which I just can't imagine him being, somehow. Then finally, of course, there's death.'

'Ah, yes, the definitive solution,' said Dunstan. 'It's a shame you can't slip something in his cocoa.'

Leonard, who was already very alert, sat bolt upright, all his antennae tuned to the screen.

'Yeah, right!' said Deborah. 'The famous undetectable poison enabling the perfect crime.'

Dunstan nodded, but his expression remained sombre. Leonard stared at him in disbelief, a shiver running down his spine, waiting for the other man to admit the ridiculousness of the conversation.

'You've always been into the medical side of things,' smiled Dunstan, 'and I've covered a few poisonings in my time as a journalist. I'm sure, between us, we could figure out something, convince the police it was an accident or suicide. Just think of all the drugs you've got in your bathroom.'

She turned to face him. 'Are you seri—?'

18

In a Lonely Place (1950)

But before their conversation could finish, the screen turned a speckled grey and the tape began rewinding automatically. For a few moments Leonard stayed in his seat, motionless. Were they planning to murder him? Poison him to death? A cold, heavy feeling attached itself to his heart. It was more than likely that Dunstan was joking, but then how could he tell, especially after all those protestations of love?

Oh, God, he needed a drink – a neat vodka or something. Dunstan's face had remained solemn throughout, but that was a habit of his, wasn't it? He'd only break his expression at the last moment, bursting into laughter.

Yes, yes, that must be – had to be – the case. It was a joke in really bad taste. There was no other reasonable—

Tap, tap-tap, tap, tap.

Eh? That was the door. Who could—?

Mrs Peavey. What on earth did she want? Could she have heard—?

No . . . No, of course not. The sound would be muffled. All the same, he could do without Filchester's answer to Baby Jane breathing down his neck just at the moment. He fumbled for the key (luckily she was only able to open the front door) and peered out into her monolithic features.

'My, it's awfully dark down here. I just came to pick up my money.'

'Oh, yes!'

Leonard fished out a ten pound note from his pocket and then started counting his change. Five more pounds to find. No way was he going to leave his post, giving her the chance to enter.

'Everything all right?' Mrs Peavey enquired.

'H'm? Oh, yeah, everything's hunky – er, fine, I mean. Here we go.' He gave her the money. 'Look, I'd like to get you something, you know, for finding that cat. Anything you'd particularly like?'

She blushed. 'Oh! Oh, that's really . . . Thank you. I don't really—'

'Well, perhaps I'll think of something, then.'

She shifted her attention to the space beyond his shoulder. Acts of kindness like this needed rewarding.

'If you like, I could go through your basement. Looks as if it could do with a spring-clean.'

'Thanks. Thanks a lot. But I'm working on something at the moment.'

He'd locked her out for the last two months, even before this recent business. She had a habit of straightening things out that was infuriating.

She moved closer to him so that he could smell her bad breath.

'I just want you to know I'm completely on your side.'

He could feel his face burning. She knew about the cameras and had probably divined his suspicions about Deborah – though she couldn't know any more than that. At a loss for something to say, he frowned as if her meaning were beyond him.

'That sort of thing's happening all the time now, you mustn't blame yourself. If you ask me, it's all down to feminism.'

The syllable 'fem' sent a warm gust of halitosis in his direction. 'Feminism?'

'You know, equal rights. In the old days men always had a bit on the side. Now it's the turn of women.'

'I'm not sure I follow.'

She shook her head. 'The way these young girls parade themselves about, I'm surprised it isn't more common. The language they use as well. Everything's effing this and effing that.'

'H'm.' You've effing lost it.

'Everyone's playing around without regard to the consequences.

Even in my day – well, that's another story – but I can tell you, I know exactly how you feel. I went through a lot with my Frank. . . .'

Her eyes left his as the sentence tailed off. Her face had assumed a dead expression, like a slab of stone. A bubble of mucus was going in-n-n, then out-t-t of her left nostril. In-n-n. Out-t-t. In—

'Disgusting, isn't it?' She was staring straight at him.

'Um— Oh, yes, absolutely. Glad you see my point of view. So! Same time next week?'

He gently closed the door, her face still locked in bleak reflection. It was all very disturbing, but it would have been very difficult, as a neighbour, to tell her that her services were no longer required – especially since she'd just brought back that cat. (Besides, when she wasn't nosing around, she actually did a good job.) After about half a minute her footsteps retreated up the stone steps, and a little later the front door slammed shut. She was gone.

Leonard returned to the couch and spent the next hour sitting stock-still, not thinking about very much at all. At least when the tape had been running, there had been new, albeit horrible, developments to discover. Even talking to 'Boris Karloff' had provided a measure of relief, since it had forced him to concentrate to some extent on what she'd been saying and then find words of his own. Now – with nothing stopping him from thinking about the Great Act of Betrayal – it was all he could do to breathe, his bearing and attitude resembling that of a mouse trapped by a cat. At least if the mouse/Leonard stayed where it was, it stood a chance of survival.

How could she?

Slowly, almost in a trance, he rose to his feet, climbed the stone steps, then the main staircase, before entering the bedroom.

Of course, everything looked the same: the cabinets, cupboards, in their usual positions, the motion detector in place, the bed sheets in pristine condition. He stayed looking at the scene for five minutes and then – because his face was on fire – retired to the bathroom to splash it with cold water. Looking through the medicine cabinet afterwards, he was surprised to find things in rather higgledy-piggledy order – a bit out of character for Deborah – but then how well did he know her any more? In any case, the water and the act of taking a couple of tablets had actually made him feel a little better, and he made his way back down to the basement.

From its previous state of abeyance, his mind had settled on the one subject and any other mental activity was out of the question. Words and images, not just from the video but further back in the past, kept coming into his head. Dunstan's best man's speech at his wedding – 'Doesn't the bride look beautiful?' Deborah's put-down last night – 'Shove your thing up me'. The sneering way she'd looked at him.

Just do it, Leonard.

Some form of action was required, for the sake of his sanity if nothing else. He walked across the room, cloaked in a familiar semi-darkness, and entered another smaller chamber.

The 'editing suite' – rather a grandiose title for just one room – was a maze of electronic equipment, the nerve centre of Leonard's surveillance operation. Lined up on a bench were two multimedia PCs, a Macintosh, a couple of printers, a scanner, three VCRs, a switcher, a receiver – as well as a great deal of junk. Leonard had recently transferred much of his film-making kit to the garage, but there were still various makes of cameras, lenses, filters, cluttering up one corner.

He watched the tape again, all the way through. With hindsight, it was clear that Mrs Peavey had spotted the camera inside the motion detector when she'd stood on the stool for a closer inspection. The second time of watching Deborah and Dunstan having sex was still extremely painful – having to regard the rapturous expressions on their faces – but at least the shock element had subsided. It was more horrible, if anything, contemplating the feelings – of love? – that lay behind the joining of bodies.

He would have to show them, both of them, these images. A few years ago a man in the States had gone even further, sending tapes of his wife committing adultery to his friends and neighbours, but Leonard had no intention of drawing attention to himself as a cuckold. In any case, it was important that Dunstan's wife, Chloe, didn't get to hear of this. (Did she have any idea already?) On the several occasions he'd met her she'd always seemed very nice, smiling up at him from her wheelchair.

He shook with the evil of it. When Shirley's health had begun to deteriorate, he'd placed all his energy into looking after her, not given other women a moment's thought. He had to do more than just show them the videotape, something to make them realize the proper extent of their crime. After all, they'd discussed his death for God's sake.

Just do it, Leonard.

He went upstairs to fix his lunch before returning to his bunker. He'd have to edit the videotape, take out the irrelevant bits. And why stop there? He could use footage from home movies he'd made over the last few years. Feed the recordings into the Macintosh, together with photographs, and paste them into a coherent whole. It was a pity in a way that only Deborah and Dunstan would be able to see the result of his labours. . . .

The real silver lining, though, was that the idea for a film for Dorry was assuming a more definite shape. Certain scenes were already playing themselves in his mind. He would definitely jot down some notes for his screenplay as soon as he'd completed his film editing.

He left the screening-room, exhausted by his efforts. There was still lots to do but the struggle of creativity had taken the edge off his injured feelings. The phone was ringing upstairs and he rushed to answer it.

'Where were you? I was holding on for ages.'

His hand, holding the receiver, quivered. It was Deborah.

'I was watching a film downstairs,' he said.

'Are you all right? You sound a bit constipated.'

He cleared his throat. He must try not to show any emotion. 'I'm fine. Mrs Peavey's found Lotte.'

'Oh, great. Where was she?'

'She was in a ditch, apparently.'

'A ditch! What, not far from the house?'

Leonard provided the rough details. No doubt he should have gleaned the whole story off Mrs Peavey.

'She's now sitting next to the fireplace.'

'Fantastic. She's still in one piece, then? No damage?'

'Well, Mrs Peavey did say she'd cleaned her up.'

'Oh, right! So she doesn't have a head, but she's perfectly spotless. Didn't you look?'

He went quiet.

'Well, it's good news, anyway,' she continued before the pause became any more embarrassing. 'Look, Leonard, I know this is a bit last-minute, but one of my researchers is having a leaving do this evening and a group of us are going along. I should be back about eleven.'

'Sure, no problem.' Go right ahead and see your boyfriend.

'OK, see you later—'

'Deborah?'

He interrupted her before she had a chance to put the phone down. There was no point in postponing the moment.

'Yes?'

'I didn't tell you I met up with Andrew Dunstan just before Cannes.'

There was a pause. 'Yeah. And. . . ?'

'Well, the last time we invited him and Chloe over must be – what? – a year ago. I was thinking of holding a dinner party.'

She coughed lightly. 'Yeah, all right, why not? You'll have to arrange it all, though.' This was evidently the only excuse she could think of.

'Of course.'

She appeared temporarily lost for words. 'Right, then. See you later.'

19

Don Juan (1926)

The weekend passed without any showdowns. Deborah was living her own life, apart from him, and perhaps for the time being it was just as well. Oh, God, how he wanted to tell her that he knew what she was up to, how just a moment's warmth on her part would have prompted him to reveal all. Yet somehow she didn't seem to notice him gazing at her a little longer than usual – having to swallow because his throat was so dry – and relations between them continued much the same as usual. Although he'd seen her in the most compromising situation, it had only served to increase her untouchable status even more.

What was to become of their marriage?

For his part – if he had any say in the matter – it was too early to think about divorce, even if that was what should be happening. Deborah was still, in name at least, his wife; they'd spent a significant period of their lives together. All he was doing at the moment was treading water, unable to contemplate the future beyond showing her the video of her adultery, supposing his feelings would be affected a great deal by her reaction to that.

Though, in any event, would he ever really be able to trust her again?

On Monday morning he called HVM and arranged to come in at 10.30. It was time to call off the investigation of Lasker. Enough money had been spent raking up the dirt on the wrong person.

111

Hedda Marshall greeted him in her office with her usual enthusiasm. HVM had managed to compile quite a dossier on young Master Lasker.

'His sex life's incredible,' she said, smiling. 'In the last three weeks he's entertained at least six women, including a call girl.'

Leonard nodded. This was probably the woman Lasker was sharing with his brother. 'And my wife's one of them?'

Although he'd been infuriated on Friday at the way HVM had misled him, he'd later concluded that they could still be right about Deborah having an affair with Lasker. Nothing would surprise him now.

'No. No, actually, she's not. I think we overrated her interest in Lasker, based on that one week.' The PI showed no sign of embarrassment, simply giving utterance to the reassuring news. 'She has been seeing him from time to time but only as a go-between. It's her friend, Kate, who's really involved. She and Lasker seem to be having quite a thing, at least from her point of view.'

Leonard gazed at the ceiling. Of course! He could see now what had happened. Because Kate's husband beat her up, she had gone to Lasker. And Deborah, very excited by the whole business (paralleled in some ways with her affair with Dunstan), had rushed from one to the other in typically melodramatic fashion, encouraging Kate on the one hand to leave her husband, while advising Lasker on the other not to worry about Kate being married. All the hand-holding and kissing was undoubtedly sincere. No wonder she'd looked so perturbed in the gym when Lasker had announced he was involved in all those other relationships. She was concerned about her friend.

Hedda Marshall proceeded to tell Leonard more about Lasker, apparently unaware that it was all a waste of time. Perhaps she just wanted to demonstrate how thoroughly her organization could perform a job as commissioned. He listened to Lasker's dealings in anabolic steroids out of idle curiosity. The man was a character from television-land, a small-time crook on *The Bill*.

His attention, though, was arrested by the photographs that Hedda placed on the desk, a line-up of the women Lasker had consorted with over the last month, all of them very elegant and attractive.

'So which one's Kate?' he asked.

'Here.'

She pointed to a photograph of a woman who was blushing, lips parted in a pant, hanging onto Lasker's arm.

'Oh, I thought . . . well . . .'

'This one's the call girl.'

Hedda indicated another photo showing Lasker accompanied by a woman who was looking disconcertingly straight at the camera. She was dressed in a smart, tailored suit, her head tilted confidently upwards. In another light she could be mistaken for a previous boss of his, though this was about twenty years ago now, a woman known for her voracious acquisition of men.

'You seem quite taken by that particular photo,' Hedda said.

Leonard was lost in his thoughts.

'Mr Fleason?'

'M'm? Oh, yes – sorry!'

'I was just saying, you seem particularly taken by that photo.'

'What pho—? Oh, um, *this* one?'

'Yes.'

'I-I . . . well, I suppose I just haven't seen that many call girls.'

'I'm glad to hear it.'

'No, you know what I mean. She just looks so—'

'Normal?'

'Yes.'

'Well, I think she's from what you might call the high end of the market. Some of these girls are very switched on, you know. Very business-minded about things.'

'H'm.'

'As well as having, of course, a more than average interest in sex.'

'Hmmm.'

'Mr Fleason?'

'Yes?'

'I think I lost you again there.'

'Sorry . . . I'm sorry!' He pulled himself together. 'This, um, lady. W-what's her name, d'you know?'

'Yvonne.' She flicked through some pages on her desk. 'Yes . . . just Yvonne. We haven't got a last name. But you're not actually thinking of getting in touch with her?'

Leonard held his hands up in a display of innocence, a gesture that only met with a frown.

'There's really no need, you know. All the information's in the file. If you were to speak to her, you might alert her suspicions. She might even mention you to Lasker.'

'I understand.'

Hedda nodded, though she still regarded Leonard with a degree of suspicion.

'Anyway,' she added, 'it's good news about your wife.'

'What! Oh, yes! Yes, absolutely!'

20

The French Connection (1971)

Well, well – what a productive conversation! Leonard really hadn't expected much from his meeting with Hedda, but he'd come away with his mind positively buzzing with activity. An idea, a new direction, had suggested itself – at the very least, it should make an interesting subplot for his screenplay. Over the next twenty-four hours, besides contemplating his real-life manoeuvrings, Leonard ransacked his memory for films with similar storylines, just to make sure his idea was original. Perhaps the closest to the mark was *Kiss Me, Stupid*, Ray Walston hiring a call girl to sleep with Dean Martin in the hope of advancing his career. But then, aside from the differing circumstances, that film was quite cruel in places. Whatever else he had in mind, Leonard had no intention of hurting Chloe – or any other innocent party. His main reservation, as he stuffed his Fred Perry shorts into a plastic bag, was that by taking things another stage further, he was becoming more and more like the film critic in his screenplay, a character Geoff Hartnell seemed to think was completely bonkers.

The next morning, having sufficiently steeled himself for the occasion, he phoned Andrew Dunstan. It was hateful talking to the man again but unfortunately necessary. How did he feel about meeting up for lunch in a couple of days' time? Dunstan said he'd be delighted. Leonard gave the rendezvous details and rang off.

Then he took a card out of his wallet, inscribed with the words,

'Accommodation for Gentlemen', together with a phone number, and picked up the receiver again.

'Hello.'

'Oh, good morning. Are you the . . . advertiser?'

'No, sir, I'm the maid.'

'Right, right. Would it be possible to provide me with some details?'

'Certainly, sir. Can I ask where you saw the advertisement?'

He was sweating profusely. He'd felt nervous when he'd first contacted HVM but this was even worse.

'In a gym – Tiptop – in Kensington.'

'Ah, yes. Well, it's a full personal service. The young lady is extremely beautiful, with dark, waist-length hair and a voluptuous figure. Her measurements are thirty-nine, twenty-three, thirty-six, and she charges a minimum sum of fifty pounds. That, of course, includes a full strip, but she does specialize for higher fees. She's here every day from lunchtime onwards but is also available as an escort on Friday and Saturday nights. Would you care to book an appointment, sir?'

'Yes, please.' It felt as if he were reserving a table in a restaurant.

'I'll give you the address, then. Twelve Jessup Gardens, the top apartment. What time would be convenient?'

'One o'clock, Thursday?'

That would be an hour before his meeting with Dunstan. Leonard already knew Yvonne's address – reassuringly close to the *Chronicle*'s offices and the pub where they were to meet – and just needed to confirm the timing. There was a pause at the other end of the line, the page of a diary being leafed.

'Yes, madam is free then. We look forward to seeing you.'

'Thank you,' said Leonard. He heard a click and replaced the receiver.

Well, that was done at any rate. Perhaps he was going a bit too far with all this, but then Dunstan should never have told Deborah he no longer looked at other women, should he? Good God, even in the canteen he'd been eyeing up a girl walking past their table. . . .

Yes, that was why showing them the video would never suffice. After all, they might say, 'All right, you caught us out, but our love is a precious thing.' This current idea of his would put the lie to anything like that. It would be hard to arrange – and he might well have to abandon ship later if things didn't work out. . . .

But then if they did. . . .

From now on, Leonard wanted all the surprises to emanate from him.

Jessup Gardens, when Leonard turned into it, was lined with plane trees, a church spire pointing to the sky about halfway down. On one side there were stuccoed terraces in the Georgian style, with high windows and pillars supporting balconies, while facing these were houses under the Victorian influence, ornate, built in red brick, with slightly smaller windows.

No reason then why he should feel particularly self-conscious, and yet, carrying a wallet stuffed with £500 in fifty and twenty pound notes, Leonard's heart was still pumping faster than usual as he entered the porch of number twelve. A young woman was on her way out with a baby in a pushchair and he held the door open to let them pass. Everything was unreal: the smell of disinfectant, the carpeted stairs. Still, the card on the third floor read YVONNE. He carefully wiped his forehead and pressed the bell.

The door was opened by a tiny woman dressed entirely in black, her face lined with age. Her voice was the one he'd spoken to on Tuesday.

'Good afternoon, sir. Did you arrange an appointment?'

'I did.'

'Please come in. Madam will be with you shortly.'

'Thank you.'

He was shown into a sitting-room that looked as if it had been furnished in the last few weeks. Neat and tidy, yet slightly cold and impersonal. Franz Marc paintings featured in the posters on the walls, while copies of *The Times*, *Le Monde* and *Newsweek* lay fanned out on the coffee table.

'Make yourself comfortable,' said the maid. 'Can I get you a cup of tea?'

'If it's no trouble.'

She came back a few moments later with a tray of tea things and a couple of hard-core porn magazines, reminding him, if he'd forgotten, that he wasn't at the dentist's. Her doleful expression unchanged, she trooped off again.

Leonard glanced down at the cover of the top magazine. A middle-aged man was tied up on a bed, his mouth hanging open in an expression of (blissful?) agony, while a leather-clad dominatrix, brandishing a whip, observed him disdainfully from a distance. He was just sipping his tea while flicking idly through the magazine – which bore the Dostoevskian title of *Crime and Punishment* – when madam made her entrance.

'Dar-leeng! We 'ave much fun, yes?'

Leonard gazed up at a woman in her early twenties – the same woman he'd seen in the photo on Hedda's desk. She was quite tall, dressed in a medium-length black skirt and a thin mauve jumper that hugged her figure – this last feature quite trim and not at all the statistical phenomenon quoted over the phone. Her dark hair was pushed forward over her shoulders.

'No, no, I haven't come here for that,' he said in a fluster. 'I've got a friend, you see. Well, not a friend any more. A colleague of mine on the paper— Oh, crumbs!' He brought himself up. 'Don't think I'm doing a story on you. I-I didn't mean— Oh, crumbs! Is it hot in here?'

Her eyes had distracted him, an exquisite violet colour, the product undoubtedly of special contact lenses.

'I know zer *journaliste*,' she said, quite unruffled. 'I 'ave met with zer reperters and zer earners.'

'Right. Well, the thing is— Sorry, did you say "owners" just then? Newspaper owners?' She must be mistaken but he just had to know. 'As in, er, Eddie Hornchurch, for instance? Would he. . . ? You wouldn't happen. . . ? Sorry, forgive my nosiness.'

She concentrated for a second. 'Is 'e zer earner of zer *Chrenicle*?'

'That's right.'

She smiled. 'I do not – 'ow you say – reveal zer names of my friends.'

Leonard's mouth swung open. Few were the moments of pure happiness in the world, when the soul is lifted to a higher plane, but he was presently experiencing one of those moments. Every year he was obliged to endure a golf match with Deborah's father,

THE DIRECTOR · 119

leading invariably to a lecture as to where he was going wrong in life. Henceforth he could always say, 'Oh, Edward! I bumped into a friend of yours the other day. . . .' And, even if he didn't resort to such extremes, the thought at any rate would do a lot to sustain him.

'No, I understand, that's very wise,' he said. 'Actually, what I wanted to propose to you involves an acquaintance of mine.'

She sat down in an armchair as Leonard briefly explained that he'd discovered his wife was seeing another man, without either of them realizing he knew of their affair.

'You are upset?' She'd obviously decided he was a talker, a fact that made no difference as long as he handed over fifty pounds at the end of half an hour.

'Yes – very. I want to show them that their relationship is a sham, that she means very little to him.'

She narrowed her eyes. Her naïvety – along with her French accent – was disappearing fast.

'I see. So you want me to have sex with him.'

Leonard recoiled. He was leading up to this but she'd commendably pre-empted him.

'I suppose, in a nutshell. The thing is, I'll give you fifty pounds now, and two hundred and fifty if you persuade the gentleman concerned to come here and have, er—'

'Intimate relations?'

'Exactly.'

She leant back in her chair, stroking her neck with her long red fingernails. 'You desire to watch?'

'No!'

She regarded him quizzically. 'You're not a copper, are you? You and this bloke aren't playing some sort of game?'

'No, no – look, I'll show you.' He flipped his wallet open and displayed his *Chronicle* ID. Her change in attitude was very disconcerting and he was beginning to feel he'd made a huge mistake in broaching the subject. 'There – see? You believe me now?'

'Huh!' She gave a cynical smile. 'Listen, honey. Never say "believe me" to someone on the game. The answer's no.'

Leonard closed the wallet and returned it to his jacket.

'The punter always comes to me, not the other way round,' she went on. 'And, even if I did agree to your idea, I'd want the money upfront, before this other bloke leaves.'

She got up from the chair and walked over to a table, picking up a packet of cigarettes. Perhaps it would be for the best if he left now. She lit up, blowing the smoke away, before addressing him in a slightly softer tone.

'You hate this bloke, right? He's let you down.'

'I was just hoping— Oh, never mind! Just that by doing this you might help my marriage.'

'H'm! I hear that a lot, you'd be surprised. Look, tell you what. Call me daft, but I believe you.' She opened her shoulder bag and took out a hand mirror, examining her fringe. 'The deal, though, is that you give me a hundred and fifty quid now, and then – if I get this guy back here – you give me the other hundred and fifty. Agreed?'

Leonard thought it over. Their present conversation was costing enough, even if he'd have paid far more to catch Dunstan out. The point was that he just hadn't given sufficient regard to handing control over to someone else.

'Your friend's a journalist, isn't he?' said Yvonne.

Leonard nodded.

'Well, let me see. How about if you introduce me as a student, doing a course on journalism?'

'Ye-es.'

'And – well, I could have the job of shadowing you for the day.'

'H'm,' said Leonard dubiously.

'Yes, follow me on this! I could say I'd written some articles or whatever, and would he be an angel and look them over. Then, when we get back here, I can just say I've left them somewhere. And – well . . .'

'That's pretty good,' said Leonard, amazed at the speed at which she'd invented a story. It was just possible things might work out after all. The key, the crucial aspect, was to avoid being too obvious.

He proceeded to reveal his intentions. He was meeting Dunstan in The Crafty Fox, about ten minutes' walk away, staying at the pub from two to three. He had his own ideas about how she should introduce herself and stressed that he'd leave a copy of the *Chronicle* on the table, which he'd pick up if he wished to abort the operation. They discussed the method of payment, and Leonard mentioned that, if everything went well, there could be more work in future. He handed over three fifty pound notes.

'All right,' she said, 'but I've got another client – a good one – at four. So your wife's lover (or whoever) is gonna have to disappear by then. 'Long as you realize that.'

21

The Importance of Being Earnest (1952)

Andrew Dunstan was already sitting in the pub when Leonard arrived at five to two, wearing a dark suit and tie. He stood up to shake the other's hand as Leonard smiled a greeting. It was odious having to be friendly to the man but there was little choice for the time being.

'Good to see you, old mucker. Drink?'

Leonard demurred, buying the first round. It was a quaint English pub, decked out in dark mahogany with a paisley carpet, the jukebox playing – ha, ha – 'Lady in Red'. They ordered food and, for the first few minutes, Dunstan chatted about his new car. He'd just purchased a Honda Prelude and was very enthusiastic about its qualities. Then, after another round of drinks, Dunstan looked around to ensure they weren't being overheard.

'So how's everything with Deborah? Did you talk to her?'

Leonard forced a smile. 'No need in the end. The gym instructor was seeing someone else. The detective agency got it wrong just as you said.'

'So you don't think she's having an affair?'

'Oh, no! Everything's been cleared up now. I don't know why I was so paranoid. I really owe you one for being there.'

Dunstan looked tremendously reassured. No wonder he'd dropped everything when Leonard visited him in his office.

'Actually,' Leonard continued, 'I was talking to Deborah about inviting you over. It's been quite a while since we saw you and

Chloe. Are you free Friday week?'

He waited for the excuse. No doubt Dunstan had been fore-warned about this by Deborah.

'Oh – well! – that's kind of you, Lenny, I'd like that a lot. The thing is, I'm afraid that Chloe's health has been getting worse lately. The left side of her body's virtually paralysed and she needs constant nursing – well, you know what it's like.' He leant forward, speaking in a quieter tone. 'To tell you the truth, old mate, she's quite different these days. Gets tired very easily, keeps forgetting things. Trouble is, whenever you try to help, she bites your head off.'

'I understand,' said Leonard. He had by no means given up, but the excuse of looking after Chloe was undeniable (however distastefully that excuse was framed).

'Don't get the idea,' Dunstan added, 'that I'm unsympathetic. Of course – *of course* I sympathize. It's just that . . .' He let out a sigh. 'Well, if I'm totally honest, I'm not very good with illness. It's probably to do with my own attitude towards feeling unwell. If I get a cold, mentally I'm giving myself the last rites.'

Leonard nodded, keeping his thoughts to himself.

'That's what happens, I think, when this sort of tragedy occurs within a family,' Dunstan went on reflectively. 'It shines a light on your character, puts you to the test, as it were. I mean, take you, Lenny. I remember being with you and Shirley, and Shirley would ask you a question, then ten minutes later she'd ask the same question, then ten minutes after that . . .

'I never knew how you managed to stay so patient.'

'I'll get another round in, shall I?' said Leonard, getting to his feet.

Dunstan's confessions of weakness were bad enough, without him bringing up Shirley – almost sacrilegious in the circumstances. Leonard walked over to the bar, returning with a couple of beers. Dunstan had never been able to hold his drink and, though there was little chance of him becoming tipsy, another one couldn't do any harm. By now they had finished lunch, it was approaching half-two, and before Yvonne turned up, there was something he wanted to discuss. He hadn't forgotten that last, cut-short conver-sation on the tape.

'Tell me, Andrew, purely in the interests of science, how would you go about poisoning your wife?'

Dunstan seemed to freeze, his hand hovering over his glass.

'I don't mean literally. I'm just thinking about writing a screenplay, that's all. You must have a few ideas, doing your line of work.'

He took a sip of his beer. 'Screenplay, eh? Still trying to become the world famous author?' A smirk had invaded his features. 'Well, I do know a bit about the subject, yeah, that's true. In fact, I wrote about a case just last month, gardener chappie who murdered his wife using paraquat. A lot depends on the job of your main character.'

They entered into a conversation about the properties and effects of certain deadly poisons. It was reassuring to hear Dunstan talk so easily – he'd surely have felt more uncomfortable if his intentions were malevolent – and Leonard allowed himself a small sigh of relief. His main worry at present was the absence of Yvonne. It was twenty to three, the pub was quite busy, but there was still no sign of her. A hundred and fifty pounds he'd handed over. . . .

Dunstan meanwhile was immersed in his lecture about poisons.

'Going back a bit, there's Dr Buchanan. Quite a character he was. Poisoned his second wife so he could remarry the first. The thing was, he used morphine, which reduces the pupils to pinpoints – which, of course, he wanted to avoid. So what he did to counteract the process was introduce drops of belladonna into her eyes. Clever, eh? Except the idiot had to brag about it afterwards. In court they proved he used morphine by giving it to a cat, then adding the belladonna while it was in its death throes. Hey presto. No contracting of the pupils.'

'That's sick,' said Leonard.

'Another case I quite like concerns this chap, Arthur Ford, who worked in a firm of chemists. He'd heard that Spanish Fly was an aphrodisiac, so he impregnated some sweets with it to seduce a woman he fancied. Except he overdid it.'

'What – you mean. . . ?'

'Yep. Afraid so. He killed her *and* he killed a friend of hers. Shoulda stuck to getting 'em drunk like the rest of us.' Dunstan lifted his glass and took a gulp. 'Anyway, you haven't told me your main character's job. I'm rushing ahead of myself.'

'He's a film critic—'

Something fell near Leonard's feet, a blue shoulder bag. He bent down to pick it up but Dunstan's hand shot out to grab it before him.

' 'Scuse me, sweetheart. I think you dropped this.'

A young woman turned round, smiling at Dunstan, her distinctive violet eyes gazing into his.

'Zank you, *m'sieur*. Zis bag 'as all my equipment.'

'Your equipment?'

'Is zat 'ow you say. . . ? My English is not so good.'

'I think you mean your valuables,' said Dunstan.

'My val . . . val . . .' She formed her mouth into a sexy pout.

'. . . u-a-bles,' enunciated Dunstan.

Leonard observed them apprehensively. Yvonne had turned up at any rate, but for some reason she'd reverted to her role in *'Allo, 'Allo!*

'Do you care if I sit 'ere?' Yvonne gestured at a stool between the two men.

'I'm sure we don't mind,' said Dunstan, briefly looking at Leonard.

'You correct me, yes? It is "mind", not "care".'

She sat down, stretching one of her legs over the other and showing a substantial amount of stocking. Dunstan cast a surreptitious glance in the direction of her hemline.

'Am I right in assuming you're French?' he asked.

'*Oui, m'sieur*. I 'ave been in England six minze. I am a student nurse at zer Chelsea and Westminster. . . .'

Leonard sat listening for a few minutes, before interrupting to get another round of drinks. It was really quite clever the way she was ignoring him, concentrating all her attention on Dunstan. Every so often she'd sweep her hair from side to side, leaving him staring at the back of her head.

He brought the drinks back – two beers and a coke – to hear Yvonne practising her English.

'My old man zer durstman, 'e wears a durstman's 'at.'

'He wears cor blimey trousers,' prompted Dunstan.

' 'E wears cur blimmey . . . cor blimey . . . What is zat? Cor blimey trousers?'

She had her hand placed on Dunstan's leg. He was laughing generously.

'One's that are pretty filthy I should think,' said Leonard, 'if he's a durst-dustman.'

'Cor blimey. Corrr bli-mey.'

Leonard suppressed a sigh. She was overdoing it. Although her accent was excellent, he hoped she really could speak French because it would look highly suspicious if Dunstan launched into his 'O' or 'A' level version of the language and all she could say in response was '*très bon*'.

'I was hoping to persuade Andrew,' he addressed Yvonne, 'to come to a dinner party.'

'*Oui, oui!*' She turned to Dunstan excitedly. Parties were obviously a good thing.

'*Non!*' said Dunstan, aping her French.

'But why?' Yvonne persisted, taking her hand away. For someone with such a kind and loving nature, being antisocial was clearly some sort of crime.

'You could do with a break,' added Leonard. 'And Deborah and I would love to see you.'

'Yes!' agreed Yvonne.

Dunstan looked down for a second, probably not too keen on mentioning his wife but not wild either about going against the wishes of Deborah.

'All right,' he replied, tight-lipped.

'Great, that's settled then,' said Leonard.

Yvonne gestured at the copy of the *Chronicle* lying on the table. 'I read zer *journal*.'

Dunstan recovered from his slight depression over the dinner invitation. 'My friend and I, we write for the newspaper.'

'You do? *Quelle chance*! Are you in zis version?'

'Not in this edition, no,' said Dunstan. 'So obviously it's not worth reading.'

'*Par-don?*' The girl appeared mystified.

'The paper is not so good without one of my stories,' explained Dunstan.

'Oh!' She clapped her hands. '*M'sieur* makes a joke.'

Leonard cringed, but he was beginning to warm to Yvonne's technique. She was so obviously over-the-top, and yet Dunstan, with all his intelligence and cynicism, was completely blind to it.

'You are so clever. I wish . . . I wish you could 'elp me.' She glanced over at Leonard for virtually the first time.

'What is it?' Dunstan leant forward, hoping to win back her attention.

'I 'ave a problem – a problem with a doctor.'

One of her elegant hands rose to her mouth. She looked quite forlorn and it appeared as if she might cry.

'Is this man harassing you in any way?' asked Dunstan.

Her mouth gaped open and she stared at him. 'You know! 'Ow did you know?'

Dunstan gave a sympathetic shrug.

She began explaining, mainly to the understanding Dunstan, what she'd been experiencing over the last few weeks, while Leonard squirmed in his seat. This was all going according to plan, but performed by such a consummate actress, apparently in a state of genuine anguish, it was almost too realistic. He wanted to leave the table and buy another round but that would have been unforgivably rude.

' 'E says I smell of garlic and I should let 'im wersh it erff.'

She paused. A barmaid was at their table collecting the glasses. She and Leonard had agreed beforehand that this mysterious doctor could make lewd suggestions but not go any further. However, no doubt wanting to provoke a greater reaction, she decided to embellish the story as soon as the barmaid had left.

'All zer time 'e touches me, pushes 'imself against me.'

Dunstan's face dropped.

'That's awful,' said Leonard. 'Truly awful.'

This was meant to be a hint to stop, but Dunstan obviously felt that Leonard was trying to ingratiate himself. He grasped Yvonne's hand.

'This is a disgrace. The man should be dismissed.'

'I 'ave told 'im not to touch me, but 'e says, if I tell, 'e will lose me my job.'

'That's crazy,' said Dunstan. 'Look, if there's anything we can do. You said it was fortunate we were writers.'

She turned to him, an incredulous expression on her face. It was amazing how he always knew what she was thinking! Leonard saw now that the French approach had been completely appropriate. It had highlighted her vulnerability.

'My friend, she says I should write to 'im, say what is wrong. But I do not know what to say.'

Dunstan smiled. He and Leonard – but especially himself – were experts in such matters. 'Well, don't you worry. I'm sure we can formulate the correct phraseology.'

She seemed a little taken aback by this sudden verbosity – as was Leonard – but his meaning was clear. It was time to pop the question and she kept up her deferential approach.

'My apartment is near. I would be so 'appy if a *journaliste* . . .'

She gazed appealingly from one to the other. Out of the corner of his eye Leonard saw Dunstan glancing at his watch. The other would find it extremely awkward offering to go with her with Leonard still there, and it was still possible that all of the (unexpectedly brilliant) groundwork might go to waste.

'Hell's bells!' he exclaimed. 'I've just remembered I was meant to be seeing Deborah at two-thirty. Sorry, Andrew. And you, too— I'm sorry, I didn't catch your name. Good luck with everything.'

22

The Great Dictator (1940)

Leonard walked straight to Deborah's office. If Yvonne had managed to entice Dunstan back to her apartment, he'd find out in half an hour's time – there was no point in waiting. So far every- thing had gone about as satisfactorily as he'd hoped, and it was time to deliver the glad tidings about the forthcoming dinner party.

Deborah didn't work in Chronicle House but in a slightly inferior dirt-brown building where most of the post-production people were situated. Here was the library, the system admin department, *The Chronicle on* CD-ROM and the offices of the weekly magazine. Leonard had fond memories of the place from his early days with Deborah, and he felt an instinctive lifting of spirits as he made his way to the second floor. Deborah's office was situated in one corner overlooking the street, and her secretary was sitting at a desk outside the room as he approached. Next door he could hear shouting – the sound of Deborah's voice.

'I've told you repeatedly, Justine. We need at least one hundred articles for each subject heading. You've managed to bring back fifty-five stories for – what? – all right, sixty-five stories for "Brave New World". The whole project depends on you at this stage. I've got developers and designers on my back, people waiting around doing nothing expecting me to hand over these articles. It's not good enough.'

Another, much quieter, voice said something. Leonard heard the words 'technical difficulties'.

'I don't care!' shouted Deborah. 'I'm not interested in your problems. How can I go to Trefford and tell him the network's playing up, or the photocopier's not working, or we don't really fancy doing all the work we're supposed to do? Does that sound convincing to you?' There was a change in her tone, alternating from anger to exasperation. 'Look, don't get upset about it. That doesn't solve anything. Just go away and don't come back till you've got somewhere. OK?'

The door opened and a young girl stepped out, looking close to tears. Leonard waited till she'd gone and then entered the office, closing the door behind him. Deborah was reading something behind her desk, and looked up.

'Leonard! I'm a bit rushed at the moment—'

'I could hear you halfway down the corridor. Do you always talk to your staff like that?'

She gazed at him as if she didn't know what he was talking about. 'Oh, *that*. Listen, Leonard, you don't understand. If I don't talk to her like that, nothing'll get done.' She shook her head resignedly. 'I've had so many problems with Justine, it's enough to make my blood boil.'

'Well, I'm glad you're not *my* boss.'

He maintained his serious expression, and she stared at him for a second, quite taken aback. Never had he addressed her in this way.

'Anyway, I won't stay long,' he continued. 'I know you're busy. I've just had lunch with Andrew. He's agreed to come over Friday week.'

'Oh . . . good.' She forced a smile.

'Perhaps you could hitch a lift together since you're so close. I'll give you his extension.'

He walked up to her desk and wrote the number on a Post-it note.

'See you tonight, then.' He kissed her on the forehead. 'Oh, and for my sake, please apologize to Justine.'

He took his leave, feeling a lot more tired than when he'd entered, a weight bearing down upon his chest. Deborah was certainly not without friends within the company, but they were all, now that he thought about it, roughly on the same level as herself. The work environment appeared to be another area of her life in which he'd been deluded.

When he arrived at Twelve Jessup Gardens at twenty to four – walking the last couple of streets in double-quick time – the maid was sitting on a bench inside the porch. Her unsmiling face looked even older, a maze of cracks and crevices, and it was impossible to gauge what, if anything, had happened.

'Hello again.' He sat down beside her. 'Sorry – I'm afraid I don't know your name. Are you Yvonne's mother?'

There was a dry chuckle. 'I used to be a friend of her mother's. I look after madam now.'

'Can she speak French? Her accent's very good.'

'Madam is studying for a degree in French. She likes to keep her hand in.'

'Oh, right, I see.' He wanted to find out more but there wasn't much time. 'So did Yvonne come back here with my colleague, do you know?'

She nodded. 'They retired almost at once to the Ops Room. I was in the sitting-room just now and your friend was shouting at the top of his voice. Personally, I think it's the height of bad manners.'

Leonard looked to see if she was serious but her withered face kept its sorrowful expression. Well, it definitely sounded like Dunstan at any rate. What an animal that man was. He glanced around him for witnesses, then handed the maid an envelope containing £200, fifty pounds more than promised. She flicked expertly through the notes and stood up. Her mouth seemed to be barely moving, her eyes dead.

'Thank you, sir. I'll give madam a sign that you've paid, so the other gentleman can leave without embarrassment. Good afternoon.'

She opened the front door and shuffled inside. Leonard didn't think he'd ever met such a strange person in his life.

He walked towards Earls Court station to catch the train home. Now that it was all over he felt a strong sense of anticlimax. It was very easy to forget his original mission. Not only had he watched

Dunstan have sex with Deborah, he'd paid for the man to have sex with a beautiful call girl. A tremendous amount of patience was required to wait until the most propitious time to reveal all these secrets. The dinner party was only eight days away.

23

Bad Taste (1987)

Leonard took the next week off work. It was unlikely Deborah would even notice, and the only person who might take an interest, Mrs Peavey, could be offered some excuse about his health. ('I've got these terrible back pains,' he'd say, and before he could finish, 'Huh!' she'd retort, 'Don't talk to me about back pains. I've had just about everything in my time. . . .') The only commitment he needed to fulfil came on Saturday – his talk at the university – which went off very well. In reply to a question about his favourite one-liner, he quoted a line from *Planes, Trains and Automobiles*: 'Those aren't pillows!'

It was crucial, though, to occupy himself, stop thinking about how things had been different with his first wife. He'd already written to Geoff Hartnell, documenting their conversation and what needed to be done to his screenplay, and although he wasn't sure even now how the storyline would develop, he could still begin to flesh out the characters. He could even think about specific shots, camera angles and so on – *not* normally included in a screenplay – yet perhaps, in this instance, in keeping with the subject matter. So far he hadn't decided on a title, but that could always be amended later. *The Dinner Party* had been his first idea, discarded in favour of the thriller-like *I Spy*.

His film knowledge, in fact, could come in handy. Making the main character, Roger, a critic, meant that Roger could be constantly reminded of how his life resembled certain films, prompting him, à la Woody Allen in *Play It Again, Sam*, to act out similar solutions. The idea for adding a filmic subtext came to Leonard the day after seeing Dunstan and Yvonne. Mrs Peavey had come over for her weekly visit and, alone with him in the study, was remarking on his vast collection of books.

'These things are just dust collectors,' she said. 'I mean, do you really need' – she picked up a book at random – '*Bergman on Bergman*?'

'Bergman is one of my favourite directors.'

She returned the book after giving it a wipe.

'Yes, yes – but you know what I mean. I bet you hardly touch some of these books.'

'Actually, you'd be surprised.'

'A lot of them seem to be about films nobody sees. I know you can't say this, but, honestly, a lot of these art-house films are rubbish, aren't they? No storyline, no action. Just a lot of talk – normally about death.'

'You've heard of Bergman's *The Seventh Seal*? The character, Death, actually appears with a scythe and plays a game of chess.'

'Good grief!'

'The thing is,' Leonard went on, 'you really can get a lot more out of these character study films. Remember that conversation we had about old people? Well, there's a beautiful film called *Tokyo Story*, directed by Yasujiro Ozu. A lovely old couple go to visit their children – who clearly want nothing to do with them.'

Mrs Peavey looked distinctly unimpressed.

'Oh, it's very depressing,' said Leonard. 'But the film stays with you after you've watched it. And, from a critical perspective, there's a lot of stylistic considerations: the use of the famous tatami mat camera angle, the lack of fades or wipes or dissolves.'

'Sounds boring,' pronounced Mrs Peavey. 'Which reminds me . . . There's a book here somewhere.' She turned and scrutinized the titles on display. 'Ahhh, yes, there it is. Trevor Horlick. *Film Essays and Reviews*. Now, Leonard, I know you wrote the introduction. But – well, really!'

'Yes?'

'Well, what a load of rubbish. I was browsing through it the other day, and the terminology he uses! Termite art. Negative space. Everything symbolizes something else.'

'Trev is very keen on semiotics.'

'Well, at least your reviews aren't like that.'

'I like to throw in the odd comment, but – yes, you're right. I have to remember I'm working for a newspaper, not a film journal.'

'Your main problem,' said Mrs Peavey, 'is that you're too nice in your reviews. Now *I* wouldn't be like that.'

'No,' laughed Leonard. 'You and a few other people. In fact, it was said of Pauline Kael that her most dedicated readers seldom watched a film.'

'I'll tell you something,' said Mrs Peavey, hoicking a thumb in the direction of *Film Essays and Reviews*. 'I wouldn't watch any of his recommendations, put it that way. He seemed very keen on somebody called Eric Rohmer.'

'Ah, well, I'd definitely agree with him there.'

Leonard began to outline the plot of Rohmer's *La Femme de L'aviateur* – about a man who suspects his girlfriend of cheating on him and decides to spy on a man leaving her apartment – but his mind was already thinking ahead to other films he could use for his screenplay. Titles could even be inserted between scenes as in the old black and whites: *Where are you when I need you, Jean Vigo?*

As for his plans for the real-life dinner party, Leonard hadn't forgotten Deborah and Dunstan's intention, whether serious or not, to poison him – and he'd decided to beat them to it.

He'd noticed from his readings on the subject that it was possible to simulate the symptoms of certain deadly drugs. It was common with most poisons to vomit upon ingestion (as the body's natural defence mechanism), but there were also perfectly natural substances or emetics, such as vinegar or mustard, that could have the same effect. Indeed, there were pharmaceutical agents available to induce people to vomit (normally employed in the event of an overdose).

This was just what he wanted for his purposes. He'd lace their teas and coffees with ipecac, the most popular medical emetic, making Deborah and Dunstan nauseous but otherwise not harming them in the least. Then, when they were at their lowest ebb, having shown them his film of their lovemaking, he'd explain how he'd poisoned them. Hopefully at that point they'd think him capable of anything.

Yes, it was tough on them, but after everything he'd gone through lately it was nothing more than they deserved.

On Monday morning he'd asked for ipecac at the chemist's and was told that although they didn't have any in stock, it could be ordered for later that afternoon. The assistant had been inquisitive as to why he might want such a product, and Leonard had replied that he was writing a novel and it would be useful for research purposes. The assistant had then made a joke about hoping he wouldn't see Leonard's face in the papers in the near future. The drug could presumably be used by bulimics to dangerous ends or by unhappy workers in their boss's coffee.

Later that day, Leonard had purchased a 500ml bottle of Ipecacuanha Tincture. From what he'd read, swallowing 15ml was all that was required to achieve the desired result in 85 per cent of cases, and another 15ml generally mopped up the rest of the population. The perfect aspect was that its effect was delayed, taking twenty to thirty minutes to work. His only real concern was how easy it was to mask the taste – if it *did* taste of anything – and with that purpose in mind, the kitchen, when he returned from the shops, had been turned into a temporary laboratory. He had no intention himself of taking more than about 5ml in his experiments.

The liquid was brown, carrying a slight, horseradish odour, but not too pungent. He'd poured out 15ml into a measuring cap and deposited the contents into a mug of coffee. Disconcertingly, the odour remained, but not so noticeably. Leonard had taken a medium-sized swig, rolling the mouthful around his palate to achieve the full flavour.

It was completely and utterly disgusting.

He quickly substituted a glass of water, but it was impossible to rid his mouth of the taste that had already embedded itself in his gums and seemed to be revelling in its parasitic existence. It was actually quite hot, tasting like coffee that had been fortified with a mouldy sort of whisky.

Leonard decided after some deliberation he'd enhance this aspect of the taste, first adding cognac, then green ginger wine and ouzo, taking tiny sips between each addition. The ipecac was finally just about indistinguishable. He'd tell Dunstan he'd added a little nip of something to make his own brand of Irish coffee. (And maybe it wouldn't be a bad idea to toss a couple more chillies in the curry as well. . . .)

He'd then gone on to experiment with Deborah's favourite herbal tea. Surprisingly, this was easier and very little alcohol needed to be added (perhaps because by this stage Leonard's taste buds had reached an advanced stage of numbness). Now that the lab work was over, he could write up the results as part of his research for the screenplay. He hadn't really imbibed enough to be ill – in fact, he felt no effect at all – but he could still describe the taste.

Strangely enough, though, as he was sitting at the keyboard, he could feel a faint stirring of the contents of his stomach. He chronicled this process in detail in his notes. It was interesting that this had to be the first stage of the emetic – it was definitely working! – and no doubt the full extent to which he'd experience its effects.

However, a few minutes later he felt a need to go to the toilet. An unfriendly presence had entered his insides and it looked as if everything was going to be expelled from the wrong end. He tore himself away from his PC.

This turned out to be a fortuitous decision. From the feeling of having just drunk a rather dubious horseradish cocktail, it now felt as if he'd just swallowed six pints of scrumpy with various Third World insects floating on the surface. The next five to ten minutes were spent continuously retching, the thought that he'd brought this fate upon himself not a particular source of comfort.

When it was all over, he was exhausted, unable to rid his mouth of the vile taste that still lingered, incredibly, the following morning. He'd even felt a trace of sympathy for his intended victims. . . .

But in any case, would he ever put his plan into action? The main worry now was that Dunstan wouldn't turn up. Deborah had said she'd phoned Andrew – he'd complained apparently that Leonard had got him drunk – and arranged for him to drive her back to Quavering on Friday week. But this acquiescence in Leonard's designs struck him as far too convenient. (Unless, of course, they had something to tell *him*.) Every day he waited for the inevitable phone call from Dunstan saying he couldn't make it. The only response he could think of to this was that Dunstan *had* to come because Leonard had prepared a surprise for him, and Deborah specially wanted him there. But naturally this was no guarantee. Nor could he rely on Deborah's appearance. She might decide she had a last-minute engagement. In this scenario, Dunstan would arrive for the evening, and Leonard would try to keep him at the house until she returned.

As for Chloe, he'd virtually accepted that if Dunstan wanted to bring his wife, there was little he could do about it. He'd just have to say that he wanted to show Deborah and Andrew a short horror movie, and would she mind very much, since he knew she didn't like that sort of thing, staying upstairs while they watched it?

It would be awkward, though. Unsatisfactory.

In the meantime it looked as if Deborah was still seeing Mr Will-it-even-fit. On Tuesday she rang Leonard to say that Justine was leaving the company and she'd been invited to her leaving do. The problem with this story was that although he could certainly believe Justine was leaving, it was highly unlikely the girl would want to see more of her boss than necessary. Leonard's reprimand to Deborah probably still rankled with her and she wanted to make a point about her staff not resenting her manner.

Well, it was time to phone Dunstan and find out his plans.

The home help answered. Andrew was out, apparently, but Leonard could speak to Chloe. There was a long pause.

'Leonard, hi, how are you?'

She had a high-pitched, staccato voice, lightly touching the words. Leonard pictured the tiny, fragile person in a wheelchair at the other end of the line.

'Fine, thanks. Andrew's out, then, is he?'

' 'Fraid so. He's got a leaving do to go to or something. Did you want to speak to him particularly?'

'No, no. Not really.'

He closed his eyes for a second. He'd assumed they were

spending the evening together, but hearing the same excuse repeated was a surprisingly painful blow.

'Andrew was saying that you'd invited us over for Friday,' Chloe went on. 'It's really nice of you, thank you. I always used to love it at your place, watching one of your films. Leonard . . .' She gave a heavy sigh. 'Is it possible to speak on a personal level?'

'By all means.'

'Well, it's Andrew. It's probably nothing, just me being silly, but he seems to spend a lot of time away these days, working or going to office functions. Now that something's come up that we can both go to— Oh, I don't know. I was really looking forward to seeing you again, but he says I can't go, I'm not up to it. But I *am* up to it, Leonard, it's not true.'

He drew in his breath. She was entrusting him with her deepest problems. Her husband was the only person she had in the world, and he didn't care for her any more.

'I'm sure it's nothing serious,' he heard himself saying. 'I haven't seen Andrew much lately, but the pressures of work can get to all of us.'

'Yes . . . yes, that's true, you might be right there.' She seemed to grasp at this explanation. 'He's told me he's been having problems at work. Is it possible to ask you a favour, though, Leonard?'

'Of course.'

'Well, just that when you see him on Friday, could you have a word with him? You know, about taking me out more? I know you'll be very tactful.'

'Sure. No problem.'

'Thanks. I really appreciate it.'

They spoke for a couple more minutes, Leonard promising to visit her and Andrew in the near future. But as soon as he put the phone down, he realized he hadn't even asked her about her health and how she was keeping. God, what a hell of a business this was. Although it appeared as if Dunstan would be arriving on Friday on his own, talking to Chloe had been a painful reminder that there were other people involved as well. But . . . well, there was no turning back now.

He picked up the phone again and dialled Yvonne's number. This would be the finishing touch.

The maid answered as before and told him that her mistress couldn't come to the phone because she was busy.

'She's still on for Friday, isn't she?'

'Oh, yes.'

'And she knows when to get here and what to do?'

'Yvonne's a very clever girl, sir. You needn't worry at all. By the way, your colleague turned up again, last Friday at lunchtime.'

'What!'

'Yvonne was with a client, so I told him she was with her boyfriend. I said I was her mother and, if he wished to leave a message, I'd pass it on. He said it was all right, he'd call another time. That was it.'

A short while later Leonard hung up. Everything was still, just about, on track.

24

Close Encounters of the Third Kind (1977)

It was Friday afternoon, a few hours before Deborah and Dunstan's arrival.

In the previous few days Leonard had been very active. He'd begun writing Dorry's script and for research purposes had borrowed a couple of books about poison from the library. His screenplay – now entitled *The Director* – was quite different from his literary efforts for the *Chronicle*. He'd discovered a power and passion that had surprised even himself, gradually drawing the reader into the depths of the protagonist's emotions.

Now, having just returned from the supermarket, he was in the kitchen preparing the meal. The hors d'œuvre was to be butterfly prawns, with chicken in spiced coconut cream as the main course. If they were still hungry after that, he'd dish up lemon sorbet. He'd removed his glasses to cut the onions and was reminding himself of his plans for the evening.

'Ipecac with cognac . . . Yes, that should do it. Oh, and don't forget to use the red mugs—'

Eh? What was that? He twisted his head to see a large pink blur wobbling in the doorway. A voice spoke.

'First sign of madness – talking to yourself.'

He wheeled round, knocking his glasses to the floor. All was confusion and, as he bent down to pick them up, he heard a crunch.

'Oh, jeepers!' The pink shape was bounding towards him. His

eyes were stung from the onions, but without his glasses he could hardly see, anyway.

'Uh-oh, one of the arms has gone skewwhiff.' She stood up and he was treated to her appallingly bad breath. 'Oh, Gawd, and the lens . . . Hold on, you sit down here. Let's see what we can do.'

Mrs Peavey took hold of his shoulders – he was still clutching the knife – and pushed him backwards onto a stool. He could hear her opening one of the kitchen cabinets and the rip as she tore off a strip of Sellotape. In a second she was back – more bad breath – and was fixing his glasses to the bridge of his nose. He gazed into her frowning features. The lens in the right frame had cracked and it looked as if a daddy-longlegs had pinioned itself to the front. It was Friday again. Why did he always forget?

'I'm sorry, it was my fault. I took you by surprise.' She was wearing a pink tracksuit top.

'It's all right,' he said.

She spent the next few minutes making sure he really didn't mind and that he didn't bear a grudge against her. Then, gazing around the kitchen, she said, 'Hell, you've made a mess. You having a bit of a do tonight?'

'A friend of Deborah's is coming over, that's all. I'm making a curry.'

'Anyone I know?' she asked, peering suspiciously into a colander containing the salad. 'I mean, from reading the paper . . .'

'Possibly. It's not anyone who's—'

'Hang on. Why are there four plates and four bowls if you've only invited one person?'

He glanced over to the counter next to the sink and saw through his cracked glasses all the crockery carefully laid out. Any reasonable explanation for this – apart from the real one – deserted him.

'Really? Is there. . . ? Oh, yes, you're right. I guess I must have made a mistake.'

'Tsk!' She went over and started collecting up the extra knives, forks and spoons. 'You writers!' she said cheerfully. 'The next thing you'll do is put cyanide in the soup by mistake. She'll like that, won't she, this guest of yours?'

'Actually, the guest we're having over is a man.'

She hesitated as she was putting a bowl away. God, couldn't the woman keep her snout out of things just for once? Was it too much to ask?

'In fact, he's Deborah's lover,' he added, 'and you're right, I intend to slip him something extra this evening. Nothing as potent as cyanide, though.'

He grinned at her gaping face. *That* would give her something to chew over. He could almost hear the neurones in her brain crackling and fizzing with activity. After a couple of seconds she wagged her finger at him knowingly.

'You writers are the weirdest.'

An hour-and-a-half later Mrs Peavey had finished around the house and joined Leonard for a coffee in the living-room. She'd remarked on a new Kenyan blend she'd seen on his shelf, wondering how it tasted, and he'd made the mistake of inviting her to stay a while longer. She was talking incessantly, mainly about the pernicious influence of television.

'The tripe they put on these days. Have you ever seen anything like it? One channel after another showing sex and violence.'

Leonard professed that he had and it was.

'No wonder everything's going downhill. I remember Frank wanting to watch *Top of the Pops*. I couldn't work it out at first. Then on came those *Pan's People* people. The filth was spreading, you see, even in those days. I used to think the only way to calm my Frank down was to give him his insulin injections.'

'H'm.' Good idea, oh mad one.

'Brisk walks, cold showers, that'd do young people the power of good. Give 'em something to think about at any rate. It's all about instant gratification, that's the trouble, isn't it?'

' "Nature, Mr Allnut, is what we are put in this world to rise above".'

'Eh?'

'Katharine Hepburn. *African Queen*.'

'Yes, well, that's right. You know, there's just no respect any more. If you ask me, schools should be teaching social skills, the little everyday courtesies we used to take for granted. Might be a shock, I know, for some.'

She ranted on. Sexual promiscuity was a heightened form of bad manners in her opinion, wanting something and taking it without due concern for others. Not a please or a thank you, just trousers down and back to the animal kingdom.

Leonard glanced at the clock. She really had to be out of the house by five – he was expecting a guest at half past – and it was already ten minutes over the hour. He held his hand up to stem the flow of chatter.

'Sorry, Agatha. Is that someone at the door?'

She shut up.

'I just thought I heard— Oh, well, maybe not. Thing is, I've really got to get on with the dinner. Do you mind?' He suddenly remembered her reaction when Deborah had used the same phrase. 'I mean, do you mind awfully? We can have a long chat next week if you like.'

He walked out of the room, leaving her no choice but to follow. He opened the front door but she lingered in the hall.

'If you need someone to talk to, I'm always here, you know.' She looked at him in her earnest manner. 'It can help sometimes, just getting things off your chest. I know my method is to record all my thoughts in a diary.'

'I'm actually doing that already,' he said. 'Writing down my feelings.'

'You are? Really? Don't you find—'

'Next week. We'll talk about this next week.'

'Yes, yes, of course. Look forward to it, Leonard.' She still made no move to leave, but fortunately the phone was ringing.

Finally, she was gone.

He picked up the phone. It was Deborah. He had this terrible premonition that either she or Dunstan couldn't make it.

'Leonard, about tonight. Is it all right if Kate comes as well?'

'No,' he said instinctively.

'No? "No", did you say? Why not, for heaven's sake? I tell you she's in a real state at the moment. I said it'd be fine if she stayed with us for the evening.'

The doorbell was ringing. All the trains on his perfectly designed model railway were derailing simultaneously.

'It – it's just impossible. I've only cooked for three.'

'Don't be a plonker, Leonard. We've got plenty of food. Besides, we can always order a takeaway.'

'The answer's no. I invited one person and one person only.'

There was a short silence. Sweat had broken out all over his body.

'Well, all right, Leonard. You win. If anyone needs help, it's you by the sound of it. Your *one* guest and I will turn up about seven.'

They said goodbye to each other and he rushed to answer the door.

25

Noises Off . . .(1992)

THE DIRECTOR

By Leonard R. Fleason

FADE IN:
EXT. M11. DUSK.

A black Ford Probe is stuck in a traffic jam on a motorway heading out of London. The camera tracks in to reveal a back-seat shot of Geoffrey, a man in his mid-forties, slightly greying at the temples, sitting next to Rhonda, an attractive, smartly-dressed woman in her thirties. He is drumming his fingers on the steering wheel but not with any sign of impatience.

GEOFFREY

Think old Roger will be getting worried?

RHONDA

Oh, yeah, I should think so. The trouble with him is he frets over the small things and misses the big picture.

She places her hand on Geoffrey's knee. The traffic begins to move and Geoffrey shifts the car into gear. Rhonda flips down the passenger's mirror and checks her appearance. Close-up of eyes.

CUT TO:
INT. BERKELEY HOUSE. DUSK.

Roger is slicing a cucumber in the kitchen. He is in his mid-forties, wearing a tweed jacket and corduroy trousers. Without being exactly handsome, he has a kind and interesting face. One lens in his glasses is cracked and a piece of Sellotape is wrapped around the angle of the frame, but otherwise he appears calm and in control. The camera slowly pans around the large modern kitchen, showing all the spices on the shelves, resting for an extra second on a bag from the chemist's, before returning to Roger. He wipes his hands on his apron, looks to check that everything is progressing nicely, and walks out into the hall. He opens a door to what appears to be the basement and shouts down into the dark.

ROGER

Everything all right?

VOICE
(heavily muffled)

Yeah.

Roger nods his head a couple of times. Then, almost as an afterthought, he pops into the living-room, a large split-level room with a table at the far end under an arch. He walks to the table and checks all the dinner things have been laid out properly. This sequence is shot in the style of closed-circuit television with the date and time recorded along the bottom of the screen. Everything is fine and he traipses back into the kitchen.

CUT TO:
EXT. BERKELEY HOUSE. DUSK.

The car is turning up the lane leading to Roger's house. It has just begun to rain. The lights of the house can be seen.

GEOFFREY
(voice-over)
Well, here we are. Hope the old mucker's prepared something hot
and spicy.

FADE TO:
OPENING CREDITS.

26

Dinner at Eight (1933)

Leonard was in the living-room opening a bottle of wine when they arrived. He heard Dunstan's voice, then Deborah's, as they removed their coats.

'M'm. Something smells good.'

'Yeah, not bad. Let's see if we can locate the *chef de cuisine.*'

The door opened and Deborah entered.

'Leonard, my God! What happened to your glasses?'

She advanced until she was a few inches from the cracked lens. She'd put on slightly more make-up than usual and was wearing one of her power suits in an eye-catching red. Dunstan stood in the background.

'It's nothing,' Leonard said. 'Just got into a fight with Mrs Peavey, that's all.'

'God,' said Dunstan. 'I didn't know working at home was so dangerous.'

Deborah shook her head, giving Dunstan a little glance.

'You sat on them, didn't you, Leonard?'

He gave them a more prosaic version of events.

'We've got this neighbour who helps out with the cleaning,' she explained to Dunstan. 'She's very thorough, I give her that, but just a teensy bit odd. Leonard likes her because she reads his articles.'

'A woman of taste and refinement,' said Leonard.

'I call her Mad Aggie,' said Deborah. 'She's got these man-eating dogs and they roam the countryside together.'

'Oh, she's not that bad,' he interjected.

'Oh, yeah? Have you seen those dogs lately? I was setting off for work one day last week and the two of them – Reggie and Ronnie – ran straight at me, yapping their heads off. I only just made it to the car in time.'

'Really?' said Leonard. 'You didn't say.'

'Well, by the evening I'd just about managed to get over it. But I tell you, Leonard, I've half a mind to report her under the Dangerous Dogs Act. They should be wearing a muzzle at least.'

'I'll have a word with her.'

Deborah nodded her approval. 'Well, anyway,' she said, changing the subject, '*I've* had an exciting day. For one thing, I've just been in Andrew's new car. Got a real thrust to it.'

'You make it sound like a sexual experience,' said Leonard.

'Huh! Well, maybe compared to one of *our* sexual experiences.'

'I was tired last night.' He gave Dunstan a wink.

'Last night . . . Yeah, right,' muttered Deborah.

'Chloe sends her love,' said Dunstan. 'Shame she can't be here.'

The other once again trotted out excuses on behalf of his wife, but for Leonard the subject was almost unendurable. It didn't help that he kept returning in his mind to Dunstan's new car, something he'd known about since their lunch in The Crafty Fox, yet which now, in front of Deborah, struck him as particularly outrageous. Had Chloe been for a drive in this wonder car yet? Was it even properly equipped for her use? What about the cost, money that could be spent on exploring new drug treatments for MS, or making alterations to their house to accommodate a wheelchair?

To make matters worse, Dunstan was currently insinuating – Leonard could hardly believe his ears – that Chloe was romantically interested in her occupational therapist. Though Dunstan himself had never met the man, according to Chloe he was wonderful – very caring, very attentive.

'Bit too attentive for my liking,' Dunstan added.

'Oh, yeah?' said Deborah with interest. 'How so?'

Dunstan replied by mentioning the amount of time the two spent together, but clearly he had very little to go on. It was all Leonard could do to stop himself frogmarching his companions down to the basement and showing them the video immediately. 'How about the level of attentiveness there then?' he'd say, pointing to the screen.

Instead, he contented himself with saying that Chloe was probably only trying to make Dunstan jealous, hoping to persuade him to take her out more. Then, before Dunstan could respond, he said, 'Anyway, how about a little snifter to get things going?'

Deborah requested a Bacardi and Coke and Dunstan a vodka and tonic.

'I've told Andrew he can stay the night,' said Deborah. 'Oh, yeah, and that reminds me. I've got a bone to pick with you, Leonard, when you get back. . . .'

He trooped into the kitchen. He could hear them in the other room discussing the porcelain cat that had been taken, then returned. Dunstan, like Mrs Peavey, was expressing his disbelief that the burglar could just leave it in the middle of nowhere, having gone to the bother of stealing it. Actually, come to think of it, it *was* a bit peculiar – at least the aspect of Mrs Peavey's discovery. Could she have seen him walking cross-country with it?

Unlikely. After all, it was the dead of night.

Oh, heck, that was another thing. In the excitement of planning this evening, he'd forgotten to buy Mrs Peavey the gift he'd promised her. Judging from her display on the video, their neighbour seemed the sort who treasured such acts of thoughtfulness, magnifying them out of all proportion. Perhaps that was part of the reason she'd been so difficult to usher out earlier in the day. She was giving him the chance to remember.

He returned to the living-room. Oh, well. He'd buy her something tomorrow.

'Right, Leonard.' Deborah and Dunstan were sitting down, a respectable distance from each other. She was looking at him through narrowed eyes. 'Give me one good reason why Kate couldn't come tonight.'

He didn't respond immediately.

'You can't, can you? Well, listen to this. I told you I had an exciting day.'

She took her drink and sipped it leisurely. She was talking to Leonard rather than Dunstan, so the latter either knew what she was about to say or it didn't affect him.

'Remember Nick, the guy who showed you the ropes at the gym?'

He nodded, handing Dunstan his vodka and tonic.

'Well, he and his brother have just been arrested. It looks as though he's gonna be charged with possessing and distributing drugs.'

'Is that so?'

Leonard was a little surprised by this, though perhaps it wasn't totally unexpected. HVM must have tipped off the police.

'Yeah, not only that. I didn't tell you this before, but Kate was going out with him – behind her husband's back.'

'Really?' He did his best to look amazed.

'Yeah. Really, really. In fact, she was so upset when he called from the police station, she wanted to stay with me tonight. We were gonna have a big heart-to-heart about it. That's where you come in, Leonard.'

'Oh, right. I didn't realize.'

They chatted on. One of the advantages of being host was that Leonard could periodically leave the room on the grounds of dealing with some matter in the kitchen. They had moved from spirits to wine and he was replenishing their glasses on a regular basis. By the time they'd seated themselves at the dining table, he was confident that Deborah and Dunstan were both at their ease. Indeed, what was remarkable was the subtlety of their relations to each other. No sly glances or brushing hands. He'd lit a couple of candles on the table and the light shone from their faces, enabling him to view the slightest discomfort, but neither of them seemed in the least embarrassed.

In fact, Dunstan was entertaining company. At the beginning of the main course he said something that gave Leonard a little electric shock.

'I always worry when I come here. Premonition of disaster, you might say.'

'How d'you mean?' asked Deborah.

'The Curse of Coggeshall, that's what I mean. Never known such a place for murder and mayhem.'

'Yeah, but Coggeshall's six miles away.'

'Ah, yes.' Dunstan raised his fork. 'But, you see, there's a school of thought that reckons there's a catchment area extending ten to fifteen miles around the village.'

'Nah,' said Deborah doubtfully.

'I once wrote about the curse,' said Leonard. 'One of my first jobs at the *Mercury*.'

Two interested faces regarded him. It couldn't do any harm to stoke suspicions about such things in preparation for upcoming events.

'Diane Jones left her home in Coggeshall in . . . July of '83, I think it was. Anyway, she didn't turn up until October, somewhere in Suffolk—'

'Beaten to death with a hammer,' said Dunstan. 'I remember that. It was the husband, wasn't it?'

'Well, that was the view of the police—'

'Oh, yeah, they pulled up his floorboards, didn't they? Yeah, yeah, that's right. They dug up the road, got frogmen to search this reservoir nearby, interviewed him for days. Couldn't get a lead on him, though.'

'I thought you'd like that story,' said Leonard.

'I remember the first time I went there,' said Deborah dreamily. 'Dad said the houses looked like Opal Fruits, so we went around, searching out all the lemons and limes and strawberries.'

'It's all down to ley lines,' continued Dunstan, falling back into his explanatory role. 'If you look at where they converge, you can see why the curse extends over a wider area.'

'And I suppose you're just a little bit outside it?' queried Leonard.

'Just about,' replied the other, smiling. 'People in the danger zone are well known for acting strangely at times.'

'That explains a lot,' said Deborah, glancing at Leonard.

'I think I read somewhere that during the Napoleonic Wars, when Coggeshall raised an army of volunteers, no one wanted to join as a private. So to get round the problem, they all had to be made into officers.'

'Sounds a bit like the *Chronicle*,' said Deborah.

'And then, of course, there's Peter Langan, the restauranteur. I don't know whether you're familiar with the story?'

'Yes,' said Leonard.

'Well, that was Coggeshall again. Threatened to burn his wife to death, did Mr Langan. All he managed in the end was to kill himself and destroy his home.'

Deborah shook her head in wonder.

'But listen, that's not all.' Dunstan's eyes were now twinkling for all their worth. 'The most amazing case concerns this American serviceman whose name was Boshears. He dreamt he'd strangled a girl he'd taken home to Great Dunmow, waking up to find – well, that he really had strangled her.'

'Oh, yeah, right!'

'The jury believed him, found him not guilty. See, it's all a bit weird, isn't it?'

'Well – yeah, if you put it like that,' Deborah conceded. 'Anyway, Andrew, whatever the strange history of this area – whatever this phoney-baloney stuff about curses – you don't really think something like that's gonna happen? To you? Tonight?'

'I'll tell you one thing, if it did,' Dunstan said, pouring himself out another glass of wine and fully warming to the subject. 'The Essex police wouldn't help any. Totally bloomin' useless.'

'Spoken like a true crime correspondent,' said Leonard.

'I'm not joking, you know.'

To illustrate his argument, Dunstan spent a few minutes talking about Jeremy Bamber – whose murders were also committed locally – enumerating the many mistakes made by the police.

'Yes,' said Leonard, 'but you've just highlighted one case. I'm sure most policemen and women do their best under difficult circumstances.'

'God, Leonard,' said Deborah, 'you're so naïve. Look at what happened when we were burgled. Absolutely nothing.'

Wow! screamed the tabloid headline in Leonard's mind. *Another Deborah Agrees With Dunstan Shocker!* He sat, fuming, while Dunstan proceeded to elaborate on his argument. The police held fixed views early on in a case; they were more worried about public opinion than catching criminals; there was a general propensity to use violence rather than mental agility.

'That's right!' said Deborah.

Clearly it was hopeless taking on the majority opinion, and

Leonard allowed the subject to lapse. How nice it was, to have a meeting of minds to match the meeting of bodies! Somehow or other he needed to keep his feelings in check, follow the plan. Up until now he'd let the conversation go into free fall, but it was time to alter the mood. The subject of other women had worked well with Lasker, and he decided to pursue the same line. Dunstan was already talking about Chloe's nurse, and Leonard, keeping everyone plied with drinks (though they were doing very well by themselves), steered the conversation from nurses to au pairs before asking the main question.

'So come on then, Andrew. What women are you into? Aside from Chloe, of course.'

'What, famous women?' Dunstan blew his cheeks out. 'I quite liked Greta Garbo, I suppose. She had a certain sophistication.'

'M'm,' murmured Deborah appreciatively. 'She was different, wasn't she, from all the other glamour pusses.'

'Any particular film?' asked Leonard.

'Well, she was excellent in *Camille* and *Ninotchka*. *Anna Karenina*, of course.'

'Didn't you feel sorry for Karenin in that film?'

'No, not really. Not the way it was portrayed. I mean, he was a bit of a stick-in-the-mud, wasn't he?'

He wasn't going to be allowed to get away with that – the good Catholic! 'But is that a good enough reason to be cuckolded?'

'Cuckolded!' scoffed Deborah.

'Well, I think her guilt was a key issue,' said Dunstan.

'*Two-Faced Woman*,' said Leonard, keeping his gaze fixed on Dunstan. 'That was her last film. What did you think of her in that?'

Dunstan confessed that he hadn't actually seen it. The conversation continued for a few more minutes, with Deborah not saying much, and then, since they'd all finished eating, Leonard took the plates out to the kitchen. Pausing at the door, he heard Dunstan say, 'Leonard's a bit sharp, isn't he, this evening? That crack about me being a true crime correspondent.'

'Forget it,' said Deborah.

He let them carry on in private. The atmosphere had altered. He'd made a mistake and overplayed his hand. The idea was to lull them into a false sense of security and any points he scored along the way were merely to lay the foundations. (Among other things, he'd been planning to ask Dunstan how he'd got on with helping Yvonne.) What was the point in trying to get one-up on both of them when he had that video waiting? The important thing was to stay calm, stay poised. Think Alan Ladd in *Shane*. Gary Cooper in *High Noon*.

27

Beetlejuice (1988)

When Leonard returned from the kitchen, Dunstan was saying to Deborah, 'I'm not feeling too great.' His left hand was pressed against his forehead. 'I get these headaches from time to time.'

Leonard studied his guest carefully. He hadn't even 'poisoned' him yet.

'Oh, no – you poor thing!' said Deborah. 'Maybe you should lie down, take it easy for a while. Or perhaps just go home. We won't mind, honestly, if you're not feeling up to it.'

'No, it's OK. I'll be all right.'

Leonard quietly let out the breath he'd been holding. Why weren't people like chess pieces, to be moved at will? He had the solution worked out – himself to play and mate in two moves – and all they had to do was take their positions.

'How about a nice cup of tea?' he suggested.

Deborah stared at him incredulously. 'Isn't that the British solution to everything? "I'm suffering from terminal cancer." "Well, how about a nice a cup of tea?" Don't you worry, Andrew.' She patted Dunstan's hand. 'I've got some paracetamol upstairs. It won't take me a minute.'

She was about to get up, but Dunstan was already standing.

'It's all right, I'll get them myself.' He left the room.

'Amazing how he knows where everything is,' noted Leonard, sitting down. He didn't want to make an issue of it, however. 'I'll put off dessert, shall I? See how he's feeling.'

Deborah was quiet. There was a small *bump* that seemed to come from under the floor.

'Hey, what was that?'

Oh, Jesus. 'What? What was what?'

'That noise just then. Shhh, listen.'

They waited for a few seconds. The only sound was Dunstan on the landing.

'It came from the basement,' said Deborah. 'Sounded like a chair or something being knocked over.'

Leonard's heart was thumping and his mouth had gone dry. 'Really? That's strange, isn't it? Oh, well, I'd better go down and check.'

He strode out of the room and hurried down the steps to the basement. His plans were already beginning to unravel. Was it too much to ask for people to just. . . ? He turned the dimmer switch on and looked around. No one was there. He closed the door behind him and walked over to the wooden alcove at the back of the room.

H'm . . . empty. That was odd.

'Aaargh!'

Something had landed on his cheek. He swung round, eyes wide with fear.

'It's me, it's me.' She looked startled as well, retracting her hand.

He pretended to adjust his glasses, needing a couple of seconds to recover. There was no sound from upstairs, so perhaps Deborah hadn't heard his shout.

'Yvonne,' he said under his breath, 'you were meant to stay here, just in this spot. What happened? There was a noise.'

'I know, I'm sorry.' She was dressed very smartly in a short black jacket, knee-length skirt and white blouse. 'It's just that I wanted the loo. I was looking round, you know, for somewhere to go. Then I knocked some tape-thingy onto the floor.'

'Tape-thingy? Right! So you managed to go in the end?'

'No. I'm absolutely killing.'

He led the way into the editing suite. He half expected to see one of the VCRs in a mangled mess on the floor, but thankfully there was only a videotape. He picked it up and read the words,

FINAL VERSION, USE! on the label. No, no, *no* – *not* the master tape! His face screwed into a grimace. Please, God, let it be all right. It was the only fully edited copy, the result of many hours' work. He should have placed it in a cassette box at least.

Storing it away safely between two of the VCRs, he looked around for an improvised chamber pot, grabbing an old *Batman* mug from the shelves.

'Here, will that do?'

She took it off him with a wry smile. 'How much longer you gonna be? It's freezing down here.'

'I'll try to be as quick as I can. I know it's hard, crouching all the time, but you've really got to stay in the booth.'

'OK, ducky. The things I do . . .'

Yes, he thought, as he headed back upstairs – for £500. At least Deborah shouldn't be too perturbed at the length of his absence because he often got distracted on visits to the basement. He bumped into Dunstan outside the living-room.

'All right, old mate? I wouldn't mind that coffee, the one you were offering, if it's no trouble.'

'Okey-dokey, coming up.' He opened the door. 'Deborah, how about—'

'What was that shout a minute ago?' she demanded.

'Oh, yes – that. Just trying to scare you, that's all.'

Her frown deepened. 'Well, ha, ha, Mr Funny Man. Wasn't quite so funny when we were burgled the other day, was it?'

'No . . . No, you're right, I should have thought. Actually it was just Ollie up to his tricks.'

'Christ, that pesky cat! Why don't we just get rid of him and have a couple of kids instead? Be a lot less trouble.'

'You really mean it?'

She rolled her eyes to the ceiling.

'Perhaps you could do with a nice cup of tea,' he added.

She lowered her gaze to stare at him. 'You're in a funny mood this evening, Leonard. If you really want, you can make me a herbal tea. That should sort me out, shouldn't it?'

'Hopefully,' he murmured to himself as he retreated to the kitchen. This was his chance, the point at which things became really serious. He switched the kettle on. Right, now, concentrate.

The first job was to place the ipecac in the mugs. (Why hadn't he done this beforehand?) He took a teaspoon out and filled it to the brim. In the other room there was a hum of chatter but no sound of movement, thank God. He'd decided to give them only 5ml per mug on the grounds that most of the stuff seemed to stay on the surface anyway, and it would help minimize the taste. Only one drink was to be used as well – cognac – to which they'd be treated to a quadruple measure.

He carried in the drinks, two red mugs for them and a blue one for him, filled with plain Nescafé.

'Hope you don't mind, I've added a little hooch.'

They weren't really listening, engrossed in yet another conversation about the *Chronicle*. Deborah was explaining how her father was hoping to plough more money into the multimedia side of things. Dunstan took a leisurely sip of his beverage while she was talking.

His expression instantly changed. He threw a pained glance in Leonard's direction, receiving a benevolent smile in return.

'Got a real kick, hasn't it?'

Deborah was the next to try her concoction.

'What the hell have you put in here?' she demanded, twisting her mouth into a spitting shape.

'Cognac,' said Leonard, maintaining his innocent expression. 'Don't you like it?'

She frowned. It was a point of honour with her, for some reason, never to admit she didn't like alcohol. In any case, before she could lodge any further objection, he changed the subject. It was important to proceed with a certain urgency now that he'd taken the initial step.

'I've got a film I'd like you both to see. We can go and watch it now if you like.'

'Just a minute, Leonard.' Deborah waved him to sit down. 'What's the big rush?'

'What is it?' asked Dunstan. 'I might have to leave if it goes on a bit.'

'Oh, Andrew!' exclaimed Deborah. 'You're really not well, are you?'

He's fine, Leonard wanted to shout out. Just had one too many, that's all. Of the two, Deborah's act was the more convincing. Showing the concern a lover might expect but staying within the boundaries of friendship.

'It's a very short film,' he said, pre-empting any debate about Dunstan's health. 'In fact, I made it myself.'

Dunstan took a sip from his coffee. 'Is this the idea you were telling me about? The one about the man poisoning his wife?'

Deborah drew herself up. 'Well, it's nice to be told about these things, I must say.'

Leonard didn't reply immediately and she went on:

'I'll tell you what, *I've* got an idea for a film. It's similar to *Rebecca*. You could call it – say, *Deborah*. It's about this woman married to a complete fruitcake who lives only for films. The mystery lies in this basement that he doesn't like her entering.'

'I let you go in—'

'For the sake of argument, Leonard, for the sake of argument. Anyway, he murdered his first wife – that's made up as well incidentally—'

'This isn't nice. Isn't funny.'

'No, listen. You haven't heard what's in this secret room. You see, he's a serial killer. He's made all these films of his victims just before their deaths.'

' 'Fraid it's been done,' said Leonard. 'You've just described the paranoid woman's film and overlaid the plot of *Peeping Tom*. That happens to me a lot,' he added, noticing Deborah's peeved expression. 'I think I've got an idea and then I remember a film that's very similar.'

Deborah addressed Dunstan. 'It's a bit sad, isn't it, that Leonard still harbours these great ambitions? He honestly believes one day he might become a screenwriter. Or even – this is his ultimate dream – a director.'

'Deborah, stop it!'

'No, I'm serious.' She looked at him calmly. 'Just tell me what critics have gone on to become directors. Go on. Who?'

'Truffaut. Godard. Antonioni.'

'Ha! There you go, then. Who's ever heard of them?'

Dunstan opened his mouth but then shut it again.

'Face it, Leonard. You're a critic. It's too late now to start on anything else. Just stick to what you're good at.'

He was very still and his eyes had become glassy. If she'd ever expressed her views so succinctly before their marriage, he'd never have gone through with the wedding.

'I intend to show you my ability,' he said quietly. 'Then you can judge for yourself.'

'Huh!' Deborah snorted. 'Hark at Spielberg!'

Leonard rose from his chair. 'I'll just get you another drink and then we'll head downstairs.'

He returned to the kitchen, fixing two more ipecac-laden drinks. Hark at Spielberg . . . Hark at— *God*, she'd really done it this time; he could hardly breathe. It wasn't enough, was it, to gouge out his heart? No. She was obviously intent on destroying his dearest, most precious aspirations.

Well! She fully deserved what was coming to her.

28

Play It Again, Sam (1972)

With Deborah and Dunstan at last on their feet (and with drinks in hand), Leonard led the way down to the basement. His senses had assumed heightened powers – eyes super-vigilant, ears super-alert – to the extent almost that he could feel the adrenalin running through his veins. One step at a time . . . He must take just one step at a time. All of his plans had led to this moment and, in spite of Deborah and Dunstan's slightly drunken state (at least in the latter's case), the film he was about to show them was bound to provoke an extreme reaction. Would he perform his part satisfactorily? Would Yvonne? He opened the door of the screening room and glanced quickly inside. Nothing. No movement at all.

'Well, here we are.' He took an extra moment to switch on the light. 'Sit yourselves down.'

He didn't want them moving around, but Dunstan, two steps into the room, loitered, gazing at the videos lined up on the shelves.

'Wow, just look at them. You must have several thousand by now. Have you expanded your collection?'

'No . . . Well, a bit.'

'That box over there.' Dunstan pointed.

'The popcorn machine.'

He carried on looking round. 'Hey, isn't that one of those

"What the butler saw" thingummies?'

'It's called a Mutoscope.'

He turned to face the alcove. 'And this wooden screen. That's where the projector is, right?'

He began walking towards it in a sort of stagger but was intercepted by Leonard, grabbing him by the arm. Things were getting out of hand.

'Let's just watch the film, shall we? We'll do all that afterwards.'

'Come and sit with me, Andrew,' said Deborah. 'You can see he's all twitchy. Grab one of those cushions and we'll make ourselves comfy.'

Dunstan sidled his way onto the couch.

'Great,' said Leonard.

He switched off the light, then went into the editing suite and picked up the master tape, inserting it into the VCR.

'Action!' he shouted.

There was a whirring sound and the tape re-emerged from the loading slot. Leonard pushed it in again. Right, just stay there this time. Good, that was—

No, back out. This couldn't be happening. Please, God . . .

He pushed it in once more, this time ramming his fingers in the tape compartment to keep it in place. No! Again! It wasn't working. It wasn't working and he was going to smash open the casing and strangle himself with the magnetic film. Yvonne must have damaged it when she knocked it on the floor. He tried another VCR, stopping it from recording for a minute. Same problem. He was getting into a panic. There were several other tapes he *could* play – and of course there was still the original – but none had the polish of this one. He tried the third and last VCR, the oldest of the group. The tape stayed in. He pressed the playback button. Steady, steady . . . Yes, oh *yes*, oh heavens be praised. Very quickly he began pulling out leads, plugging them back into other sockets to connect the third video recorder to the projector.

'Just going to the toilet. Be back in a sec.'

Dunstan poked his head round the door.

'All right. Nearly there.'

Leonard looked up, very flustered, but Dunstan was already

heading off and he returned to the job at hand. Why couldn't the stupid lummox have gone beforehand? Oh, Jesus, now he'd turned the light on. Surely he could have make his way up the stairs without additional help. The whole world was ablaze with a sickly brightness. It only needed Deborah to start moving around and she was sure to come across Yvonne. How ridiculous would it look if he were to rush in there now and turn the light off? No, no. He had to sweat it out. Deal with this first. . . .

'This tastes a bit off, Leonard. Did you clean the mug?'

She was framed in the doorway, peering suspiciously into her tea.

'What? Yes, of course I did.'

He was trying to sort out a tangle of flexes but also looking at her in case she became distracted. If she turned her head 120 degrees the wrong way, she'd almost certainly notice Yvonne's legs.

'I don't know. It's just a bit . . . Here, you try it.' She held out the mug.

'It's all right, thanks. I don't like your herbal teas.'

She screwed up her face. 'I feel like something's definitely got to me. I'm not feeling all that well.'

'Oh, no, really?' Just one more cable to attach. . . .

'Yeah, my stomach feels really tight.'

Done! Everything was connected. Now he just needed to get Deborah and Dunstan back into position.

'Ready!' Dunstan shouted obligingly from the other room.

'Oh, well, see how it goes,' he said.

She looked at him for a moment and then walked back to the couch. He came out after her and discovered Dunstan standing in the middle of the room, eyes glazed over, looking in spite of his summons as if he'd forgotten his purpose for being there.

'Over here.'

He guided him towards the couch, turned the light off, and then went back to the editing suite.

'Right, here we go then. Everyone settled? Annnd . . . action!'

He was sweating from head to toe. Breathing heavily, he pressed the playback button. There was a little whirr and the tape ejected itself from the loading slot.

'Oh, God, have mercy on me,' he moaned.
He pushed the tape back in and tried again.
It worked.

29

The Last Picture Show (1971)

The strains of Mendelssohn's 'Wedding March' filled the room. The church of St Luke's appeared on screen in a soft filter.

'That's where we got married,' said Deborah.

Leonard moved over so that he was directly behind her, laying his hands flat on the back of the couch and taking a deep breath. The opening credits would come next.

'I'm in it,' said Deborah on cue. 'And there's Mum fiddling with my hair. Leonard, you took this from our wedding video. That's cheating.'

Dunstan's name appeared on screen but the shot stayed on Deborah's preparations.

'You could've made yourself second billing, old mate,' said Dunstan. 'It was your big day, not mine.'

The camera moved in for a close-up of Deborah's face.

'Uurgh, my nose! This is embarrassing, I don't want to look.'

The music ended and the picture faded to a medium close-up of Deborah during the wedding service as she pronounced her vows.

'Oh, no, not this all over again. You swine, Leonard!'

She was burying herself into the couch, looking through her fingers. The film cut to Dunstan's best man's speech.

'You've all noticed these delightful bridesmaids.' He gestured with his arm. 'I'm sure you'll agree with me just how much they complement the beautiful bride.'

The camera panned to Deborah who looked down. One of the

167

guests shouted out, 'Creep!'

'Leonard's certainly a lucky man,' Dunstan continued. 'A lot of women might have preferred someone younger like myself. . . .'

There was a shot of Chloe smiling indulgently at her husband, before the film switched incongruously back in time to the church service and the vows.

'For better, for worse,' said the bride. 'For richer, for poorer. . . .'

'Hey, this is all wrong.'

Deborah twisted round on the couch and looked up at Leonard. He kept his gaze straight ahead, his hands curled into little balls by his sides. She glared at him for a full second before reluctantly turning to face the screen. The bride was holding a wedding ring.

'Take this ring as a sign of my love and fidelity love and fidelity love and fidelity love and fidelity.'

'It's stuck in a groove,' said Dunstan.

'Leonard, what's happening?' Deborah demanded, turning round again. 'Why aren't you saying anything?'

He still ignored her, his stomach tightening into the most stubborn of knots. A snippet of Dunstan's speech was being constantly replayed.

'Beautiful bride beautiful the beaut-beaut the beautiful bride beautiful bride.'

'That's a pretty bad stammer,' said Dunstan.

Suddenly the screen went black and they were plunged into darkness. For a second or two there was silence, then the sound of moans, low in pitch, filled the room. The screen was slowly clearing and it was possible to distinguish the edge of a bed, a chest of drawers, and the outline of a couple of figures.

'There'd better be a point to all this,' said Deborah.

Leonard's heart seemed to rise in his chest until it lodged somewhere in his throat. He could still rush into the other room and turn everything off. No damage would be done. . . .

The sound increased in volume and the picture became defined. The 'point' evidently occurred to her over the next few seconds, and she put her hand up to her mouth.

'Oh, God,' she said quietly.

She turned to look at him. Her eyes looked enormous, bright

even in the diffused light from the projector.

'Is this the wedding night?' said Dunstan.

'You were filming us. There was a camera in the bedroom.' She glanced at the screen and then back to him again, her face suddenly crumbling. 'Oh, Leonard, stop this! Stop this filth!'

'I'll turn the volume down.'

His voice sounded a little throaty. He stepped next door and muted the sound. He had to be strong. *They* were the ones who'd been dealt the shock.

Deborah had her head in her hands when he returned, murmuring, 'This is awful, just awful.'

'You think it's filth?' he asked, immediately conscious of the stilted nature of the question.

She opened her mouth to reply, but Dunstan intervened.

'You got a twin, Debs? This woman's the spit of you.'

They both looked in Dunstan's direction for a second, amazed at his lack of perception. He clearly wasn't paying attention to the man in the film at all.

'I don't know what to say,' said Deborah quietly. Her eyes were wider than ever, burning into his. 'What made you think we were. . . ?'

Dunstan started laughing, giving Deborah a nudge.

'Hey, that's a bit unfair, isn't it, darling? Having a close-up of some bloke's willy, then superimposing your dad's face.'

She looked at him in astonishment, briefly glancing at the screen. Leonard could tell from her profile that she was appalled.

'Profound, though,' added Dunstan.

'It was sensible of you to use a condom,' said Leonard, not giving her time to recover. 'I know how you hate getting messed up.'

She clutched at her stomach, making a grimace.

'I can't believe you could do this, go to these lengths. We could have talked.'

'All right, then, let's do that. Let's talk. Tell me – I don't know . . . Tell me how it started.'

He knew his face must look silhouetted with the light behind him, that he could still appear in control of his emotions. She gazed at him desperately, almost on the point of tears.

'OK – OK, I will, if that's what you want. It hasn't been—'

Dunstan was tugging at her sleeve. 'Debs, check this out!'

She rounded on him, exasperated. 'Shut up, Andrew. Don't you understand? That's you up there. You and me. Having sex. He's filmed us doing it.'

Dunstan calmed down, blinking in incomprehension. 'I'm a bit tiddly, I'm afraid.'

She gave a little shake of her head, then turned her attention back to Leonard.

'I'm not defending what we did, but – well, we were both unhappy at the time. You know we hardly speak to each other, Leonard.'

'Are you in love with him?' he asked.

'Oh, God, look, I don't know. Everything was working out just . . . OK, then, yes, what the hell, if it makes you any happier!'

He looked down. He'd been hoping for another response but there was always that chance. Possibly their marriage was already over. She had made up her mind.

'And faithful to each other?'

She frowned. 'Andrew knows I sleep with you, if that's what you mean.'

It would have been appropriate, perhaps, to ask Dunstan for his opinion, but the latter's head was now resting on the back of the couch.

'What about him? Who's he sleeping with?' asked Leonard, gesturing towards the recumbent figure.

He was planning to build up to Yvonne's introduction – 'Because I'd like you to meet someone . . .' – but his surprise guest pre-empted all this.

'I'll tell you who he's sleeping with!'

30

The Running Man (1987)

Yvonne appeared out of the darkness and strode over to the light switch. The room was suddenly filled with a dazzling brightness, temporarily obscuring the screen.

'I'll tell you who he's been sleeping with!' she sobbed. Streaks of black mascara ran down her cheeks.

'Yvonne!' said Dunstan, waking up.

'You scumbag! You lying piece of garbage!' She wrestled with her shoulder bag and brought out a note. 'How could you write this, telling me how special I was, how I was the only one, when all the time you were having sex with her?'

Leonard looked at Deborah who was completely motionless, agog.

'Yvonne,' said Dunstan. 'What are you doing here? Your accent—'

'Just look at that!'

She gestured towards the screen. It was just possible to make out Deborah on her knees in front of Dunstan.

'What letter?' asked Dunstan, still trying to catch up.

Yvonne glared at him as if he were the devil. 'Oh, you complete pig!'

She walked over and started pushing his head, still holding the note. Leonard rushed forward to guide her arm away.

'No, no! Stop! That's not the way.'

She broke off, crying convulsively. Then, pulling herself

171

together a little, she tearfully addressed the figure slouched on the settee.

'It's over. It's over between us, Andrew. I knew about your wife. I could just about put up with that. But her, too. I just feel sick.'

The object of her spleen stared at her incredulously. Deborah was looking terribly pale. Her cheek twitched slightly.

'You know what,' said Yvonne, switching her attention to the other woman and raising her chin to preserve her dignity. 'You know what, you can keep him.'

She thrust the note back into her bag and, adopting a brave face, left the room in a similar manner to the way she'd entered it. A moment's silence elapsed, as at the sudden end of a concert performance, and then Leonard addressed the two stuffed dummies on the couch.

'Stay there.'

He rushed to the top of the steps and, almost shaking with joy, locked the door. Yvonne was standing by the front door, her make-up still a mess, grinning from ear to ear.

'How was I?'

'*Magnifique*,' he responded.

'The bit about the letter, was that OK? I knew he was drunk, so I thought, give it a go.'

'You made that up?'

He reached into his jacket pocket and handed over an envelope containing £250, the second half of her fee. It would be petty-minded to tell her there was no need for embellishment.

'Brilliant. You were brilliant,' he assured her.

'The look on your wife's face!' She clapped her hands excitedly. 'Talk about death!'

Doubtless they could have gone on chatting for some time, but her part had been played. He opened the door. It was raining quite hard.

'Crikey. Just look at it. Here, Yvonne, take this.' He fished out an umbrella from the stand. 'I've left the garage door open. Have a safe journey. Oh, and thanks again.'

'Gimme a call, OK? I wanna know what happens.'

She ran out into the rain and he closed the door, enjoying a little oasis of calm. It didn't do any harm to let Deborah and Dunstan sweat on the revelations of the evening. Whatever they were talking about was being videoed using the motion detector down there. The business of introducing someone else had been the riskiest part of the endeavour and it had worked extremely well.

Now there was only one scene left to play. The process of lacing their drinks was well under way and it was time to provide the 'antidote' – a double dosage of laxative. They both looked dreadful, particularly Dunstan, and with any luck would fully believe that they'd been given something poisonous. Deborah already had her suspicions.

He went into the kitchen to pour the magnesium hydroxide out into a long glass. It certainly looked clear and healthy enough. Probably more palatable than the ipecac he'd given them. In any case, for the purpose he had in mind, it didn't matter whether the taste was repulsive. Probably better, in fact.

Oh, God, the old weakness was returning, doubts he'd vowed to banish forever. Was he going too far with all this? Being unnecessarily vindictive. . . .

No. No, of course he wasn't. Don't be silly now, come on! Remember the deception on their side, the lack of concern for his feelings and Chloe's. Besides, he wasn't really harming them. Just giving them a taste – ha, ha, yes! – taste of their own medicine. Actually, that was quite good. Perhaps he could use that in his screen—

Ah, yes, *that* was another reason why he had to keep going. The screenplay! He was almost forgetting!

He added some water from the measuring jug and stirred the solution. Amazing how affected Dunstan had been by a few drinks. Those pints he'd had in The Crafty Fox probably accounted for his behaviour there to a large extent. Being taken in by Yvonne and then—

'Open the door! Open the door!'

Deborah was shouting from downstairs, accompanied by a loud banging. He took the glass of magnesium hydroxide into the hall and placed it carefully on the carpet. Incredible how she still expected him to be at her every beck and call.

'Leonard, *please!*'

Her tone was different now. Disturbing. He hurried to retrieve the key. The next second there was a gurgling sound. As quickly as possible, his lethargy swept aside, he unlocked the door.

Deborah regarded him from the middle of the stone steps looking an awful colour, her face drawn with strain.

'Too late,' she said laconically.

He looked down at a pool of sick a couple of steps in front of her. For a ghastly moment he'd thought she really might be unwell.

'Deborah, could you go back inside?'

His voice sounded calm and authoritative. She stared at him.

'Believe me, it's for your own good. Go back or I'll lock the door again.'

She retreated. He picked up the glass and trooped down the steps, avoiding the puddle on his way.

Both of them looked wretched when he entered. Dunstan had climbed to his feet but was using the edge of the couch to prop himself up. Deborah's hair had lost its shape and her arms were wrapped around her body. Leonard walked across the room, warily observed by both of them. The film wasn't playing any more. One of them had managed to turn it off.

'What about the mess?' asked Deborah. 'Don't you think we should clean it up?'

The 'we' at least was an improvement on the 'you' employed when Oliver had been sick.

'Later,' he said.

He left the glass on the bench in the editing suite and came back into the room. Odd that he should have felt so tense before. His nerves had completely restored themselves.

'Yvonne's gone,' he continued. 'I did my best to calm her down.'

'She was hysterical,' said Dunstan. 'I didn't know what she was going on about.'

'Really? She knows a lot about you. I happened to bump into her a couple of hours after we met in the pub. She told me your interest in her nursing career was very short-lived.'

'I don't think she is a nurse.'

'Oh, she might supplement her income by other means. Not all that surprising on her wages. But she actually thought she'd found someone who really cared for her.'

Dunstan pointed an unsteady finger at him. 'I don't want to hear these lies.'

'Imagine how she felt when I revealed that not only were you married, you were having an affair with my wife. She just didn't believe it. The only way I could convince her was by showing her the video. If you thought the scene just now was painful, you should have seen her the first time. Pulling at her hair. Screaming at the top of her voice.'

'But I hardly know her.'

Deborah was gazing at him, shaking her head.

'She's a lovely girl, you know,' Leonard continued. 'Real credit to the profession. Although she was very upset about everything, she also felt sorry for me. She was particularly shocked when I played her the end of the tape.'

Leonard looked meaningfully from one to the other, receiving two blank expressions in return.

'When both of you were talking about how to poison me,' he clarified.

They both appeared horrified at this, looking at each other for enlightenment. Memory seemed to dawn on Deborah first.

'You don't mean that silly chat we had, the one about death and divorce? Jesus, we were just messing about. You must have realized that, Leonard?'

He gave a wry smile. 'Obviously not. And nor did Yvonne. We only caught the start of the conversation, but both of us had the impression, apparently mistaken, that you wanted me dead.'

'This is madness.'

'You've got it wrong, old mate.'

'Ah,' said Leonard.

They both looked very much in earnest and he felt the last weight of suspicion lift itself off his shoulders. Of course he could stop now, but he had them just where he wanted, where he could do anything. They might not have been planning his murder but he'd teach them not to joke about it, either.

'Well, as I was saying, Yvonne's a lovely girl and she wanted to help me out. Truth is, she felt very strongly about the whole issue. She even felt she might be next on your hit list if you did away with me.'

'What!' exclaimed Deborah.

Dunstan was staring at him doggedly, swallowing hard.

'Remember, Andrew, the conversation we had about poison? You said a lot depended on the murderer's job. Well, it struck me that here was a nurse. Someone with access to lots of drugs.'

'What are you saying?' demanded Deborah.

'Well, just consider. That funny taste in your tea. It *was* suspicious, wasn't it? How often have you been sick recently?' He turned to Dunstan. 'And your headache, Andrew? You feel a little hung over, but that doesn't quite explain the cramp in your stomach.'

'What have you given us?' She raised her voice angrily.

'Poison,' moaned Dunstan, clutching his neck.

'Yes. Got in first you might say,' said Leonard calmly. 'In reply to your question, I used a drug called digoxin.'

'That's for the heart,' said Deborah, pursing her brow. 'Something to do with the heart.'

'Absolutely right. Heart failure specifically. Hearts that don't beat as strongly as they used to. Ironic, don't you think?'

No, that was too glib. There was no need to embroider his tale.

'I'm going,' said Deborah brusquely. 'I'm not listening to any more of this. Coming, Andrew?'

The other man stood his ground, staring at Leonard with terror in his eyes.

'Before you rush off to the nearest poisons unit,' Leonard continued, backtracking quickly, 'there're a few things you should know. Seriously.'

He held Deborah's eye. A look of desperation crossed her face.

'I didn't have to use digoxin. I wanted a drug with a delayed effect. Unless something's done now, the symptoms will get worse – much, much worse, I assure you. To my calculations, you've both been given about five milligrams each. The lethal dose is between five and twenty-five milligrams. I don't think the drinking tonight will have helped, either.'

He glanced at Dunstan.

'However, looking on the bright side, I wanted to give you something with a specific antidote. Yvonne also got hold of a drug called Digibind. It's a very safe way, apparently, of nullifying the poison. Every 40 milligrams of Digibind binds 0.6 milligrams of digoxin.' He appeared to do a quick mental calculation. 'Which means that for each of you about 340 milligrams of Digibind should do the trick. You'd feel better in half an hour, and after three hours you'd be fine.'

He walked into the editing suite and retrieved the glass, holding it aloft.

'And this, if you were wondering, happens to be 340 milligrams of Digibind. This would totally cure one of you. An equal measure each would give you both good chances of survival.'

'How can we be sure that's what you say it is?' asked Deborah.

'True enough. We could go and examine the phials (nine of them, by the way). Or I could try some for you. (It's completely harmless, apparently.) Or you could phone for an ambulance, I really don't mind. All I can give you is my word that this,' he lifted the glass again, 'will make you better.'

'It's not good enough—' began Deborah.

But before she could continue, Dunstan grabbed the glass and proceeded to pour the contents down his throat, a drop of the liquid running down his chin. Breathing heavily, his eyes filling with tears at the speed he'd quaffed the mixture, he handed the glass back to Leonard and shambled off towards the door.

'Where are you going?' demanded Deborah.

'Toilet,' he mumbled over his shoulder.

She made a couple of steps in pursuit, but Leonard took hold of her shoulders.

'Coward! Call yourself a man!' she shouted after him. 'Let go of me,' she said to Leonard. 'Let go of me!'

She struggled briefly, then went limp. He released his grip and she fell on the couch.

'I don't care any more!' she sobbed.

Leonard sat beside her. For the next minute or so she was crying, unable to stop. It was quite odd, the way things had worked out. He really hadn't expected Dunstan to strike out on his own like that. This was meant to be the moment when he informed them they'd been given a laxative to drink, that he'd been making it up about the poison. It just went to show that lying to people was a tricky business. You really didn't expect them to take you quite so seriously.

'You're not going to die,' he said quietly. 'I didn't really poison you. I just wanted to see how you'd react.'

She brushed the tears away from her cheeks. 'You've got some more of that stuff?'

Leonard smiled. 'You wouldn't want that, believe me.'

He briefly outlined the substances he'd given them that evening. There was a drawn-out silence. Eventually she spoke, phrasing her words carefully.

'Telling me I could die was meant to be a joke?'

'Well, I must admit my sense of humour suffered while listening to your discussion with Andrew. It's not a nice feeling, is it?'

'Oh, God.'

She relaxed into the couch, rubbing her face with her hands. Everything had changed over the last few minutes. He'd asserted control, got his own back, but what should he do now? The future was still pretty vague but perhaps it was time to take a risk. Put the bitter feelings to one side.

'Look, Deborah, I know things have been difficult for us lately. I haven't been the best possible husband. . . .'

His sentence tailed off. She'd taken her hands away from her face and seemed to be indulging in her own private thoughts.

'That woman – the one who came out of nowhere. She must have been hiding in the projection booth.' She twisted round to view the alcove. 'Who was she? How did you know her?'

He explained how he and Andrew had 'bumped into' Yvonne in The Crafty Fox. (The truth could be postponed, perhaps indefinitely.) She regarded him with a quizzical expression.

'That note she was waving about – it didn't look much like a personal letter. It looked more like an invoice or something.'

Leonard shrugged. There was no answer to this. In any case, he wanted to talk about *them*, himself and Deborah.

'Where's Andrew?' she asked, looking towards the door. 'He should have come back by now.'

'I expect he'll be in the toilet for a while longer.'

She ignored this attempt at levity. 'When he comes back I want him out. I don't ever want to see him again.'

He nodded. They appeared to be making progress. 'I'll destroy the tapes tomorrow.'

She looked at him, apparently on the verge of saying something but unable to find the words. Eventually she said, 'You're a strange man, aren't you? Cold. Very cold. You go to such lengths to humiliate me, and now, I honestly believe, you want to patch things up between us. Just like that.'

He kept his own counsel. If he'd wanted, he could have revealed certain facts about Yvonne and Deborah's father, her hero among men, news of which would crush her further. If he was truly cold. . . .

'Well, I'm not the same as you,' she continued. 'I can't switch my feelings on and off like a tap. I know what you were thinking. That I would instantly realize my mistake and come crawling back, all penitent. But think about what you've just done. You've just invaded my privacy in the most intimate way possible.'

Her words filled him with dismay. He hadn't realized how much he'd wanted her to react in another way. What she was saying wasn't even true. Yes, he'd been partly motivated by revenge, but hadn't he also accepted his share of the blame? The point was that if there was a lesson to be learnt, she'd forgotten it. What about *his* feelings?

'You only wanted me when you found out I was having a relationship with another man. But I was actually serious about him, Leonard, fool that I was. I wasn't playing a vindictive game. I'm not joking either when I say that if anyone else sees those tapes – however many you've made – I'll kill you.'

They stared into each other's eyes. The whole ethos of her argument repelled him. She may have made some points in her own defence, but she'd shown a complete lack of remorse. There was no acceptance of her betrayal of their marriage. Just excuses.

'I'm going to bed,' she said, standing up. She walked out of the room.

31

An Inspector Calls (1954)

Leonard collapsed on the couch and took a long, deep sigh. It was over. He'd done it. How he'd managed to keep himself together all that time, God alone knew. The only question left now was how to spend the remainder of the evening. Following Deborah to bed was obviously unthinkable and, though there were other beds upstairs, perhaps it would be better tonight if he kipped down here.

You're a strange man. Cold.

What was that about? Just because he didn't scream and shout the whole time didn't mean he was bereft of feelings. In any case, *she* could talk. Look at the utter lack of affection she showed towards him. The victors in the love stakes were the ones whose feelings were reciprocated and, by that yardstick, he had suffered a crushing defeat. Perhaps she'd been right in saying he should have talked to her first. That way he could have discovered her true sympathies without resorting to the pyrotechnics of this evening.

But hold on. That wasn't true, was it? At least his chosen method had put the mockers on Deborah's relationship with Dunstan. The latter had really shown himself in a bad light, not just with his extramarital activities but with hogging all that laxative—

That was a point. Leonard lifted his head off the cushion. Where was Dunstan? Not still in the toilet, surely? He'd better search the house, then dump him into a taxi. It wouldn't do to have him roaming around during the night. He left the screening-room and came face to face with Deborah's vomit. Someone had trodden in it and there were traces, growing fainter, progressing up every second step. How long would it have to remain before *she* did something about it? He went to the kitchen, leaving the empty glass in the sink, and grabbed a floor cloth. It took ten minutes to clean up the mess, a task that made him recall the job he'd done with Oliver's sick almost with affection. Then he checked the toilet on the ground floor to see if Dunstan had taken up residence there – but without any joy. No doubt if the man had gone upstairs there'd have been some unpleasant noises from Deborah by now. Opening the front door to the downpour raging outside, he could see that, yes, Dunstan's car had definitely gone. The idiot must have slipped away in a half-drunken state. Well, that meant the evening was over. Apart from Deborah's unrepentant remarks before going to bed, it had been a success.

Leonard wandered down to the basement and resumed his position on the couch, closing his eyes and replaying scenes from the evening. Both Deborah and Dunstan had certainly been humiliated – both had undoubtedly felt in peril of losing their lives – but had he really been fair? All of the lies, the deceptions?

Leonard didn't feel like analysing that aspect particularly. Part of the reason he'd gone to such lengths was because of his ambitions to write a screenplay for Dorry. That was why he'd filmed the whole evening – to ascertain exactly how everyone would behave. . . .

Oh, God, that was right! He'd filmed the whole evening!

Sleep was now out of the question. Ideas were already beginning to surface, improvements on the conversations that had taken place, the ending in particular. The real-life Deborah might not be very pliable, but her fictional counterpart, Rhonda, had far greater potential. He could use the most useful scenes from the evening, applying his own unique gloss, and then weave in a few more plot strands. He went into the editing suite to view the rushes. Better to relive the experience while everything was fresh in the mind and he could write it down. Besides, he'd promised to destroy the tapes the next day.

It was well into the early hours of the morning but, rather than feel tired, he felt invigorated, possessed. Yes, he'd been rebuffed, but there was no reason why he might not be reconciled with Deborah eventually. It was just too early to assess the long-term implications of events. Everyone was a bit overwrought, quite understandably. In any case, he had the chance to create something truly wonderful. The keyboard was his palate and, with the fury of a great artist, he plied his trade, stopping every so often to examine an expression or study a gesture from the tapes.

INT. BERKELEY HOUSE. BASEMENT.

Roger and Rhonda are sitting on the couch. She is silently weeping, occasionally dabbing her eyes with a handkerchief.

RHONDA

I trusted that man. I thought that both of us were locked into unhappy marriages. I can't believe he could do that to me.

ROGER

I think he did feel for you in his own way.

RHONDA

But to make another woman pregnant! And then to write to her saying she should have a termination!

ROGER

He denied that.

RHONDA

Oh, but his face, did you see his face? It was written in every feature. Oh, God, I wish you really had poisoned him with arsenic.

She bursts into tears.

ROGER
(standing up)

This business has been painful for all of us. I'll destroy the film of you and Geoffrey in the morning.

Rhonda's expression is one of revelation. Her attention has been drawn away from Geoffrey's betrayal and she regards Roger as if she were meeting him for the first time.

> RHONDA
> *(grabbing at his sleeve)*

Oh, Roger, you're so good. You've been really hurt as well, haven't you? I've just been so selfish. A bitch. I'll do anything, anything to get you back.

> ROGER
> *(sitting down)*

I'd like to forgive you, I really would. But I can't turn my feelings on and off like a tap.

> RHONDA
> *(burying her head in her hands)*

I've lost everything.

> ROGER
> *(determinedly)*

If there's any hope left for us, Rhonda, we'll have to start all over again. Tomorrow.

She breathes again, reaching out to clasp his hand, but then, not wanting to appear presumptuous, draws back.

> RHONDA
> *(whispering)*

Tomorrow.

FADE TO:
CLOSING CREDITS.

Leonard was bathed in a feeling of euphoria. The Muse had descended into his dark sanctuary and shone her light on his offering. Never had he felt so inspired, so in tune with the great writers of old. He read through the whole script, more to remind himself of how beautiful and witty it was than for any other reason. In the odd moment of high excitement he'd written Dunstan's name instead of Geoffrey's, but otherwise very little needed to be altered.

Now, though, it was vital to send the script off to Augustus Dorry as quickly as possible. The famous film director would probably forget about their arrangement unless his memory was refreshed fairly soon. Besides, now that his masterpiece was written, Leonard was desperate to show it to a wider audience. As the printer whirred into action, he gazed at his watch for the first time. Ten minutes past eight in the morning! He must have been writing for over six hours without a break! If he was quick, he could catch the first post.

He penned a brief covering letter, mentioning his meetings with Dorry in the past and his hopes about making a film together. Then he carefully bundled the screenplay, together with the note, into an envelope and wrote the director's Surrey address on the front. Outside, when he finally emerged from his den, it was a lovely, clear day. It had rained during the night, but the sun glimmered off the dew, endowing everything with an almost unnatural brightness. This was the first day of Leonard's new life, a life bereft of problems and upsets. He placed the package on the passenger seat beside him and made his way into Filchester.

There was a long queue in the post office and a twenty-minute wait. One or two people were giving him strange looks, probably because his glasses were still cracked, but Leonard merely treated them to his most gracious smile. The only opinion that mattered was Dorry's, and he could picture, as if he were there, Dorry chuckling away, unable to suppress his mirth, the laughter turning to a lovely warm feeling at the end. *Leonard, this is wonderful . . . privileged to be the first to read it . . . already had talks with various people. . . .*

'First class,' he said to the assistant when he arrived at the counter.

What a wonderful, wonderful day! He left the post office and walked down the high street, mystified as to why all the other shoppers should look so gloomy. Surely life wasn't all that bad? Popping into the opticians, he was told that his lens could be fixed within half an hour. They could also supply him with another pair of the same frames for half the price of the originals. Leonard was delighted and said so, beaming at the assistant whose day had immediately improved with the introduction of a radiant Leonard into his life.

Then he squinted his way over to the newsagent's. A large box of chocolates for Mrs Peavey was in order. He picked out the most luxurious confectionery on offer and then bought the ingredients for a huge fry-up from the supermarket, trotting back to the opticians to pick up his glasses.

Now home – to Deborah. In this new spirit of generosity he didn't even bear a grudge against her any more. Or even Dunstan particularly. They had been catalysts in his career after all. There were other, more important things to think about now, such as who would play the part of *him* in the film. For some reason the name Tom Wilkinson popped into his head, Tom Wilkinson wearing a pair of specs and a tweed jacket. It was definitely an idea at any rate.

As he turned into the road leading up to the house, he noticed a couple of police cars, together with a third car, parked on the verge. A group of men were milling around, a couple in uniforms, another man dressed totally in white. They let him pass, but one of the uniformed officers closely scrutinized his face.

What was going on here then? Silly, but even though he'd done nothing wrong, his hands were clammy on the steering wheel. Perhaps he should have phoned Chloe last night. Ascertained whether Dunstan had arrived home safely. No, no, there had to be some other explanation. Loads of kids hung around the area in the evenings, didn't they? More likely something had happened to one of them – a drugs overdose, for instance.

Oh, *no*. A Ford Mondeo with yellow stripes along its sides and a bank of lights perched on the roof was sitting in his drive. He climbed out of the car, collecting up his shopping. Deborah couldn't have phoned the police, could she? No, that was preposterous. And what could Dunstan complain about? Nothing. Absolutely nothing. Just the same, he felt the need to swallow to relieve his dry throat. *It was a joke, officer. The whole evening was a joke. No harm done, eh?* He pushed his key into the front door but it was opened from within. A middle-aged man in a grey flannel suit, about the same height as Leonard, with short grey-black hair, addressed him.

'Mr Fleason?'

'Yes.'

The man nodded slightly. He had a very immobile face, his thin lips hardly moving as he spoke.

'Sorry for the intrusion, sir. My name is Detective Chief Inspector Boswell of the Essex County Constabulary. I'm investigating the death of Andrew Philip Dunstan, who was discovered in his car this morning.'

A loud explosion had gone off near Leonard's head and his brain sang with the reverberations. Everything for a moment – sight, sound, feeling – was a blur.

'Mrs Peavey down the road called us to report the matter,' Boswell continued. 'I believe you knew the deceased quite well.'

Behind the chief inspector, Deborah, clad only in her nightdress, was being ushered, or rather supported, out of the living-room by a WPC. As soon as she saw Leonard, she pointed towards him, her face blotchy with tears.

'You murderer! You killed him!'

The WPC tightened her grip on Deborah's arm, in case she lunged at him, but there was no need. Completely overcome, she collapsed on the floor in a flood of tears.

PART THREE

32

A Matter of Life and Death (1946)

Leonard stood pale and motionless by the door as Boswell and the policewoman helped Deborah to her feet and escorted her into the kitchen. The day wasn't so sunny any more, the dew not so bright, and the people going around with miserable faces were, if anything, understating their case.

Dunstan. Dead. The whole thing was inconceivable. Perhaps in his haste to leave the house he'd crashed his car while driving under the influence. But why then should Deborah accuse Leonard of murder? There'd be enough awkward questions to answer without her sticking her oar in. Think, think. What else could have happened? Suicide? Dunstan's last evening hadn't been the happiest, but how had he gone about killing himself unless he carried a revolver in his glove compartment? Oh, this was just hopeless. Nothing made sense.

Boswell returned from the kitchen, smiling at Leonard and opening the door to the living-room.

'Let's go in here, shall we?'

Leonard followed the chief inspector, dropping into one of the armchairs.

'Perhaps I should explain what we know so far,' said Boswell, sitting down on the sofa. 'Mr Dunstan was found dead in his car this morning, at the turn-off to your road. I've spoken to the police surgeon, and his opinion, from first appearances, is that death

187

might have been caused by poison. Now we know from Mrs Peavey – and your wife – that Mr Dunstan spent last night with you. Do you recall him taking anything, um, suspicious during the course of the evening?'

'No. I, er . . . No.'

'You don't sound very sure.'

'I really can't think of anything,' he replied more confidently.

'Your wife seems to have taken Mr Dunstan's death very badly,' said Boswell, pretending to remove some lint from his trousers. 'Her reaction when she saw you just now, for instance.'

'Well, she's in shock, I suppose. We both are. Deborah . . .' Was he really going to tell him straightaway? 'If you must know, Deborah and Andrew were having an affair.'

The chief inspector's eyebrows rose a quarter of an inch. He extracted a notebook from his pocket and scribbled something down.

'I see. And she believes you killed him out of jealousy?'

'I-I've no idea. Look, is it all right if I have a drink of water?' Guilty, my lord. . . .

The WPC appeared in the room, closing the door behind her and lowering her voice.

'Sir, Mrs Fleason wishes to leave the house. She's asked if she can collect a few clothes and things and go and stay with her parents. She says she doesn't feel,' she glanced at Leonard, 'safe.'

'All right, Cathy,' Boswell consented after a moment's thought. 'Go with her, and if she feels she wants to talk, do your best to encourage her.'

Leonard's face was beginning to flush. *She* didn't feel safe? *She'd* been the one discussing ways of poisoning *him*. Had the police already made up their minds about her innocence?

'This is mad, I haven't done anything,' he said to Boswell as soon as the WPC had left the room. 'I want to tell you everything, exactly what happened.'

The chief inspector gave a satisfied little nod. 'Good. I'll get you some water and we'll take it all down.'

Over the next hour Leonard attempted to narrate the events of the previous evening. Judging from all the head-shaking and eyebrow-raising coming from Boswell, the other didn't have much sympathy with his plight. Still, Leonard was determined to tell the truth. Apart from anything else, he was frightened that any lie could be found out later. Real life was so much more physical than the synthetic emotions displayed in films. It was about adrenalin and sweat, and a heart beating at an unhealthy rate.

One point of interest was why Deborah had been sick. Boswell wanted Leonard to show him exactly where on the stairs it had happened. Crouching down, he couldn't detect any sign of vomit but, as he pointed out, that would be for the forensic team to ascertain. Leonard said there might still be some residue on the floor cloth he used to clean up the mess.

Shortly after they returned to the living-room, another man with a crew cut and boxers' eyes arrived and was introduced by Boswell as Sergeant Aylott. He was younger and more casually dressed than his boss, with his tie loosened and the top button of his shirt undone.

'The body's been taken to the mortuary, guv. SOCO are still at work on the car.'

Boswell nodded. 'Get them over here when they've finished to examine the basement. They might find something interesting.'

His whole tone and body language implied that they had their man. All the other bodies were buried downstairs.

Aylott disappeared into the hall to make a phone call, returning as Leonard was in the middle of explaining how he'd videotaped the whole evening. Boswell had already been astonished to discover Leonard had filmed Deborah and Dunstan having sex, but this new revelation seemed to take him aback completely. The tapes, Leonard added, were in the basement.

'Are you some sort of voyeur?' the chief inspector asked eventually.

'I just like to know the truth of things,' said Leonard.

This sounded a little pompous, but the real reason for the tapes – his screenplay – seemed inhuman in the light of events. Not to say that if the police raised the issue later on, he wouldn't be open about it.

'You're not filming us now?' asked the sergeant.

'Good point,' murmured Boswell.

'No. No, I'm not.'

A little later, five men entered the house, two of them in uniform, including the bald-headed Toms who'd investigated the burglary. They trooped down to the basement, followed by Sergeant Aylott, leaving Leonard alone with Boswell. He was just explaining – again – the purpose of the ipecac and the laxative when Aylott returned, holding in gloved hands the mugs of tea and coffee Leonard had made for Deborah and Dunstan.

'We found these next to the couch, guv. One of them's full, the other's empty.'

'Is the full one coffee?' asked Leonard, leaning over to take a look.

Aylott hesitated before placing his nose to the liquid. 'It might be.'

'Ah, right – well, Andrew was drinking coffee. That means he couldn't have swallowed any more ipecac – and *that* explains why he wasn't sick. Whereas Deborah – I remember now – complained about her tea and was sick not long after.'

'There's lipstick on the rim,' said Aylott, holding up the empty mug.

'Right, right. So that was Deborah's,' said Leonard as the sergeant showed his discovery to Boswell. 'Actually, I was forgetting, anyway. It's all on tape. That will prove it, won't it?'

He looked at one frowning face, then the other. Finally Boswell turned to Aylott.

'OK. Check out every video—'

'The one you want is in the second VCR. It's unlabelled.'

'Check out *all* the videos, Aylott.'

'You any idea, guv, how many he's got?'

'Well, check the ones without labels first,' responded Boswell with some irritation.

'Hold on!' said Leonard as the sergeant hovered in the doorway. 'The only time I gave Andrew something Deborah *didn't* eat or drink was the laxative. The glass is probably still in the kitchen – in the sink. I don't think I washed it.'

Boswell rubbed his face. 'All right. While you're checking the tapes, Aylott, send one of the forensics boys up to the kitchen.'

'Perhaps somehow or other I gave Andrew something that was

contaminated,' said Leonard, voicing his thoughts. 'That would be unlikely, though, wouldn't it?'

There was a knock on the front door which the sergeant, still holding the mugs, left to answer. The chief inspector settled back into his chair.

'You think the laxative might be the poison?'

Leonard replied that he had no idea, he was merely guessing. He hadn't even bought the magnesium hydroxide himself. The medicines were kept in the bathroom upstairs and, in spite of his earlier remark, he couldn't see how that bottle, or any other, might have become contaminated.

Aylott returned, wearing a frown. 'Guv, that was a chap from the *Mercury*, wanting to know what's going on.'

'Jesus,' muttered Boswell. 'You'd better set up a roadblock at the bottom of the lane. We'll brief the press this afternoon.'

Constable Toms appeared at the door of the room. Like Aylott, he wore gloves, holding aloft a couple of books.

'I don't know if these are relevant, sir. *Deadly Doses* and' – he checked the other title – '*Poisons and Poisoners.*'

The chief inspector gave Leonard a quizzical look.

'They're library books,' he explained. 'I wanted to find out more about poison so as to scare my wife and Andrew. It's just as I've been saying—'

He paused. Three sceptical faces stared back at him.

'The *Poisons and Poisoners* book seems to fall open on page thirty-five,' continued the constable. 'The entry for arsenic.'

'Arsenic!' Leonard's voice rose in pitch. 'What are you saying? That I poisoned Andrew with arsenic? How could I get hold of arsenic, even if I wanted to? Anyone could have bent the spine open on that page.'

'Some sentences are underlined,' said Toms.

'I *never* write in books.' Leonard's face was bright red.

'Being inert,' the constable read out, 'elemental arsenic is not toxic when swallowed because it is absorbed into the system. Compounds of arsenic are quite a different matter, however.'

The chief inspector's expression remained inscrutable. 'Well, let's hope it's elemental, my dear Watson. Anything else, Constable?'

'A mug left on the floor in that little hidey-hole – you know, where the projector's kept. It appears to contain urine.'

Boswell turned to Leonard, the beginnings of a smirk appearing on his face. 'Didn't make it on time then, sir?'

'Some of it went on the floor,' interjected the constable.

'Looks as if our aim could have been improved as well.'

Leonard proceeded to explain it was Yvonne, not him, whose aim was in question, but inwardly he was kicking himself. He should have remembered to clean up Yvonne's little job last night – or at least told the police in advance.

'H'm. Well, we'll have to talk to her,' muttered the chief inspector.

'Another thing, sir,' said Toms. 'In the bin downstairs we came across a few scrunched-up pieces of paper. Looks like some sort of play.'

'Is that all, Constable?' asked the sergeant a little peevishly.

'I think so. . . .' Toms glanced round the room, his eyes alighting on the hearth. 'Hey, your cat, Mr Fleason! And another one, too!'

'Real stroke of luck,' said Leonard with a sort of morbid jollity. 'Mrs Peavey found it.'

He briefly explained the circumstances to Boswell, producing from the latter a comment about a cat burglar.

'Well!' said the chief inspector, clapping his hands on his legs and standing up. 'We're learning new things about this household all the time, aren't we?' He turned to Aylott. 'Let's have a little chat in the hall. You as well, Toms.'

The three men filed out of the room, shutting the door behind them. Leonard stared after them for a couple of seconds and then fell back in the armchair, closing his eyes and breathing out. What a palaver. Really, Dunstan had shown amazing prescience when he'd spoken about strange deaths and the Coggeshall Curse. And what about his criticisms of the police? Leonard had never experienced a murder investigation at close quarters before, but somehow he'd expected . . . well, not so many interruptions for a start. Everyone was rushing about and there seemed to be a haphazard quality to it all. At least he'd given them his version of events and much of his account could be proved. Whatever they were discussing . . .

But hold on. Words were filtering through from the hall, little snatches of conversation. The hairs on the back of his neck stood to attention and the blood began to pump a little faster.

'There are just so many possibilities,' said Boswell's voice, 'and he's in control of all of them.'

Aylott agreed. His voice was much quieter and he was probably facing away from the door. 'He's a control freak . . . videoing everything. . . .' He said something else that seemed to involve the ipecac and the laxative.

'He's clever, all right,' responded Boswell.

Another man joined them, presumably arriving from the basement, and the quartet moved further along the hall and out of earshot. Leonard ran his hands through his hair and sighed heavily. He'd endeavoured to help the police as much as possible, consenting to a search of his house, answering all their questions. Yet right from the start, inspired by an Oscar-winning display by Deborah, they'd assumed he was guilty, only letting him talk in the hope of incriminating him further.

The door opened and Boswell and Aylott came back into the room.

'We've decided, Mr Fleason,' said the chief inspector, 'that it'd be best if we carry this conversation on at the police station. From what you've been telling us, it's important we seal off the house for forensic investigations. I hope you understand.'

For a moment Leonard almost wanted to laugh. Were they still making out he wasn't a suspect? No doubt if he didn't agree to their suggestion, he'd be arrested anyway.

'You find something amusing?' asked the chief inspector.

'No, no,' Leonard replied hastily. 'Of course I'll go if it will help.'

Straightaway he was led outside. Another patrol car was waiting in the drive and he was directed onto the backseat.

'Oh, no!' he exclaimed. 'I haven't fed my cat.'

Boswell had his hand on the car door, about to close it. He frowned heavily.

'Don't worry. We'll take care of your little moggy.'

He slammed the door and had a word with one of his colleagues

194 · THE DIRECTOR

just inside the house. Then he climbed into the front passenger seat and they set off down the lane. Everything seemed to be happening at breakneck speed.

'It's possible,' Boswell said, not looking behind him, 'we might have to put you up overnight.' They turned the last bend before the bottom of the lane. 'Oh, hell. Keep your head down, Mr Fleason.'

Leonard placed his head between his knees. A moment before, he'd seen a group of photographers and local reporters, one of whom he recognized.

There was a short wait – which felt like an hour – while the police removed the traffic cones. Then the car sped away, hardly pausing at the junction.

33

The Wrong Arm of the Law (1963)

Leonard spent the next hour in a sort of daze. On arriving at the police station he was escorted through the back entrance and booked in, before being guided along a corridor and down a flight of stairs to the fingerprint room. Then he was led back upstairs to an interview room. The point of his being there appeared to be one of convenience. Boswell and Aylott had more important engagements – the former arranging to attend the postmortem, the latter to interview Yvonne – and it was left to Toms to look after Leonard.

Over the next few hours he became very familiar with the miserable room with its peeling yellow paint and stark neon ceiling light. Apparently, so he was informed, a case like this came along about once a decade, and it would be a grave disappointment to Superintendent Wallace, presently on holiday in Scotland, if he couldn't lead the investigation. Toms, very open about internal politics, rather thought that Boswell was deliberately delaying the moment the superintendent was informed, hoping to crack the case himself and gain all the credit.

Leonard could manage only the merest show of interest. Whoever was in command, an arrest would surely follow. At long last he'd be in the media spotlight but, rather than being fêted by his peers, he'd be reviled, the image people would carry of him one of gormless bewilderment as he stared into a police camera. Having been charged and remanded in custody, an inquest would take place succeeded by Dunstan's funeral. . . .

Something Shirley once said popped into his head. Funny how it hadn't occurred to him before, although this must be ten years ago now. Dunstan had spoken to Shirley about an assignment he'd been given that involved interviewing an incredibly flirtatious sixteen- or seventeen-year-old girl. Nothing had happened between them, according to his story, but the point was that Dunstan had been 'tempted', in his own words, 'to have a fling'. Indeed, he'd been so het up by the experience that when he was with Shirley a very unusual thing had occurred: he had broken down and cried. Both Leonard and Shirley had interpreted this as a sign that even the thought of adultery racked him with guilt; but, on reflection, what if the 'fling' had really happened? That would provide more justification for the tears and perhaps – who could tell? – Dunstan had been having affairs for years, feeling less and less guilt each time. It certainly fitted in with his personality – easy-going on the surface, one of the few men to hit it off with both Shirley and Deborah – but then where was his moral core, his sense of decency? (Or did his libido always win the day?) In any case, it wasn't quite as simple as that. Leonard recalled that Dunstan had written a lovely letter after Shirley died, and he'd really felt at the time that Dunstan had understood something of his situation. . . .

Oh, Lord, that was a point. Forget about himself for a minute, what about Chloe? How would she survive now? What sort of life would she have? No doubt she'd already learned about her husband's affair with Deborah and that Leonard was responsible for Andrew's death. God only knew what she'd make of that. Moreover, her debilitating illness would give the story an added dimension from the human interest point of view. Reporters would want to know all about her domestic life. . . .

Leonard slumped forward in his chair until his forehead was resting on the table. This was terrible, an absolute nightmare. Why had he arranged that whole stupid evening in the first place? Why? *Why*? WHY?

'Taped interview,' said the chief inspector in a monotone. 'June the fifth, 2004. Nineteen twenty-two hours.'

He gave the names of everyone present, then reminded Leonard that he was still under caution and that the interview was being recorded and might be used as evidence in a court of law.

'Do you understand that?'

'Yes,' said Leonard, clearing his throat of the logjam that had developed over the last couple of hours. Boswell sat opposite him, Aylott to one side, chewing gum, and Toms stood guard by the door. The chief inspector paused after his introduction, leaning back in his chair and tapping his pencil lightly on the table. He was looking directly at Leonard, apparently weighing up the best way to proceed.

'We now know the cause of Andrew Dunstan's death,' he began. 'According to the pathology report, traces of phenobarbitone, a barbiturate, were found in a urine sample collected from the deceased. The drug depresses the central nervous system and should never be taken with alcohol which exacerbates the process. Now we've already searched Mr Dunstan's home, spoken to his GP, and found no indication of phenobarbitone, or any reason, in fact, why it should have come into his possession. His wife, because of her illness, has been prescribed various drugs, but no form of depressant – nothing, in other words, that could have caused her husband's death. The first question I have to ask, therefore, is: Have you ever heard of phenobarbitone?'

'No.' The name sounded vaguely familiar. Perhaps – no, definitely – he'd come across it during his recent reading on poisons, but it would hardly help to volunteer such knowledge.

The chief inspector leant forward, his elbows on the table, his face about a foot away from Leonard's.

'Think very carefully. Your wife remembered the name and seemed to think you knew rather more about the subject.'

Leonard shook his head dumbly. Good old Deborah. Without her, those female spiders, scorpions and mantids – renowned for eating the male – might feel that they were being singled out.

'We found a bottle of Gardenal in your bathroom, one of the brand names under which phenobarbitone is sold—'

'Ah, hold on!' Why hadn't they given him the brand name in the first place? 'My first wife took Gardenal to help her with her epilepsy. I must have kept hold of it after she died.'

'The bottle was empty,' said Boswell. 'We had it examined at the lab to check it previously contained phenobarbitone – which it did.'

'Ah, well, then!' Leonard beamed at his interviewers, not receiving a smile in response. 'Andrew must have taken Shirley's medicine, that's what must have happened ... Oh, God!' He clutched his head as another thought occurred to him. 'He went upstairs at one stage to get something for a headache. Perhaps he picked up the wrong bottle by mistake.'

Boswell frowned, but Aylott made a disdainful 'tuh!' sound. 'You don't think he'd recognize a packet of paracetamol?'

Leonard gave a shrug. He didn't like Aylott's aggressive manner. The chief inspector instructed Leonard to go through his entire story again, from the point where he'd first suspected Deborah and Dunstan of having an affair and contacted HVM to investigate the matter. Every detail was discussed, but now that Boswell and his team had spent the day investigating the circumstances behind Dunstan's death, the chief inspector was able to interject occasionally with points of his own.

'We've talked to Yvonne Smith, the call girl. She told us that when she first met Mr Dunstan, he was talking to you about poisons. Would you care to tell us what the two of you were discussing?'

Leonard was tired, extremely tired. Although he'd spent the greater part of the day doing nothing, he'd used up every ounce of nervous energy he possessed. As he was explaining that he wanted to find out more about Deborah and Dunstan's plans to poison him, Boswell reached down into a briefcase by his side and pulled out a sheaf of papers.

'*The Director*,' he read, squaring the bundle in front of him into a neat pile. 'You see,' he smiled at Leonard, 'it occurred to the detectives who found those few pages in the bin that there might be a file somewhere, on a computer, that would provide us with the whole magnum opus. And here it is! Not only have we had to watch a fair few videotapes today, we've also had to plough through this.'

'Load of tosh,' muttered Aylott.

'Each to his own, of course,' said Boswell. 'I was going to

congratulate you on your vivid imagination, but then how much of this' – he picked up the bundle of papers and dropped them back down on the table – 'is based on fact?'

Leonard was quiet.

'Well, shall I use my own imagination?' continued the chief inspector. 'OK . . . OK, then, let me see. I could imagine, for example, that such was your desire to write a convincing plot, you decided to kill someone . . . you know, just to see how it felt.'

'No! No, you've got it all wrong.'

'Quite a clever idea in some ways. You tell them they've been poisoned – having given them something that replicates the necessary symptoms – but when it's time to deliver the antidote, *that's* when you offer the poison. You don't mind who takes it – the greedier, more selfish of the two. The point is, justice has been administered.'

'Are we still talking about my screenplay?' asked Leonard.

'You tell me.'

Leonard took a deep breath. 'Roger Berkeley didn't poison anyone. And I never intended to if that's what's happened. Why would I film everything? Why didn't I clean up afterwards?'

Boswell gave a little smile. 'You're a writer, aren't you? You must be familiar with hubris, the vaulting arrogance and ambition that leads to the transgressor's downfall.'

Leonard felt he'd endured enough questioning without being patronized as well. 'As displayed by whom?' He turned on his accusers. 'Look, am I a suspect or a witness? Because I've been trying my utmost to help. I've allowed you to tape-record this conversation. I've told you repeatedly my version of events. I've waited patiently in this room while you conducted your investigations in the hope that this matter might be resolved as soon as possible. And yet at no time have you reminded me of my rights or whether I'm entitled to a solicitor.' He looked from one detective to the other. 'I think I'll go now.'

'Sit down.' Boswell gestured, not in an unfriendly manner, for Leonard to stay. He turned to the constable who'd been standing all this time by the door. 'You can go home now, Pete, you've put in a long day. We'll sort this business out.'

'Yes, sir.'

He faced Leonard again. 'I'll get us a nice cup of coffee and we'll have a chat about things.' His chair scraped back as he stood up. 'Interview halted at twenty-three eleven. Chief Inspector Boswell leaving the room.' He pressed the stop button on the tape recorder and followed Toms out of the door.

Leonard shifted in his seat. What was happening now? He was conscious of Aylott's stare, the man's large arms folded in front of him. There was an awkward minute or two before Boswell returned, a strange smile on his face. Toms's presence had been reassuring, but now Leonard felt unprotected. Shouldn't the tape recorder be switched on again?

The chief inspector placed the tray of coffees in the middle of the table. Then he walked over to a corner of the room, his hands in his pockets. Leonard looked into the face of Aylott who seemed pleased about something. For a minute or so no one said anything, and then Boswell spoke. The hope that he was going to discuss Leonard's complaints was immediately dashed.

'I'll give you my theory, shall I? Of what I think happened last night.' He turned round to face Leonard. 'I think you were deeply, deeply upset by your wife's infidelity. Who wouldn't be? Especially since your best friend was involved. You didn't know who you hated the most, him or her. It was a double betrayal, and you must have played that videotape over and over, thinking about how to get your revenge.'

He walked over to the table, placing his hands on the back of his chair.

'Many men, most men perhaps, would have reacted differently. Beaten the other man up. Lost their temper with their wife. But you weren't like that. You were essentially passive, a non-violent man who nursed a terrible grudge. In spite of everything I think you still loved your wife, deciding after a lot of thought that you wanted to save your marriage. You still wanted to humiliate her, of course, but by now a plot had nurtured in your mind, a mind unable to divorce fantasy from fact, which involved you eventually forgiving her for her lapse.'

'I didn't murder Andrew,' said Leonard. 'That is all I have to say.'

Boswell drew back his chair and sat down opposite. The

sergeant sat broodingly next to him, his fists resting on the table.

'All right, Mr Fleason, I'm going to be honest with you. Place all my cards on the table as it were. In my opinion you've been feeding us a pack of lies. You're a sick and twisted individual. You have to possess and control people, monitor their behaviour in your absence. Your ego is so enormous you cannot abide rejection. You genuinely believe yourself to be a great artist and will do anything to accomplish your ends. Other people are only characters in your melodramas.'

Boswell stood up and moved at his leisure behind Leonard, leaning over so that his mouth was an inch away from Leonard's right ear.

'You killed him, didn't you?'

Aylott calmly smiled across the table.

'I told you,' said Leonard, his voice taut with emotion. 'I didn't do it. That is my last word.' He wanted to retreat into a make-believe shell, dismiss what was happening to him as a memory.

'You think you're above all this, don't you? So clever, such a brilliant mind. "Oh Roger, no. How could you? . . . You'll never get away with it, old mate. . . . Oh, won't I? I think you place too much faith in PC Plod." Well, one way or another, you're going to confess. I'm even telling you in advance.'

Leonard was stock-still, blinking a couple of times. Boswell stared at his profile for another second and then pulled away.

'I said we might have to put you up, didn't I? Well, now I'm keeping my promise.'

He made a gesture to Aylott who stood up and grabbed Leonard's arm, forcing him out of his seat. The latter was then frogmarched down to the charge room, booked in by the duty sergeant, instructed to remove his tie, belt and shoelaces, and then thrown into one of the cells.

34

Saturday Night and Sunday Morning (1960)

A thin stream of light filtered through the bars, highlighting the whitewashed walls, brown in places with grime. The only fixtures in the room were a toilet with two wooden blocks attached to the bowl, fulfilling the function of seat rests, and a bedstead with a blue plastic mattress and pillow. It was cold and there was a faint smell of urine.

Leonard knelt down by the bed and placed his hands together in supplication. It was impossible to calm down. His pulse was racing and his body shivered with anxiety. No prayer came to mind – he wasn't religious – and in any case Aylott might be watching through the observation window. He punched the bed a couple of times, then lay down, exhausted. God, he'd been so naïve. He'd actually believed that when the police had said they'd put him up, they'd meant a hotel. Now, even though he hadn't slept for at least forty hours, sleep seemed further away than ever.

What had really happened last night? There had to be a way of determining the cause of Dunstan's death. After all, phenobarbitone was now known to be the means. He rested a hand on his chest to calm his fast-beating heart and closed his eyes, taking a few deep breaths.

The police hadn't said whether they'd analysed the remains of the glass containing the laxative but, assuming Dunstan hadn't poisoned himself intentionally, that was where the phenobarbitone must have ended up. It was ironic, really. The laxative had originally been bought to help Leonard with his constipation. Deborah had nagged him more than once to stop complaining and take his medicine. . . .

His eyes sprang open and his body tensed. Of course . . . Of *course*! He'd been so stupid! The interrogation had turned everything towards him, and naturally he'd tried his utmost to defend himself, but the solution to Dunstan's death lay in a completely different direction. Deborah had provided the clue when she'd told the police she'd heard of phenobarbitone and volunteered that Leonard would probably know more about it.

He sat up in bed, sweat pouring from his brow. Dunstan *wasn't* the intended victim. He, Leonard, was. Deborah and her lover had been trying to poison him after all.

The shock was almost too much to assimilate at once, but it was quite clear – yes, perfectly – that he'd found the key to the mystery. The conversation between Deborah and Dunstan after the tape had ended *had* turned to how they were going to dispose of him. Deborah, in response to Dunstan's comment about drugs, had racked her brains and recalled the medicine used by Shirley – pretty powerful stuff by all accounts. At this point they'd have needed to get out of bed – a pain but then it was for a good cause – and gone to investigate. . . .

Ah, yes, and there it was, Gardenal, hiding away at the back of the cabinet. And yes, because Gardenal according to the medical dictionary was really phenobarbitone under a different name, it was indeed very dangerous. Well, great – just perfect. But then how to put it to use? It was Dunstan, probably, with his crime writer's mind, who'd thought of the idea of pouring Leonard's laxative away and substituting the Gardenal. 'Has Leonard tried his laxative before?' Dunstan would query, and the answer would come, 'No, he'll probably trust the label.'

Leonard rocked up and down on the bed with the excitement and shock of his narrow escape. Everything lay before him in perfect clarity.

Deborah would encourage him to take his laxative, the magnesium hydroxide, every time he complained of constipation. (Hadn't she done just that when he'd first suggested going to the gym?) She wouldn't make it too obvious, but when the subject arose she'd be her usual forceful self. Eventually, of course, he'd succumb, then returning from work one day with him lying dead on the floor, she'd only need to do a couple of things. First, get rid of the magnesium hydroxide bottle. It would look as if Leonard had swallowed the contents of the Gardenal bottle, either by accident or on purpose. ('I knew he was depressed, Inspector, but I never thought . . .') Then she'd need to place the empty Gardenal bottle, still containing trace elements, in Leonard's hand – ensure at any rate that it was covered in his fingerprints.

Oh, God, that was the plan. He was the only person likely to drink from that magnesium hydroxide bottle and consequently the only person likely to die. But by an amazing quirk of fate it had all backfired. Without knowing it, he had offered the poisoners their own poison.

He climbed out of bed. He must inform Boswell and Aylott straightaway. He was about to bang on the steel door when he checked the momentum of his fist. How likely were they to believe him? Up till now they'd resented every suggestion he'd made, believing he was telling them how to do their jobs. They'd hardly be happy if the duty sergeant phoned at this late hour to say that the prisoner wanted to talk – and no, it wasn't a confession.

He slumped back to bed. For the time being there was nothing he could do. Resting his head on the pillow, he fell asleep immediately, not even bothering to remove his glasses.

'All right, wake up.'

Leonard was with Cindy Crawford, the female protagonist on his latest film. She'd invited him back to her hotel room in London to discuss her role and thrown herself at him, discarding many of her clothes in the process. He'd mentioned in passing that he was married, but she'd insisted he make love to her, feed her incurable sex addiction to greying middle-aged men with love handles. Now she was lying beside him, whispering softly in his ear.

'Come on, wakey, wakey.'

Strangely, Cindy's voice had lowered a few tones, sounding almost butch, and rather than stroking his hair or massaging his back, she was poking him in the chest.

'Oi! The superintendent wants a word. Get up.'

The superintendent? Ooh, you kinky thing, Cindy. This room was really cold, though. Couldn't be a hotel. The bed was hard and all his bones ached. Hadn't he killed someone and they – the forces of law and order – were punishing him for it? But who could have died? Deborah? Dunstan? Drugs were involved, weren't they? Perhaps he was drugged up now. . . .

'Right!'

Arms – strong arms – were pulling him upwards. He opened his eyes and gazed into the face of the duty sergeant. Sleep . . . sleep, please. Somehow or other he was on his feet, but his brain and most of his internal organs were still around his knees. Now he was moving, moving out of the door and towards the stairs. Dave Crawford, that was the duty sergeant's name. He hoisted him up the stairs, Leonard's feet sliding over some of the steps.

Sitting across the table in the interview room was a little man of about sixty-ish with tired eyes and stubble on his chin.

'Mr Fleason, sir,' said the sergeant.

'Sit yourself down,' said the man. 'Dave – coffees all round. Cheers.'

Leonard took his place as indicated. Either his ears had acquired a new sensitivity as a result of his early awakening or the superintendent spoke in quite a loud voice. His jacket looked a couple of sizes too big, his shirt needed ironing, and his tie, judging by the discoloration at its tip, looked as if it had come into contact with liquid at some point.

'Sorry to drag you out of bed. I realize you've been through a lot lately, so I'll try to keep it brief. My name is Superintendent Wallace. I'm heading up this investigation, taking over from DCI Boswell.'

Good. Whatever political camp he was in, Leonard was for the time being a supporter.

'The chief inspector has been debriefing me throughout the night – from not long after you were taken down to the cells – and I've just told him to go home and get some rest. Now.' He rested his thin, bony hands on the table. 'This story you're telling us about poisoning your wife and her lover . . . but not really . . . and then one of them dies.'

'It's the truth.'

'Pardon?' Wallace leant forward.

'It's the truth.'

'What's the truth?'

'I just wanted to scare them, that's all.'

'Just wanted to. . . ? I didn't catch that last bit.'

The duty sergeant returned with the coffees and Leonard took a sip of his, waking himself up a little. Brilliant, wasn't it? The old tramp he was banking on to rescue him from that Rottweiler Boswell was deaf.

'I just wanted to scare them, that's all,' he said, raising his voice.

'Ah,' said Wallace.

Leonard proceeded to give his theory about Deborah and Dunstan, not just to the superintendent but to half the street outside. Thank God that here was a man who appeared to listen (at least when he was shouted at), and even appeared to sympathize. At the end, Wallace admitted that Leonard's problems with constipation might be a critical factor – 'certainly worth investigating' – but in fact he'd already managed to compile several pieces of evidence that seemed to absolve Leonard from guilt.

'If you'd really killed Dunstan, I don't think you'd give him ipecac. That's for people who've had overdoses. Also, it's not clear who you were trying to poison. Difficult for a jury to accept you didn't care. *And* you offered to drink from the glass.'

'That's right!'

'The other thing is, why would you transfer the contents of the Gardenal bottle to another bottle? No reason. In any case, your fingerprints weren't on the Gardenal bottle. That fact alone would probably be enough to release you.'

Leonard blinked. 'You're letting me go?'

'We certainly don't have enough evidence to make an arrest. We'll probably want to talk to you over the next few days, but now that we've finished examining your house, you're free to leave. Here's my number in case you want to get in touch, or you remember anything else.' He wrote down the details on a sheet of notepaper and handed it over. 'I'm sorry for all the inconvenience we've put you through.'

'Well, you've just been doing your job.'

'Sorry, what was that?'

'Thanks very much! Goodbye!'

No trial. No prison sentence. No Deborah even to worry about. Just home and a nice, warm bed. He'd lock himself in, away from the prying lenses of reporters, and enjoy a long, relaxing sleep.

35

It's a Gift (1934)

He was dropped off at The Elms. It was still incredibly early, about 7.30, and the day's brightness seemed even more vivid in comparison to the bleakness of the police station. He'd come to the conclusion while they were booking him out that there was still a question mark over his involvement in Dunstan's death, and that one of the reasons he was being released was because of the factional dispute between Wallace and Boswell ... But on the other hand, so what? He'd survived, kept his cool during that interrogation last night, and now could even manage a salute to the patrol car as it pulled out of the drive. No more police, at least for the time being.

He opened the front door and picked up an envelope lying in the hall, addressed to LEONARD. Not in Deborah's handwriting. Before he had a chance to read it, though, he was joined by a cat who gave every indication that his hunger had reached a state of national emergency. He trooped into the kitchen and fed Oliver, then ripped open the letter, written in a large slanting script.

Dear Leonard
I called round this evening and was disturbed to hear that you'd been taken away by the police to be questioned. Heaven knows when you'll get this, but I want you to know my thoughts and wishes are with you in this trying time. It was a

terrible, frightful shock to find that man dead in his car, but I
know you could have had nothing to do with it. I'll testify on
your behalf if necessary! Anyway, I hope the police are taking
good care of you.
God bless
Agatha

'One supporter at least,' Leonard murmured. Mrs Peavey might
be a touch eccentric but at least her heart was in the right place.
He walked into the living-room, throwing the letters onto the
coffee table. Mrs Peavey's present, the box of chocolates, was still
lying there from yesterday. He'd planned to go straight to bed but,
strangely enough, now that no one was taking charge of his movements, felt himself to be waking up again. With the press probably
gathering at his door later this morning, it would be as convenient
a time as any to pay a visit on his neighbour.

The day was pleasant, if a little fresh, so after donning a large
woolly sweater he set off down the road with the box of
chocolates under his arm. Amazing – and disturbing – to think that
Deborah and Dunstan really had been planning to kill him all
along. And they'd looked so innocent when he'd first accused
them! What a narrow – very narrow – escape it had been. Waving
that poison around and even offering to drink it to prove it was
harmless. . . .

Just a minute, though. Just a minute. He'd told Deborah it was
only a laxative. He'd actually explained to her . . . God, yes, he'd
completely forgotten. And, if anything, she'd calmed down at that
point – calmed down when, if she'd really doctored the laxative,
she'd have been thrown into a panic. The chances were that she
hadn't been planning to kill him after all, and he'd just unfairly
maligned her to the police. . . .

Huh! Well, it made a change at any rate. Even so, he'd better
call Wallace when he got home just to keep him abreast of things.
Lack of sleep had no doubt affected his memory.

Mrs Peavey's cottage was now in view, a traditional, thatched,
two-storey building, with a small, picture-postcard garden.
Surprisingly, the front door was ajar and there was no response
when he knocked.

'Agatha! Agatha, are you in?'

He stepped into the hall. She couldn't have had an accident or anything, could she? He opened the door to the living-room. Everything looked immaculate, apart from what looked like teeth marks in the arm of the settee. Ah, yes. She must be taking those pesky hounds of hers for a walk, as she did every morning. He'd just leave the chocolates on the television with a note.

Uurgh, my giddy aunt! There was a strange and somewhat gruesome photograph on the TV. Mrs Peavey was pictured staring at the camera while the man beside her – Frank? – was half in, half out of the frame. It was difficult to tell whether the effect was deliberate, but just the look in her eyes – and the fact she'd recorded it for posterity – made Leonard wonder anew about his neighbour. He tended to switch off whenever he was with her, but when he had time to observe and reflect, as with her video performance, for example . . . well, perhaps Deborah had a point about 'Mad Aggie'. This house, now that he looked around, was quite dark, not matching its chocolate-box exterior.

Anyhow, he needed paper to write a thank-you note. A large green notebook, bound with a tartan strip, lay on the couch, next to several different coloured biros. He went to pick it up, then hesitated. What if it was her diary or something similarly personal? He shouldn't really be in her cottage in the first place, never mind nosing into her possessions. He looked out through the large bay window that faced the front garden, listening out for any sounds, then opened the book.

A splurge of colour confronted him. She'd obviously been writing with each of the different biros. There were little pictures, words twice the height of others, sentences underlined in triplicate, much of it written in such a severe slant it was impossible to decipher. In fact, it was all very confusing, the only clear aspect being that it was indeed her diary, breaks occurring every so often to record the events of a new day.

Leonard was going to put the book back to its original position, but at the last moment a phrase, 'a curse on humanity', caught his eye. She was obviously off again. So what had invited her spleen on this occasion?

Thursday, April 15th

Drat and double drat. Left the washing in the machine overnight and found that my whites were still wet in the morning. (You'll forget your head some day, Aggie!) It went clean out of my mind because I became so wrapped up in a film last night, My Beautiful Launderette. *I was looking forward to it enormously because it starred Daniel Day Lewis, who was wonderful in* The Age of Innocence *and plucky, if less attractive, in* My Left Foot. *(Do you remember Dublin, Frank? Do you?) Well, what a shock I received! I was hoping he might play another romantic role – and deliberately avoided reading the review in case it spoilt my enjoyment – but it turned out that he was acting the part (if 'acting' is the right word) of one of THEM. I can hardly say the word.*

In tiny faint letters she'd written 'poofter' on the next line.

Doesn't anyone under forty have any sense of morality? You, the director of My Beautiful Launderette, *are a curse on humanity. And as for you, D.D. Lewis, erstwhile hero, you can shove it.*

Leonard was completely engrossed. It was akin to listening to Mrs Peavey normally, complaining endlessly about something she'd blown out of all proportion, except that here she was letting rip to her full Shakespearean range of emotions. He turned over the page.

Friday, April 16th

Something's afoot chez Fleason. This is the third week on the trot he hasn't allowed me in the basement – and after I did such a thorough job of clearing out the rubbish mouldering away in there. I started to wonder whether he'd noticed one of his vases was missing and suspected something. Although – HELLO! – that was an accident for God's sake!

Perhaps that shrew of a wife spoke to him. That woman thinks she's so pretty. (Shove off, pretty!) Thank God, though, he's all right. (Why is it the nice ones always end up with such awful cows? I could do so much for that man!) Today we talked about films – about which he's a real expert – and he agreed with me about everything! (Agatha Jean, you could have been a film critic, y'know!) He said some of my views reminded him of Christian fundamentalist attitudes in Midwest America. Well, hi-ho, Silver!

Leonard recalled very well that conversation and could picture her now, the granite-like head with its dank, grey curls, her right forefinger stabbing out the points. She had argued that Hollywood had lost its moral perspective and that it was high time for a return to basic values, akin to what happened in the thirties with the Hays Code. ('So, for instance,' he had jokingly enquired, 'a kiss shouldn't last longer than ten seconds?' 'That's right,' she had answered.) His remark about her reactionary outlook had meant to be a gentle dig – referring as well to the increasing tendency in her speech to include Americanisms – but he'd wondered at the time whether she'd taken it as a compliment.

He read on a little further but she'd changed the subject, moaning about the weeds in her garden. He flicked through the pages. Wouldn't it be fascinating to read her version of the argument with Deborah, the one he'd videoed? Very shortly he was on the day itself. Difficult to miss, really. It had been allocated three pages, all of which had been given a deckle edge in black. She'd almost worn through the paper with the pressure of her pen.

<u>Friday, May 14th</u>
A black day.
Leonard is in Cannes at the moment and, for some reason which she wouldn't reveal to me, HER ROYAL HAUGHTI-NESS was at home. Skiving, probably. Anyway, I was in the master bedroom, polishing the dressing-table mirror, when I noticed this motion detector thingy in the corner. I got up on the stool for a closer look and could just about make out this circular shape inside. It took me a couple of seconds to realize what it was, but there was absolutely no doubt.
A CAMERA for God's sake! A WRETCHED CAMERA!
Aren't there any lengths to which they won't go to make

sure I'm doing my job? Do they honestly believe I'm pinching things? Because it could be arranged, you know! That wasn't the worse of it, though. A few minutes later I was just putting one of Leonard's books in his bedside drawer when SOUR-PUSS comes into the room.

'Is it really necessary—' she says, all uppity, 'is it really necessary to clear out those drawers?'

Naturally, I was completely stunned.

'I don't know what Leonard's told you,' she went on in that hoity-toity voice of hers, 'but I'd prefer it if you left the bedroom cupboards and drawers alone. Do you mind?'

Well, honest to goodness, I just couldn't speak, couldn't begin to express my feelings about this totally unwarranted reproof. I mean, just imagine! To address me like that – in such a snippy way! She then turned her back and flounced off, not bothering to wait for a reply, but I swear, if I had a mind to, I could have said one or two things myself. Just because I can't – I just can't – be rude to people. Just because I'm too nice, too well-mannered. . . .

Even so, she'd just incensed me so much, I wanted to do something at least. I went in the bathroom and surveyed the rows of medicines and drugs. I wanted to give that hypochondriac something to really worry about, show her what could happen if I really decided to meddle! I took the pills out of one bottle and swapped them with another, tipped away the contents of a third and poured in something else. I carried on this procedure four or five times until I felt purged. It might not have much of an effect, but it's all she deserves. He probably won't suffer – not being so prone to every virus and malady that comes along – but if he does take something, that will be his punishment for marrying her.

Leonard stared at the page, reading and rereading the words, almost unable to take in the full implication of what she was saying. Suddenly Mrs Peavey wasn't a figure of fun any more. Over a petty argument she'd got it into her head to tamper with the medicines in the bathroom, leading eventually to a man's death. The diary, which he'd picked up completely by chance, was the evidence.

He looked up, letting out a deep sigh.

Something about the room was different. There was a shadow on the carpet leading to the window. The sunlight was streaming through and it took him a while to make out a dark shape on the other side. Was that a face? It was completely unmoving, looking as if it had been painted to the window. He gazed at it for a few moments before realizing it *was* real. A shudder ran through his body. Somewhere a dog barked. The eyes on the face were staring at him.

Mrs Peavey had returned.

36

Fierce Creatures (1997)

She was wearing the same angry expression he'd seen on the videotape, now directed straight at him. How long had she been there? Could he get away with saying he'd only just picked up her diary but not read any of it properly? In a moment she'd moved away from the window, striding purposefully towards the front door.

Oh, dear God. Why, oh why, hadn't he been more careful? He scrambled away from the door, reaching the other side of the room just as she swept in with the dogs, coming to a stop beside the settee. She was breathing heavily, still staring at him, apparently attempting to keep her emotions in check.

'Agatha! Hi there! I just came over to give you—'

He gestured to the present on top of the television. The dogs were circling him, tails wagging furiously. Mrs Peavey didn't even bother to avert her gaze. Nor, unusually, did she say anything. Instead, she ran the dogs' leads through her gloved hands, her face exuding hostility.

'I was just going to write you a note. I picked up this' – he held up the notebook – 'by mistake.'

She stared back at him intently. Her face flushed angrily, her lips tightening.

'I didn't think you were the sort to invade someone else's

privacy,' she said, her voice sounding a little tremulous.

'I-I'm sorry. I didn't mean to—'

'You know everything, don't you?'

'No, no. Really, I hardly read—'

'You know what happened, don't you? How he died.'

Leonard took a couple of breaths, sweat breaking out on his forehead. 'It was an accident – an accident, that's all. You didn't mean it.'

She gave a cynical shake of her head. 'Are you saying you won't tell anyone? Is that what you're saying?'

'No,' he said carefully. 'I-I can't promise that. I don't want anyone else to get into trouble. It was just . . . It was just a mistake.'

'You know I murdered Frank.'

'What!' He gave a little jump.

'You've just read about it, haven't you?'

'No, not that. I didn't know that. I've forgotten it already.'

She gazed around the room with a sour expression, apparently looking for inspiration. The dogs had retreated from Leonard and were standing in front of her awaiting orders. There'd been an inquest, hadn't there? Accidental overdose or something. She was always going on about Frank, the insulin injections she gave him— Oh, dear Lord.

'Still, it's only your word against mine,' she continued, almost to herself. 'Give me my diary back and that'll be that.'

She took a step forward but he clutched the journal to him tightly, hardly knowing what he was doing.

'I can't. It – it's too valuable. Look. Look here.' He opened the diary, playing for time. 'Friday, February 14th. Bright and sunny. Took the dogs for a walk and contemplated sending a Valentine's card to that little whore of Frank's, telling her—'

'Give it to me!' she raised her voice. 'I'll get my dogs—'

'Wait! Wait!'

They stood staring at each other for a couple of seconds. Leonard licked his lips, desperately racking his brains.

'I killed Andrew,' he blurted out.

'Andrew?'

'My wife's lover. I poisoned him.'

She stroked her chin with the back of her hand, gazing at him speculatively. 'You did say something on Friday. You weren't joking?'

'I had to do it, I had no choice. He and Deborah were planning to kill me.'

He'd definitely rattled her. She took a couple of paces to her side and sat down in an armchair, joined by one of the dogs who plonked its paws in her lap.

'Get down. I know you're hungry.' She looked up at Leonard. 'You really bumped him off?'

'I couldn't stand it. Couldn't stand being cheated on any longer. The thought of them laughing behind my back.'

She had another think.

Could he make it to the front door? No. No, impossible.

'Why not *her* then?' she queried. 'Deborah?'

'I tried. Just bad timing, that's all.'

She shook her head. 'I don't know what to make of this. I never thought. . . . Not you.'

'I know. I never thought with you, either. It's a bit of a shock.'

She sat on, still shaking her head. Perhaps now was the time. . . .

'Shall I make us a cup of tea?' he suggested. 'We can talk about it some more if you like.'

For a moment or two she didn't respond, and then she suddenly rose to her feet. 'No, I'll do it. You stay here. Mufty!'

One of the dogs followed her, the other lying down on his side and surveying him languidly. He still had the diary. He could still get away while she was in the kitchen. He tiptoed to the door, watched by the remaining canine presence, and stepped into the hall—

Eek! Mufty was lying sprawled out on the doormat, blocking the exit.

Backtrack. Perhaps there was a patio door or something. . . .

Damn. It was locked. Now what?

Ah, the phone. Just sitting there on a little table by the couch. He hurried over to the living-room door, mindful not to unsettle Treacle, and shut himself in before fumbling in his pocket for Wallace's number. Returning to the phone, he slipped the diary under the couch and knelt down, dialling away with feverish fingers, cupping his hand over the receiver. Come on, come on. . . .

'Hello,' said a voice.

'Wallace, thank God,' he said in an undertone.

'No, this is Baker. Can I ask who's—'

'It's Mr Flea— Leonard Fleason.'

'I'll pass you over.'

'Yes . . . quick.'

Something was on the move near him, padding its way over. Now it was right next to him, breathing its hot, rancid breath down his neck.

'Wallace here.'

'Wallace, it's Leonard Fleason. I'm at my next-door neighbour's house.'

'Speak up. I can't hear you.'

'I'm at my next-door neighbour's house.'

'You haven't got a next-door neighbour. I thought you were quite isolated.'

'No, no, get off, get off.' Treacle was nipping at the shoulder of his sweater. 'I have got a neighbour. She's down the road a bit. She's got me trapped. She's the one you want.'

'You're growing faint again.'

'I said, "She's the one you want." She's responsible for—' Wet sandpaper scraped its way up the side of his face as he was treated to a long, luscious kiss. 'Look, just get here quick. Please.'

The door was opening. Leonard sprang to his feet, replacing the receiver just in time to hear Wallace say, 'Where d'you say you were again?'

'Who were you talking to?' Mrs Peavey demanded, looking at Leonard and then out of the window. 'Who should get here quick?'

'Your dog. I want a cuddle.'

Treacle had sloped back to his mistress, dropping to the floor where he was presently eating one of his front paws.

'You want him to come over?' she queried.

'Well, perhaps best not to bother him.'

'If I say the word—'

'No, no. If he doesn't want to come, he doesn't.'

'Jeepers, you're all red in the face. Are you all right?'

'Fine. Just . . . you know . . . I've been under a great deal of strain lately with this murder. You're the first person I've told.'

'Ahhh.' She looked almost wistful. 'Well, I just wanted to know how many sugars you take. I couldn't remember.'

He gave his requirements and she disappeared again after telling him to keep the door open for the dogs. He sat on the couch as the sweat fell off him. Could he try the phone again? No, she'd hear him. Mufty had just bounded into the room. Another big, powerful brute. They both were. There was nothing for it but to sit tight. Whatever else he'd heard or didn't hear, Wallace must have picked up on the franticness of his tone, must have heard his directions correctly in spite of his query at the end. It should only take a few minutes for him to get here. . . .

Mrs Peavey strode into the room bearing a couple of mugs and placed them on the coffee table before sitting down at the other end of the couch. Then she turned to face him, wearing a somewhat disconcerting smile. A section of her grey hair was sticking to her scalp.

'There we are. I've just been thinking about things, out in the kitchen. It's a tricky situation we have here, isn't it? I really appreciate you telling me about this business with your wife.'

She reached forward and gave him a pat on his knee. Just two neighbouring psychopaths enjoying a cuppa.

'You know, you and I, we've got a lot in common. We've both been wronged by our spouses. We both did something about it, to which society takes a dim view. We've both got a lot to lose.' She held out a mug for him to take. 'Here you go. I hope that's all right.'

He placed the mug on the other side of him, next to the phone. Something was very wrong here. This was the point at which she was meant to set the dogs on him.

'The way I see it,' she continued, 'is you've got to trust me from now on – hope I don't go blabbing to anyone – and I've got to trust you. So how can we ensure that that happens?'

He smiled wanly, not seeing the relevance of what she was

saying. She smiled back and even blushed.

'How can we make it impossible for either one of us to testify against the other? You see what I'm getting at? Have the insurance of knowing we'd be safe from prosecution. You couldn't say anything even if you wanted to and neither could I.'

'I'm sorry, I don't quite follow.'

'I know it's a leap year. Even so, I don't think it should be down to me . . . to pop the question. . . .'

She beamed at him. She was like a human version of Treacle.

'Oh!' He gulped. 'You're talking about marriage, husbands and wives. But I-I'm already married.'

'Silly. I know that. You'd have to get a divorce, I'd wait until then. But what d'you think? I know your work better than anyone. You know mine. We've both got an interest in films. We get on well together.'

'Well . . . um . . . I'm flattered. Very flattered. I just need some time to think about it.'

'All right,' she said, her face falling a little. 'I think you'll find it's the only way, though. Neither of us wants to go upsetting the other, do we?'

'No . . . no.' Wallace, for the love of God. . . .

'Where's my diary by the way? I nearly forgot. What have you done with it?'

'And I nearly forgot your present,' Leonard announced, getting to his feet and heading over to the television.

'Never mind about that. I want to know— Oh, who the hell's that?'

A car had pulled up outside. Mrs Peavey went over to the window.

'Two men. Never seen them before in my life. Stay there, Leonard.'

She closed the door behind her, leaving him with the two dogs for company. A couple of seconds passed and then he heard a man's voice, followed by a shout of 'No! Get out!' from Mrs Peavey. There were a few scuffling sounds, but his attention had become riveted on the dogs, both of whom were sitting up and growling, showing their teeth. In the next moment there was a scream from the hall. The dogs dashed over to the door, scrambling furiously away before turning back to face him. There was a slight pause, and then they launched themselves. . . .

EPILOGUE

Leonard could still remember everything clearly two years later. A policeman had rushed in and done his best to coax the dogs away from his prostrate and helpless form, but the animals were intent on demolishing the box of chocolates he was clutching to his chest. Over the next minute or so he'd endured all of their licks and slobber, somehow emerging unscathed.

A couple of months later he and Deborah had begun divorce proceedings. The inquest had cleared him of any greater involvement in Andrew Dunstan's death, but it was clear that Deborah at least blamed him for all the adverse publicity she'd received. Not that he particularly cared any more. *The Chronicle on CD-ROM* had collapsed and all the staff made redundant, yet unlike everyone else Deborah had been relocated to the weekly magazine. She seemed quite different, almost alien, to him now, conducting their relations in such a stiff, businesslike fashion that it was hard to imagine they'd ever been married. Perhaps time had softened her outlook but, if so, she certainly didn't intend to give anything away. Leonard had once asked her how she felt about Dunstan's death, but she'd simply stared at him and told him the subject was closed. She and Leonard had never discussed anything really important, so why start now?

As for Dunstan's wife, Chloe, Leonard had written to her twice, expressing his deep regret over events and offering whatever help he could provide. At first this had met with no response, but at Christmas she'd sent him a card with her best wishes, passing on the glad tidings that she'd recently become engaged to her occupational therapist. Really, she had coped with events better than anyone else closely involved. Bad things happen to people,

222

but perhaps because she was living with a bad thing – MS – it gave her a greater sense of perspective. Certainly, Leonard had overreacted to Deborah's affair with Dunstan, and the criticisms of Chief Inspector Boswell (he could see now) weren't totally without foundation. He did, on the other hand, compare favourably to Mrs Peavey whose 'moral' stance placed her completely outside the loop. From what Leonard could gather, Mrs Peavey had been very much affected by her father going off with another woman, leaving her and her mother, and had plagued Frank incessantly about his relations with women until he'd done the one thing she dreaded.

Leonard sold The Elms, and he and Oliver moved to a village in Hertfordshire, not dissimilar to Quavering but well away from Coggeshall and its infamous curse. Deborah's father, Eddie, in a surprisingly generous settlement, offered Leonard early retirement from the paper (Sue Latchford taking over his former position), and his most amusing reviews were collected together in book form, receiving much critical acclaim.

As far as his film script was concerned, though, he wasn't so fortunate. He'd tried to get in touch with Augustus Dorry but discovered that he'd recently died. The loss of someone he liked was far more upsetting than the stunting of his professional aspirations. In any case, he'd reread *The Director* and, while not concurring with the view of Sergeant Aylott, he'd completely changed his opinion of its worth. It was incredible that he'd actually believed, albeit at about eight in the morning after the most emotionally charged night of his life, that his critical faculties were still capable of functioning properly. Especially taking into consideration his years as a journalist. Going over the script again, it had read like a second-rate soap opera.

Nevertheless, he'd concluded that writing – specifically *non*-fiction – was what he should be doing for the rest of his life. In the last year-and-a-half he'd been living on his own, spending a considerable amount of time in his study. In fact, he'd nearly finished what he considered to be his *pièce de résistance*. Two or three publishers had already shown a great interest and, based purely on his agent's promotion of the sensational subject material and Leonard's unique perspective, looked set to start a bidding war.

And now he was sitting at his desk, as Oliver lay to one side on a blanket, paws up in the air in an undignified pose and mouth hanging limply open. He switched on his PC and watched as the title page appeared on the screen, the first page of his insightful study into the mind of a psychopath, with extensive references to her diaries.

Mad Aggie: The True Story of Mrs Agatha Peavey.

The subject herself, none too happy about her life sentence, had warmed to the idea of working with him (the deciding factor being his efforts in finding a good home for her dogs), and all his research and hard graft had paid off, delving into her background and talking to relatives of Frank's. This would be the first work in his new profession as a true crime writer. There was just one last addition to make on page two and then it would be complete. He gazed for a moment at the framed photograph of himself with his arm around his first wife and typed:

Dedicated To Shirley.